PENGUIN BOO1

THE WIDENING OF TOLO HIGHWAY

Lucy Hamilton grew up in Dronfield, a quiet town in the north of England. She lived briefly in Australia before moving to Hong Kong, where she began work on her first novel, *The Widening of Tolo Highway*. The novel is a semi-fictional account of expatriate life in the New Territories, set against backdrop of the 2014 Umbrella Revolution. While writing *Tolo Highway*, she also trained as a Behaviour Analyst, dividing her time between the USA, Asia and the UK. In 2019, she completed a PhD in Creative Writing at the University of Sheffield, where she had previously studied English Literature as an undergraduate. She now teaches in Stylistics at the University of Nottingham Ningbo, China.

ADVANCE PRAISE FOR *THE WIDENING*
OF TOLO HIGHWAY

The Widening of Tolo Highway is a Hong Kong novel that explores the city as
political and mental space at a key and violent juncture in the city's history,
the Umbrella Movement student protests and clamp down. It is also about the
intricacies of time, its dimensions, subjective feel, and paradoxes, complicated
by the double consciousness that memory and the imagination foster when we
return to a place we powerfully experienced as a younger body and mind. This
is a sharp and intense study of hauntedness: how we are haunted by violent
history, how the city at violent breaking-points in its story shapes desire and
the unconscious, and how the traces of empire and colonial ideology also
haunt the social politics of our time.

–Professor Adam Piette, Professor of Modern Literature
at the University of Sheffield and author of *The Literary
Cold War, 1945 to Vietnam*

Lucy Hamilton's *The Widening of Tolo Highway* is a powerful, fast-paced,
sometimes breathtaking, exploration of loss and return set against Hong
Kong's 2014 Umbrella Movement protests and their aftermath. The novel's
use of psychogeography offers the reader a fresh narrative voice; the actions
and thought processes of the characters seem to feed off the crowded streets
and futuristic cityscapes of this iconic city. For the first time in a full-length
English novel, the young Hong Kong protesters of the Umbrella Movement
are remembered. *The Widening of Tolo Highway* is a captivating psychological
thriller in which a young woman's quest for clarity over the disappearance of a
lost friend is constantly being derailed by her own mental struggles and by the
elusive geography of Hong Kong.

–Michael O'Sullivan, Writer and academic based in
Hong Kong and author of *Lockdown Lovers*

The Widening of Tolo Highway

Lucy Hamilton

PENGUIN BOOKS
An imprint of Penguin Random House

PENGUIN BOOKS

USA | Canada | UK | Ireland | Australia
New Zealand | India | South Africa | China | Southeast Asia

Penguin Books is part of the Penguin Random House group of companies
whose addresses can be found at global.penguinrandomhouse.com

Published by Penguin Random House SEA Pte Ltd
9, Changi South Street 3, Level 08-01,
Singapore 486361

Penguin
Random House
SEA

First published in Penguin Books by Penguin Random House SEA 2022
Copyright © Lucy Hamilton 2022

10 9 8 7 6 5 4 3 2 1

ISBN 9789814954136

Typeset in Garamond by MAP Systems, Bangalore, India

www.penguin.sg

For Carole, Ian, and Gaynor,
without whom, for very different reasons, this book wouldn't have existed.

Prologue

A camphor-skinned youth is lying on his back, overlapping the border where the curb retreats into a layby. What remains of his face is still and angled straight at the sky. The girls twist to see through the window of their taxi. They think he is in shock. He wears a high school uniform: sand shorts and white shirt. Several others who stand around him are dressed the same. One peers down over his friend in the road, his back to the stream of traffic. Though his face is obscured, it is clear he is no longer speaking but stands like a reflection in a motionless pool. He now waits with the rest for the sirens, arms holding back an invisible crowd, the hordes that have not yet come to help and probably won't.

The girls' taxi follows the traffic as it curves to the right to avoid the green minibus, doors fixed open, jutting into their lane. Its passengers have reformed a queue and avert their eyes from the boy, as they glance down at watches. It is 8:47a.m. These minutes are precious. Framed in the near-side mirror, their faces diminish, but Anna knows their expression: urgent dissatisfaction.

A sudden jolt pulls her back to the present; her elbow has slipped, knocked from the armrest. The crunch of slow traffic melts into the hum of the aircraft's engines. Anna shifts in her seat, leaning back against the headrest. This trip will be different. Deadened with purpose.

'There's this,' a voice offers from the window seat beside her, 'but it's still half full.'

She recognizes the accent immediately, the American bounce with British Council vowels. He reminds her of a boy she hasn't seen in two years. When the stewardess leans across Anna to take his cup, she smells like a long shift and duty-free perfume, uncomfortably close. When she leaves, the smell lingers. Anna glances at the student. He smiles, but Anna stretches her lips and looks quickly away.

'You're a student too?' he asks.

She shakes her head.

He nods at her laptop, 'Studying?'

'In a way—Hong Kong.'

'Studying Hong Kong?'

'I used to live there. *Here*. I'm sort of an expat.'

'My dad is an expat,' he baits, half-suspicious.

'Mine too,' Anna lies, 'we moved here when I was nine.'

The student settles back in his seat and plugs in his earphones. Anna is about to do the same when he leans forwards again.

'You left—when?' He asks her.

'2015.'

'14?'

'15.'

'15.' He echoes. 'So, you were there for the . . . '

'Yes. Were you?'

He nods. 'Me too, from the beginning. And now?'

'Now?'

'You're coming back?'

'Just for a trip—two weeks.' And as she speaks, she feels those weeks stretch expectantly ahead of her.

The student replaces his earphones and closes his eyes. A minute later his lips begin to twitch. He seems to be appreciating the lyrics.

She slips the laptop into the pocket and tries to concentrate on the screen on the headrest in front. The film is something like *Cast Away*. But the brightness is too high, and the contrast is all wrong, and Anna finds herself unable to settle. Caught somewhere between a reclining seat-back and a memory, the monotony of the cabin pulses in her ears: a gyrating thrum, a higher pitched vibration, and the cackle of an acrylic window. The ticking sound pauses, and the buzz from the student's earphones fills the void. The sounds begin to swell. The air pressure squeezes tighter.

It is already too late; two hours since take-off, a familiar anxiety is seeping into her pores. She wonders if the other three girls still remember it: the boy by the roadside, the commuters checking watches, that twitching impatience. Anna once shared it. In the two years since, she has shed it. But already, she is beginning to feel the itch of its regrowth.

She glances at the student, remembering Cheuk Yiu's flashcards, and a phone recorder, blinking between slats of a bookcase. She is inches from searching her footwell for surveillance, disguised as the punt in her miniature wine bottle, concealed in the gunk of a countersunk screw.

She'd felt ready to go back, to begin from the start on her own terms, her own time, but now she finds herself powerless against something drawing her in—back to Tai Wo, to the boy in the road, and a feeling of sickly nostalgia. Concentric ripples surface in her cup. A seatbelt sign pings then pulses overhead.

Chapter 1

Polythene hoods hide their faces, slick with rain. They crush into the corners of a zigzagging blockade, the line of steel triangles that stretches the length of the side road. This time, they are careful; there can be no points of weakness. Someone distributes zip- ties. Three others drag a crowd control barrier onto its side. Together, they heave it up into the air and bring it down on top of two others. The girls hope it will hold. Their bodies stand resolute with the rest, identical, expectant, their sodden black T-shirts cloaked in thin plastic. When rogue drips breach the coverings, bare skin feels exposed, they stare out beyond the barricade at the wide empty lanes and taste the prickle of tear gas they pretend isn't there. This will be the stronghold; it is just a matter of time.

When they emerge from the tunnel, Anna recognizes mountains: tower blocks and penthouses, clutching the hillsides. She seeks out the names she doesn't know she has forgotten: *Tung Chung* and *Tai Lung* as they merge with Route 8. A bridge in the distance frames a sign for *Tsing Yi.*

For a while, she's distracted by each fresh recognition, drawn out through the window by some feature she half-remembers. But soon, the traffic slows, and the air inside the taxi becomes stifling. Her skin sticks to the peeling leather. She can no longer ignore the closeness of the present.

The space between exit signs begins to grow longer. Route 8 stretches endlessly in front and behind them. Duplicate *Tsing Yi* signs flash at every junction.

The road dips and they descend, a tunnel through foliage, and they burst into the dust-cloud of Lantau Island city blocks. Their windows are countless, peering down as she passes, scorning her for leaving, and whispering that she's back. She tries to focus instead on the taxi's interior, on the door frame where the glass meets the chassis, but she can see their eyes reflected in the curvature of the metal.

A *Tsing Yi* sign appears again. They are going round in circles. She itches for an exit, feeling like a fly caught on the wrong side of the window.

The highway straightens, and they slip into the shadow of sound-barriers. The driver checks his rear-view mirror. Their eyes meet for just a second. For the first time, she is conscious of their mutual silence. It isn't yet uncomfortable but a noticeable presence, magnified by their synchronized swaying around corners.

The towers shrink into apartments of three or four storeys, squat above shop fronts. Anna looks for Kowloon. Grass spouts in the gutters. Roadworks collapse around pits that gape open. Anna feels at home for the first time since the flight. From a distance, the north of Kowloon is rich tartan. Jade hills that stud a lattice of highways, with bright yellow sand paths that snake up their sides.

Closer to the road, it is concrete and rubble. Some houses are trimmed with Fai Chun and dracaena, but, still, two years later, many remain empty shells. Clad in webbed bamboo scaffold, they squat between sludge tracks.

The driver snarls at a barricade. Anna nods and copies his expression of annoyance.

Then a familiar junction takes her by surprise.

Welcome to Tai Po. She'd read it most nights.

Anna relaxes for a while and sits back in her seat. But before long, a new shade of trepidation creeps towards her. It stalks her from the shadows of black thorns and ashes. It isn't like the panic of that first Mong Kok evening, nor the thud of her pulse when her eyes meet the driver's. It is something much deeper.

The taxi slows as they approach the Lam Tsuen wishing trees. The stalls are all shut, it is clear from the road, but the driver seems expectant that she will ask him to stop. When they have almost passed the turn-in, he speaks.

'Tree closed, ah? Bad time.' He goes to turn in the driveway.

'No, no. Go straight on.'

'Here—Wishing Tree.'

'No Wishing Tree. Go straight.'

'Straight, ah?' He checks her direction with a forward-chopping motion. She copies his gesture. They crawl on along the corridor of aspens, too slowly, the silence heightened by their mutual glances. She avoids his gaze in the mirror as he pretends to watch the road. She remembers Lottie's warning, the knife below the dashboard.

They're getting closer now, creeping through the dimness towards the layby, hovering on the edge of Anna's recurring nightmare. The space had felt more real when she had dreamed it on the plane, more vivid, more definite. The evening light is too thin. But as they pass the spot, Anna is forced to turn away. The driver stamps on the pedal.

'Here, la?!'

But it isn't. Not quite. They advance a little further.

'Lido,' she says softly. *San Tong Village* is obscured by a creeper and cobwebs. She reaches forwards with the money.

'Mm-goi.'

'M̀hgòi,' the driver nods and slides the notes from between her fingers. She waits for him to pull the lever to open her door. He reaches towards it, but stops and scans the entrance to the village. His hand lingers above the lever. Anna pulls her own handle, but the door stays shut. She tries again, harder, struggling against the lock. The driver ignores her. He is surveying the empty path. It is almost dark.

'I used to live here.'

She tries to sound assertive, but her voice is thin and unsure, like the words aren't really hers. She jerks the handle and lets it snap back in the frame. He snaps out of his reverie. There's a clunk, and the door swings open. Then another for the boot.

'Mmm goiy!' but he doesn't hear.

Green metal slams shut, and she watches him disappear. Now, she's alone again. For a moment, Anna stands with her suitcase by the roadside, heat from the pavement seeping up into her soles, torn between the imminent present and the past. It is a past she feels at home in. Part of her stays put, enticed by its permanence, before the rest of her remembers why she's come back. She watches that part of herself turn towards the village.

'San Tong,' she breathes and hopes the house hasn't waited up.

Chapter 2

A searing pain where her back meets the buttock: Anna springs from the wall and grapples with her waistband for a pin that has come unfastened or a sharp wire thread. As she twists, it stabs her again, and this time the sting buries into the muscle. The pain is intense. She thrashes to locate it, stretching the fabric away from her body, but it doesn't go away.

Then she sees it. A bull ant, half the length of her little finger. Black against the skin. Shiny and armoured, it grips the flesh with cruel pincers.

She hits it with her palm, but the ant's grip holds firm. Another agonizing pang. The muscle clenches instinctively. Anna grips its writhing body between her finger and thumb and pulls, but the pincers cling on tight and pull the skin with it. She strikes again, harder, a swipe with the knuckle, and the ant drops to the ground.

She's since heard that they don't bite, but sting like scorpions. She remembers its body, turgid and juicy. She leaves her suitcase by the wall of a new property, a little way into the village. She won't be long. No one will take it. They used to sit here while they tried to flag a taxi to work, taking turns to brave the sunlight and the multiple rejections, until Anna learned the hard way that it was safer to stand. As she moves away from the wall, she rubs the flesh where it had stung her. The red line has long since faded, but the skin still tingles at her touch.

Something moves to her right. She stares up at the window, but the house, like the road, remains silent. Two years ago, this new home was a shell: gaping sockets in breezeblock, rusting iron stiches. Now, the grey bricks are clad; a family must live here. She surveys the yard. There's a scooter and work boots, signs of lives that don't know her. She looks back up at the window. She hopes it will be dark by the time she returns.

The evening is dank, the air stagnant, she can taste it. She'd forgotten that smell. Back then, she was used to it. They'd called it 'The Swamp'. She remembers damp cardboard; a kitten-sized casket. The path up through the village is steep and uneven. She climbs a little quicker. The humidity is thickening. By the time they'd returned from Dumaguete, her mother's jacket was mouldy; the blue dots would fade, but never disappear entirely. Denim sticks to Anna's skin, every step she feels it dragging.

It wasn't the middle but the very edge of nowhere. It was always just a little too still. They'd kept their voices low at night, unsure exactly who they were hiding from and what would happen if they were caught. There were shadows of rumours and the snakes in the reeds.

Beyond the completion of the house at the entrance, San Tong hasn't changed. The raised path winds through the allotment, cleaving the village in two. It is a patchwork of pipelines and lazy repair jobs, and fragments of spilled cement crunch underfoot. Anna's footsteps echo across the plots of bare earth and tangles.

As the path climbs higher still, the mosquitoes grow thinner, buildings grow denser, black windows blink down. She can see the wrought iron fence now, protruding above the wall. The spikes are aligned, which means the gate is closed, but Anna knows they never lock it. *Are you safe here?* Her mother had asked.

She reaches through the bars and feels for the catch.

Inside the gate, her confidence falters. Other houses share the yard; she must be absolutely quiet.

She is almost past the second property when a loud click sounds behind her. She jumps and scans the courtyard. The evening light is almost gone. But over by the gate, she sees the shadow by the grate. A rat, maybe, and then she is alone again.

She turns back to the old house; a few more steps and she'll reach it.

The sound comes again, louder.

Anna jolts forwards, grabs the handle, wrenches it open. Inside the stairwell, she jams the metal back into the frame. She shakes the handle until it latches and peers back out through the pane. The patio is still deserted. The gate is closed as she left it. Every window remains in darkness. Above the hum of tiny wings, she listens hard. The clicking seems to have stopped. But as her pulse begins to steady, Anna hears a gentle tapping, much softer, more regular than before, somewhere close by. And then she remembers; the man next door kept a terrapin. Across the yard, she locates the tank in the shade below his window. Inside the murky, green water, a shadow nudges at the glass. Anna's terror subsides, but the feeling of unease still glows in her stomach.

For a while, she stays motionless, fingers pressed to the glass, watching the creature fade into the blackness. How constant its world must be, knowing nothing but the heating and cooling of water, the paleness of its perimeter, convinced of its entirely. She waits until the light is too weak to trace its outline, then drags herself away.

The stairwell is stifling. She takes a breath and begins to climb. The air is thick in her throat, and she can feel the mosquitos already at her neck. At each floor, their wings grow more frenzied. There is one apartment on each floor. At the third, Anna pauses outside a familiar door. There are scratches, still, around the lock where she'd fumbled with her key. She remembers the panic, those late nights towards the end. She leans closer to the panels, listening for voices. All is quiet, but she senses there are bodies just beyond it. This time, Anna is the intruder.

On the fourth floor, the padlock of the roof door hangs open. As she slips it free, the bolt clangs loud against the bracket. The clang echoes back down the three flights of stairs. A baby wails, but nobody comes. She pushes the warm glass.

Out in the open, black mountains surround her, she can make out their peaks across Lam Tsuen Valley. She leaves the door wide open and steps out onto the terrace. Anna scans the neighbouring rooftops, close enough to climb from one to the next. That story had stayed with her; the switch knife and the woman who screamed the whole village awake. She moves away to the far side; she shouldn't scare herself with stories. In the still evening air, she looks out across Tai Wo. There is no place like somewhere that once felt like home.

The city air heaved, but up here she feels a breeze. She remembers how the sun used to slip behind the mountains long before it set, but how the blue it left behind seemed resistant to the evening. Hong Kong Island was draining: its tunnels and its traps, the vertical streets that were impossible to map; secret walkways springing up between walls lined with tree roots that lead her back to where she'd started, hot and impatient.

Though the house is only three storeys, up here on the rooftop, Anna always felt higher. From here on the hill, she can see beyond the fields to the neighbouring village and its network of pathways. From here, she can see both entrances to the village, at the front by the parking lot, and the other eastern path, a shortcut to Tai Wo station. She had walked it many times.

She tries to pick out his house. Whatever entrance he chooses, he will have to pass by the pond at the centre of the village where the two paths converge. Anna squints to see it now, a darker rectangle in the black panorama, but the night has closed in. Only distant lights are visible, way out at Tai Po market. But tomorrow, she'll be down there, waiting in the daylight.

She takes a final deep breath and turns back towards the door. It is shut firmly in the frame; someone has followed her.

Chapter 3

There is violence in their faces, more real than cardboard slogans. 60 days without pay and no promise of an ending. The black T-shirts outnumber the button-downs two to one, but the workers are angrier; they are fighting for the present. This side of the barricade, students swell behind fencing re-purposed from roadworks, and a second line of policemen who hold back the aggressors. The danger is closer now, there are new borders to contend with. The students' chanting is dwindling, uneasy now, wary, they've been warned against provoking them, and the fierceness of the workers is difficult to ignore.

An older protestor loses his patience and makes a grab at the barrier, two others rush to aid him, and both sides erupt. They grapple with the steel, faces contorted, while others hurl indistinct threats across the chasm.

Already on the fringes, Anna and Lottie pull back. For a moment, there's the fear they'll get caught in the crush. A gap opens. They move towards it. There's a sudden flash of silver. Pink cartilage blossoms as an ear is cleaved open. There's a moment of calm, before red suddenly rushes. For several seconds, the student doesn't realize it's his own. Anna doesn't know him but knows exactly who it could have been.

The student stares at the blood on his T-shirt, and then the pain hits. He crumples forwards into the crush of bodies. A girl screams and recoils. Panic erupts; there's a traitor amongst them. Two friends grab the injured boy by the armpits and drag him, disappearing into the masses that part to let them through.

The blade is passed sideways and rolled into an apron; it will later carve pineapples or liberate mangosteens.

Anna didn't look up to see the man who had wielded it. If she had, she might never have had a reason to come back.

Three years later, she hurries through the crowds of Ladies Market, retracing every sidestep and every half-forgotten turn. She imagines Lottie ahead of her, always just out of sight. Only, this time, Anna can't lose her.

Lottie ploughs forwards, colliding with strangers without an mm-goi or sorry, ignoring trinkets and jade chess sets she's seen too many times to care. The crowds shrink back around her, like bark around a knot, tutting, 'Aiy ahhs' and scowling at her entitled stampede. Anna stumbles after her through the terraced tarpaulin, past the papercuts and wraparounds of imitation silk.

It was here that her mother had bought a tea set from the lady who'd covered the crack with her palm as she sold it. And the brown leather journal that leaked dye around the edges and stained Anna's bag a burnt orange when it rained.

She keeps her mind fixed on Lottie and looks for gaps in the crowds.

She takes a left down a grocery street, off the main strip. The air smells of sawdust and roughly butchered meat. The average age shifts. Faces pass, and she forgets them; hardy middle-aged women who survey each other's stalls, bare-armed grandmothers muttering to anyone who will listen. She catches wafts of old armpits, skin hanging loose over muscle, and shopping bags bulging in clusters from fingers. Polythene splits and tomatoes take grazes from gravel.

'Aiy ahh!' The woman scrabbles in the mulch of old cabbage.

Anna hears a phlegm splat on the pavement and she pivots.

A bald, lethargic figure is reclining in a deckchair. He spits again with more force and Anna sees herself grimace. The faded canvas of his chair is distended entirely so that he is resting on the road. Unconcerned by the grime, he rubs at his temples, recovering from the nap and wishing he were back there. His toenails are milky, curling down into sandals.

The man pats his shoulders, loosening the muscles, and looks around at a congealing pot of sui mei beside him on the curb. On his other side is a cage, where a lemonish budgie flits from its perch to the rafters and back again. The man covers it with a cloth, condemning it to darkness.

He catches Anna's eye and holds it.

Slowly, he raises his hands to his eyes, shapes his fingers into glasses and watches her through them. His lips curl back into grin and his throat echoes a dry sound that might have been laughter. Anna turns away quickly.

The memory falters.

She looks around for Lottie, but she too has disappeared, back into the past.

The birdman's gesture had seemed to follow her, and it follows her now, through the years in between them, tracking her along the streets. It is as though he could see what she couldn't have then, that she'd be back three years later, searching for someone she hadn't known she would meet.

The grey pavements are patchy, their flagstones like static on an untuned TV. Every second, in every flag, separate lives are united. Soles share the dull concrete slab for just a moment, before a sidestep reroutes them—so many almost-collisions, so many tiny diversions. As Anna traces Nathan Road, she recreates the near misses that had guided her to Kallum.

Last night, she'd tried to call him. Cross-legged on her bed and losing hope that the aircon was working, she found his number in her contacts. She never liked phone calls, too intimate and immediate, but last night, on the rooftop, she'd felt a connection rekindle, a closeness that—she knew—wouldn't last until morning.

Amongst the names she knew from home, Kallum Cheung looked out of place; not the spelling of the surname, but the feeling that it belonged in some separate timeline. She couldn't link the two together. And there in the hotel room, listening to the wall unit's slow, painful whirring, she wasn't sure exactly which one she felt more at home in.

She tapped his name but found herself unable to go further. If she hit the number, and he answered, this whole thing would be over. But it was almost too simple, like escaping a bad dream by deciding to wake up. And, if he didn't, that sharp recorded message would be all too familiar. She hovered above the number; she wasn't sure she was ready. Voices in the corridor; her thumb jerked and tapped the number. She raised the phone to her ear. There was a silence of several seconds as she waited for the ringing or the voice mail instructions, listening to her pulse. But then a faint, empty clicking, and another woman answered, her voice a harsh, robotic scraping. Not the mailbox this time, something different. Anna didn't know the Chinese words but knew exactly what the voice was saying. The pre-recorded message unsympathetic, almost scathing: number no longer in use; she was unable to connect them.

Anna tried again, a little bolder, since she learned that the number wasn't working. The same unfeeling voice. She hung up before the beeping.

This morning, she obliges the urgent beeping of walk signs, following street signs she and Lottie might have not even have followed, and retracing crossings they might not have taken. These myriad turnings are all equally probable, but each new street she arrives at seems equally unlikely.

Thick traffic chokes the air. She remembers it was hotter, then, than she had known it could get, and it is hotter, now, than she remembers it. She loops around blocks, doubling back at random as though trying to lose a stalker. But she is already lost. Last night had unnerved her. Someone followed her to the rooftop, she was certain. Though, here, amongst the afternoon crowds, it seems less so. Back inside the stairwell, the building was still silent, mosquitos barely stirring. And when she'd made it back to the road, her suitcase was right where she'd left it.

In between two shop fronts, an overhang drips down the back of her neck. She looks up at the source and finds herself at the bus stop she'd been trying to find. Beyond it, the thousands of windows stare back. A dubious bamboo platform clutches a ledge high above her. She remembers how the sight of it had made her shiver, and how everything had seemed just a little too balanced, a sustained, frantic energy threatening to burn out.

The bus comes too fast and too close to the pavement, they always do, but back then, she'd been yet to find that out. She flinches at the rush and the stink of hot rubber and remembers the jab that made the panic so much worse.

A jab on her shoulder and she swings around. A whole queue of passengers is glaring at her. She shuffles back along the curb into a space that can't fit her, muttering apologies. She is new, she doesn't know.

She squeezes in after them, just before the doors clamp shut, and pays the same coins as the woman in front. The woman turns to survey her, as a man with no expression offers her his seat. Anna hovers for too long, unsure whether to take it. The man's expression hardens. As she pushes to the back, his frown catches and spreads amongst the other standing passengers. She finds a rear-facing seat.

After several stops, she notices the student sitting opposite watching her through the reflection in the window. For a moment, her eyes meet his. He saw her in the queue. Humiliation shifts to anger. She is new, she doesn't know.

When the bus turns out of direct sunlight, the student's reflection brightens in the glass. His lips are slightly parted, self-consciously pensive, and there's a mark on his nose from the glasses he's removed. His eyes flick back and forth between the shops of Argyle Street, as though he's looking for her too.

But when the junction untangles, his reflection fades, and this time it doesn't reappear. The seat opposite her is empty.

Chapter 4

The girls said 'Fan-*Leng*' in taxis because it got them there sooner, but this far out from the New Territories, she decides to take the train. Anna crosses Nathan Road and descends into the station. She moves quickly through the atrium and joins a neat queue. *They think you're from the mainland if you cut in the line.*

Their bodies filter into the carriage.

As the train pulls away, a family draws her attention. Lottie and Hope notice them too. The family are too glossy, over-preened, and polished, hair oiled and careful, set like a photograph. Hope stands with her back to them, but she and Lottie keep watching.

Some invisible glue holds the family together and apart from the other passengers. Cousins tease one another through the legs of uncles, until mothers snap something like stop, and they do. The word the mother uses is Mandarin, because when Hope says, 'mainland,' Lottie nods to show she's already figured that out. Anna hasn't.

'It's weird how you can tell, isn't it?' Lottie has seen her staring.

Alone now, Anna passes right through them to a space beside the doors, opposite where they'd stood, where she and Lottie had watched them and wondered, searching for the signs.

Three years later, Anna can't unlearn what to look for, but is less convinced than ever that the telling details exist.

Fanling has the grime of a New Territories district. Everything is sun-bleached, dusty, and sad about it. Dragonflies travel further than most. In those first few months, before the riots, Anna had the sense of something fading in Hong Kong, an absence different to the one she feels now. Fanling *was* that feeling, an apathy almost. They had settled too easily, and Anna craved a tension, something to remind her that here was different from home. Like the taste in the air when the triad men passed them, she'd wanted more of that friction she didn't understand.

Fanling station is crowded, just as she'd hoped. He'll be harder to pick out, but so will she, which reassures her a little. She's about to cross the footbridge when a grandmother stops directly in front of her. Face to face, they stand in each other's path for several seconds until Anna steps around her and she continues on her way. Here, people stare because this isn't the Island. At first, the girls had liked it, they enjoyed being the novelty, blonde hair was called *yellow*, and they'd listened out for *hou leng* when the school Aunties discussed them. They dreaded hearing *fei*. But now, every glance, even the ones that slide over her, makes her twitchy and self-conscious, like they know she's trying to hide. She tries to slip into the crowd, and a suitcase catches her heel. Anna turns to apologize, but the owner hasn't noticed, and a surge spins her sideways into the stream of commuters. She is carried a few paces, her backpack wedged between the bodies of two overweight businessmen, before she pulls herself free and ducks behind an ATM. She re-scans the crowd for any faces she has missed. They're too quick and too many. Her strategy is ridiculous. Anna pushes towards the exit.

They think you're from the mainland. Hope's comment had stayed with her. Today the bus queue is short, the school rush is finished. The bus is afternoon-empty, so much vacant grey leather. As they pull away from the station, she tears her eyes from the footbridge and places her fingertips against the window. The glass is only slightly cooler than the air inside the bus, and when she closes her eyes, the skin forgets it is there.

She keeps them closed and traces the bus's progress in her mind, feeling her weight shift at each roundabout and junction. Soon, half of her forgets that any time has passed at all. The space around her fills with bodies.

Kallum doesn't see her. He grips the handrail by the door at the front of the bus, listening in earnest to a friend's excited monologue. He looks younger than before, a school uniform, square glasses, but she recognizes the way he pulls the hair below his eye. She nudges Lottie to point him out.

There's a ripple in the tarmac and a screech of glass in a metal frame, and the jolt shakes the scene like an etch-a-sketch. She opens her eyes.

Alone again, Anna presses her fingertips harder on the window, a thin barrier, marred by the grease of old foreheads. From this side, the outside is only an image on a screen, impressions of flower beds and steep cobbled verges. The glass dislocates her, removes a dimension. At the next corner, the bus will loop back towards the station. She knows the circuit well, though, when she pictures herself alighting at the stop beside the school, she realizes she doesn't. It was only ever that stop, the meter or so of tarmac between the bus and the curb, twenty strides to the steps, twenty steps up to the school. The rest was a slideshow, glimpsed through a window, her mind already preoccupied with thoughts of destination. Perhaps the alleyways she glimpsed weren't really cut-throughs at all, but would lead her into a matrix she might never get out of. She couldn't have placed it on a map.

A powder blue dragonfly bisects the inertia. For several seconds, it keeps up, tickling her window with frail, frantic wings. Anna and the insect share a moment of stasis before it dives and shrinks away into the dust of Fanling.

The bus stops beside the school, too far from the curb, just as it used to. The doors clunk open, and she steps off, the step too high above the road, just as she remembers it.

Anna hadn't really planned to come here, but there was a lot she hadn't planned. She'll approach the school from around the back.

In the space behind the classroom that used to be Lauren's, domestic helpers are lounging in the shade beside the flower boxes. These long afternoons are better in summer, though the children are more difficult. She crosses the quiet patio and peers through the window. The classroom is deserted; the children must be elsewhere. She's about to turn away when something stops her. In the dimness, her reflection inhabits the space. It loiters beside the worktop, staring back as she stares in. On the outside, Anna lets her eyes fade out of focus, and the reflection turns away.

Inside the classroom, Claudi enters the frame, and together they begin to paint stars on crimson flags, struggling to get the yellow paint to show against the card. She and Claudi glance up periodically through their own internal window, over at the office across the entrance hall. From the inside to the outside, every corner of the classroom they share is exposed.

Claudi puts down her paintbrush and points to Anna's phone. Anna unlocks it, opens pictures, and hands it to Claudi. Claudi can't remember her own trip to the mainland; she'd been too young to know she should, and she flicks through Anna's photographs with curiosity and concern. She clutches the phone, pinching and enlarging an image. Stretched diagonally across the screen from a lens flare in the corner, the Great Wall rises and falls along snow-dusted hills. Anna remembers how they'd struggled through the dirty glass to glimpse it, to be the first to see it, and how they'd spoiled the surprise. Though, they would pretend that they hadn't. They'd forget about the potholes and how the headrests pulled their hair, and spend the next few weeks telling each other how beautiful it was; refusing to believe it looked better in the photograph.

'Wah, so beautiful!' Claudi agrees, hypnotized by the shrinking and growing masonry between her fingertips.

Her head jerks suddenly from the screen: 'Miss Gladice coming!?'

She drops the phone, instinctively.

They stare together across the foyer. The blind twitches but stays shut.

But Claudi picks up the paintbrush and dips it in the yellow, nudging the phone out of sight, behind a basket.

The Local Teachers are scrutinized; Native English Teachers, *NETs*, are quietly critiqued. Anna couldn't exactly say that the recruiter hadn't warned her. After the interview, Lauren had asked her what they'd asked. Her own interview was later, and she'd wanted to know what kind of candidate they wanted. 'Nothing really,' Anna shrugged. 'Just the usual. No real tips. Though the interviewer told me it helps that I'm blonde.'

Back inside the classroom, Anna watches her double turn suddenly towards the window, as though aware of the phantom staring in at the past. Their eyes meet for a moment inside her reflection, then Claudi jabs her with a paintbrush and she turns back towards the office.

'I think she's busy with the banner,' Claudi is saying, 'with Cherry and Mr Michael. They don't see if I - your phone.'

'They're obsessed. I doubt they'll notice, but if they see it, just say it's mine.'

Claudi giggles.

'Miss Gladice so stress about National Day ceremony. Always like that. Even last year.'

She goes back to Anna's photographs of her mini-break to Beijing, flicking past group shots and snaps of duck pancakes. Anna watches her scrutinize the still frames of day trips, spending longer on some, as though trying to remember. Claudi pauses on one: a wide square and the silhouette of a palace in the background. Anna shrinks away from the photograph, remembering the question she'd asked the guide as she took it.

'So, why is it famous?'

The square had stretched around them, pale inside the smog.

Lauren and Hope stare as Anna asks the question; she's warned them she will. Not because she doesn't know the answer, but because she does. There is a silence. Anna squints through the bitterly cold mist of the morning. She recognizes the roofing of the Palace and the flagpoles from the photographs of the incident she'd heard about and guessed how to spell. She stares at the gate that stands squat, chest inflated, and at the three-generation families scattered around them. Tour guides grow impatient and blow whistles at grandmothers, who ignore them and don't worry that they are being left behind. But, in spite of the bickering, a stillness cloaks the square. Anna wonders how many of them know what she is asking.

Their own guide is pretending she hasn't heard Anna's question, so she asks it again. This time, the guide feigns confusion.

'You means . . . the Palace or the Monument?'

'The Square.'

Anna speaks confidently, but the sound of her words out in the open makes her nervous. She is fearful of how far she will let herself push it. For just a second, she feels the weight of the sky. Lauren looks away; she isn't part of this. Hope follows Anna's gaze back towards the guide.

'Because it's very big. The biggest square in China.'

The interactive part is over. As they trail towards the ticket booth, Anna says nothing, more satisfied with her own dissatisfaction. She can take it away with her, and will.

As Claudi hands back the phone, she returns accidentally to the image of the Wall.

'Really, cold—on the Wall?'

'Yeah, especially at the top.'

Claudi shivers again and hugs herself: 'Here also, so cold when Director is coming.'

They knew her only as The Director, and that she came from the mainland, and that her husband owned the school. The title matched her reputation—she was cruel to Local Teachers and cold towards the NETs. And Anna had no reason to doubt the rumours of her severeness. For at least a week now, in anticipation of the Director's visit to the school, disinfectant had choked the corridors, and the air conditioning was cranked to an unbearable setting; the atmosphere must be crisp and unforgiving. The Director, Claudi hinted, might not even be there in time for the ceremony. But the National Day banner was re-straightened every hour.

A voice behind her.

'Miss Anna!'

She turns away from the dark classroom. It takes a moment for Anna's eyes to re-adjust to the light, then she locates the woman reclining against the flower box opposite the playroom. Behind the sliding glass doors, the playroom is also in darkness. The woman's expression is somewhere between confusion and amusement. As Anna crosses the patio towards her, she doesn't shift from her position on the tiles.

'Miss Anna, I don't recognize you!'

Anna smiles, uneasy about how long she has been watching. Josephine nods at the empty classroom.

'You try to get inside the school?'

'No, I just came here, to Fanling, for something else.' She looks back at the window; 'Just remembering, really.'

'They are there, I think, on the roof.'

'Who?'

'The childrens.' Josephine looks at her strangely.

They sit side by side on the patio and talk to one another's reflection in the glass.

'Miss Anna, we miss you.' She unlocks her phone and begins searching for the still frame. Anna had taught Josephine's toddler to catch. Where babies are interviewed before they can walk, and refused admission to kindergartens if they show off or shit themselves, the photograph is paramount, its credibility increased by the western face in the background. The mask Anna became was always bright, always smiling. The toddler was kept awake with a refrigerated flannel.

In her very first lesson, Josephine had approached her: 'Where are you from?' The child was sleeping in her arms.

'From England.'

'Ah England. From London?'

'No, North.'

'North,' she copies again and nods, as though it means something to her.

'Have you been there? To London?'

'No, never, but I want.'

Anna has begun to mirror the woman's swaying, and their smiles stretch too wide as they struggle to keep the conversation flowing.

Three years later, Anna finds she isn't struggling for questions, but wrestling with the many she wants to ask but can't.

'Do you still live in the village?' she asks instead.

'The village? Ah, Tai Wo?'

'Yes, your family. The family you work for. Next door to Christine—and the children?'

'Ah yes, Christine! The children. You're the tutor, I remember. I arrange it for you. And you working also with the eldest here, in the class.'

'Yes, Claudi,' Anna nods back at the classroom, as if they're still inside it. 'How are they—all?'

'No, no. I don't see them. My family move. The daddy's work change—so, we moved to Tsuen Wan.'

Anna's heart sinks.

She asks about the new district and is nodding mutely at the answer, thinking up a reason to leave, when another woman rounds the corner. Josephine exhales, almost a sigh. The sunlight is in Anna's eyes, but she squints politely in the woman's direction.

'Teacher! You are back here! Can you remember who is me?'

A second later she does.

Chapter 5

She and Jenny are facing one another on the carpet. Anna doesn't know her name yet; she won't think to ask until it's useful to know it. They are passing a ball between themselves and her child, who shrieks each time he catches it, his smile mirroring his mother's, when a slap echoes across the gym from the corner. Their eyes swivel towards the source of the sound. In the shadow of the play slide, a two-year-old writhes in the grip of his grandmother. White finger marks linger, but they pretend not to see.

Jenny's own child, Patrick Phillipe, is startled by the slap. Still gripping the ball, he freezes, eyes wide open. He hasn't learned, yet, not to stare. Jenny smiles to reassure him; he is not the naughty boyahh, and she stretches her arms forward to distract or embrace him. He flings back the ball and hollers, his excitement too loud in the nervous suspension.

In the corner, the grandmother's forehead is damp. A fuchsia flower has slipped a little in over-permed hair. Her forearms are strong, but she is growing too old for this kind of battle. She hopes the maids and Missy won't see that she is struggling and resolves to keep up with her exercises.

Jenny joins Anna and Josephine by the flower box.

'We think they're on the roof.'

As they talk about Anna's visit and arbitrary flight times, Josephine nodding between them to show she's already asked and is familiar with the answers, the three women look through the glass into the dim, deserted playroom. Behind their reflections, Anna sees Jenny remembering too.

'You remember the naughty boy?' Jenny asks her. 'You are happy you go home in the end? Yes, I know it.' They all laugh. The women understand.

It was a few weeks into the Autumn term when the maids had called Anna over. They were perched around a table in the tiny yellow classroom at the back of the school. Jenny called her first, parroted by the others, Josephine sitting uncomfortably in the middle. At this point, Anna might still have been calling Jenny 'Patrick's Helper' instead of his mother. *She says she gets that all the time. And you can tell that the other Filipino women treat her differently. An easy mistake to make.* But it was Anna who had made it, and Hope wanted her to know that. And yet, the more time Anna spent watching Jenny with the others, those long afternoons of playgroup, the more Anna came to see that Jenny *encouraged* the distinction. The other women were only working here; their Hong Kong families weren't their own.

Across the tiny table, Jenny thrusts a photo on a phone screen towards Anna. The other women lean in closer to see her reaction. The photo shows a woman pouting at the camera, pink lipstick, almost neon, and a manicure displayed against her cheek.

'You know who?' Jenny asks. The others crowd even closer. Anna smiles but shakes her head.

'She!' The women point across the table at Josephine, who blushes as shakes her head, as though she can't believe it is herself in the picture.

Jenny thrusts the phone into Anna's hand so she can have a closer look, and she notices, below it, several filtered and edited versions also have been saved. Anna smiles and hands the phone back.

'Beautiful, right?' says Jenny. 'But now she never wears the make-up! Why!?' Jenny is teasing her, now. It is something more than playing.

But Josephine only shakes her head.

The morning after Fanling, Anna emerges onto Nathan Road, blinking in the sunlight.

Families are beginning their National Day holidays. Fireworks across the harbour will draw them to the waterfront, but, for now, they block doorways and flood into shopping malls, suitcases clogging up the pavements. It has rained, and brown puddles splash lace that looks expensive. For a weekend, Hong Kong becomes a playground for the tourists of which locals speak proudly but secretly despise. This time, Anna is one of them, but she isn't here for the fireworks.

She moves into the shadow of Isquare, a bright sterile sanctum bisected with escalators, and settles in a coffee shop on the ninth or tenth floor. From here, she can look down on the oblivious crowds. The glass kills their textures, and she's too far away to tell one face from the next, but the city doesn't care. It won't accommodate her interest.

Hong Kong emanates from some unplaceable centre, reclaiming land that the ocean never knew it had stolen, tree roots woven through masonry, as though neither came first. Like the city that always was. Hong Kong people never talked about the highways, expanding beyond edges that don't believe in themselves, nor the fierceness of the mountains, jagged teeth piercing the surface of the water. As though Hong Kong is the blueprint, the taken-for-granted. For all their claims of marginality, Claudi spoke as though the matcha of Japan came from Central, Korea's beef from Mong Kok barbeques, English curriculums from Kowloon schools.

This self-confident bustle frames Anna's laptop. A map fills the screen. She stares at the lines, railway lines and dotted districts, tracing routes to dead ends—San Tong, Mong Kok, Josephine at Fanling. *No, no. I don't see them. My family move.* And then beyond it, through the window, the same impenetrable maze. The window stretches without frames from ceiling to floor across the entire side of the shop. If she stares hard enough, for long enough, the thick bolts disappear, and Anna can almost kid herself that she's out in the open air. Anna catches her reflection, hovering above the streets.

Her gaze drops to the road. Four identical taxis and a fifth one that joins them. She leans closer to the window and sees an endless line of others. She wonders how many thousands have come and gone since she left, hundreds of thousands. She's heard that, in her absence, the number of drivers speaking Mandarin has doubled, but she is yet to find a source; it might just be anecdotal. The line of taxis ends at the junction before the station, where crowds cluster at the crossroads that connect to Chungking Mansions.

The Golden capitals above Chungking Mansions are grubby. It is likely they always were, but she'd remembered them shining.

Each floor of the mansions is a grid of grimy stalls, cash booths, and news agents. Their names are uninspiring, their punctuation careless: Shamas Trading, Kamal Shop, Punjabi Provision's, their owners once proud of the late-nineties font. Their products are too cheap to be ashamed of their quality: phone chargers, carry fans, and stale biriyani displayed side by side behind the same milky glass. From the awnings hang lanterns and ancient potato chips, rusty crocodile clips gnawing at the packaging. The pattern repeats after every third stall.

Just inside the entrance, journalists have gathered, clogging up the few metres of walkway before the stalls. There are rumours of a story, and, if they can't find it, they will make one. A rape or a stabbing. A beating at least. An hourly, probably. A miscommunicated price. They fight for an interview with the most vicious-looking of the traders. A timid man with childlike dimensions lurks behind them, ignored by their microphones. Until a question provokes him. Their cameras swing to pick him out of the rabble, tangling the mic wires. His opinion is garbled, but it's the soundbite they're after.

But from up here in the coffee shop, Anna can see beyond the edges of the distraction. Dark uniforms moving with purpose catch her eye. Four armed policemen slip past the front of the mansions, unnoticed by the crowd. Anna's eyes search for their batons. An instinctive aversion. She still thinks of their tear gas and riot shields, and a grubby yellow ribbon tied around an arm. They approach a side-entrance and disappear into the chaos. They'll emerge again later, diffused and disappointed.

Anna returns to the map, zooming in over Tai Wo. It takes several seconds to come into focus, then she slides to the west and zooms in closer over San Tong. Again, she's forced to wait for the pixels to clear. Switching to Street View, she digs out the village, tracing the eastern path back towards the house. She finds it and dives lower, enlarging the tiles—a sand-coloured blur, but it is there all the same. She sinks deeper and deeper, until the lens is suddenly stopped by some invisible forcefield metres above the roof. It refuses to take her further, but Anna finds herself drifting through the barrier of the screen.

'Um . . . Scared-ing?'

'Almost,' she tries again: 'If you are scared someone might harm you? Then what would you be?'

'Threat-end-ing!'

'Exactly, yes!'

Anna praises Cheuk Yiu loudly, careful to let Christine hear her daughters progress from the study. The girl beams.

'Let's try one more.'

Anna watches her take another card from the pile and stare blankly at the word, printed in marker pen. While Cheuk Yiu mouths the letters, Anna checks her phone. The minutes are dragging.

'Can you read it?'

Cheuk Yiu nods.

'Have we done this one before?' Anna can hear herself growing impatient. 'Is it something to do with . . . ?'

Cheuk Yiu shakes her head. But Anna knows that it is; her own felt-tipped letters are showing through the card.

'You need to try. Sound it out.'

'Dem-oc-ra-cy.'

'Right, and do you remember what it means?'

'Like government?' The girl offers.

'Could be. It's when the people decide who represents them in the government. It's a word from your homework,' she adds, a reminder to Christine that she is following the curriculum.

Anna watches herself listen for a sound of approval from the office, knowing now what she didn't then: that Christine is too distracted to notice. He said he'd be home by now.

When the office stays quiet, Anna checks her phone again. 18:32 p.m. She stands immediately to leave. Ordinarily, she'd disguise her eagerness, but tonight, she can't help it; she's already wasted two minutes.

Anna can't remember how she first heard about the protests. She had woken up yesterday, the morning of National Day, and by the evening was refreshing South China Morning Post *every minute for mentions of tear gas. Claudi was not planning on joining the protesters. She said she didn't know, though she said that about a lot of things, and stashed the question away with the trays of coloured paper. But Anna couldn't leave it.*

She'd brought it up again when the children were settled with a video on the carpet. Claudi had pretended to think for a moment, still sorting flags into piles, and said her parents would worry. There was another reason too. She'd never say it but didn't have to. The school's official position was yet to be established, and, for local teachers, contract renewal was far from guaranteed. The Director was from the mainland. China. *China. Hope said you can tell she wore a corset.*

Anna had asked again as they sorted Tuesday's handbooks.

'I still thinking. You will going? With Miss Lauren?'

'Yeah, we're planning to. And Lottie. Tonight, after tutoring—if the crowds are still there. Do you think they will last?'

'Last?'

'Stay. Still be there.'

Claudi handed Anna a finished stack of books and started counting paper straws into bundles, flagpoles for the ceremony they'd recreate in the foyer. She was used to Claudi's silences, but this time it felt hostile.

'But why you will go it? And tonight is my sister's lesson?'

Anna shrugged, '—to support. It's important. I'll go after the class.'

'And all the NET teachers?'

'I'm not sure.' And she wasn't.

'Is it strange that you will go it?' It wasn't really a question, but not quite an accusation. 'My brother, he was saying . . . it can be part of the problem. Just the ideas—the impression, maybe—something like that. Like Hong Kong still depending. Don't know. Only thinking.'

A tension settles, Claudi's brother's words hanging open. It was as though they weren't arguing with each other but with his presence in between them, holding them apart. By the middle of the morning, the atmosphere was stifling.

But Claudi's questioning had only made her more determined to join the protests. She'd spent the afternoon screenshotting MTR stations, directions from Tai Wo. She couldn't cancel Cheuk Yiu's lesson, but she'd meet the girls as soon as she possibly could.

18.32. Anna is so rushed that she forgets about the payment and collides with the maid in the middle of the room, crumpling the notes in her hand. Startled by the sudden closeness; their sorrys are shrill. She delays now, making small talk, and helping Cheuk Yiu clear the books away.

Anna cringes at the memory, the image of herself, oblivious to all but her own over-politeness, no idea that every second she was getting closer to meeting him, to tangling herself inextricably in his life. By then, he'd be stepping off the bus beside the koi pond. A minute later and he'd have rounded the corner to the houses.

She aches to go back there, to reach through the screen, to drag herself out, down the steps, across the car park, and never look back. She wonders, now, if she still could have made it in time.

When she finally drifts into the stairwell, she is still reeling from the collision with the maid when it almost happens again, this time with a boy dressed entirely in black, coming up the stairs towards her. Anna sidles to avoid him, but he steps the same way. She apologizes and he reaches out and stops her by the shoulder.

'You.'

For a moment she doesn't know him. His long fringe is sweaty, and a yellow ribbon hugs his skinny bicep. They stand opposite each other on the steps, each expecting the other to speak.

'Can you remember? From the bus?'

Three years on, she can't forget.

'Oh. Right. Yes, I think so.' She stares, trying to place him. 'Do you live here?'

'Yes, my family.' He nods to the ceiling.

'I tutor a girl here.' Anna copies his nod.

'Yiu Yiu- She's my sister! So, you're the teacher, really?' He doesn't wait for her to confirm. 'Been in Central, all day. I skip the classes—all

of them. My teachers just say: 'Why you do that? Very crazy!' But we have seen it—how we are living—we have to do something to change it.'
He had practiced that last line and would use it again.

'In Central? At the protests? Actually . . . '

'Okay! Is okay. We just have to do it! Tonight, I will go back there. Tonight will be bigger.'

' . . . No, I mean, I know. Tonight, I will go there, too.'

'You will go? To there?'

'Yes. I'll go there now.' She gestures down towards the exit of the building. 'I'll meet my friends and then we will go there.'

For a second, he is uncertain. His eyebrows curve like Cheuk Yiu's. Then, the frown melts to excitement. 'Ha! Then you will be helping us.'

He dashes past Anna and bounds up the remaining stairs towards his family's apartment. When he reaches the door, he calls back down the stairwell, 'Maybe I will see you! But just first, I take a shower.'

A light touch on her shoulder.

'Is okay if I . . . ?'

A boy hovers beside her, gesturing at the seat.

'Ah . . . '

He nods an apology and starts to leave, glancing at the pixelated rooftop on her screen.

'Ah, no! I mean, it's fine. The seat isn't taken.'

He apologizes again for the misunderstanding and sets his laptop beside hers. His smile is polite and unfamiliar. And as he settles, she realizes he is older than she'd first thought, already a graduate. His stubble is deliberate, and his HKU T-shirt clings too tightly to his shoulders. It isn't Kallum, but he looks like someone who Kallum might have wished he could be.

Anna remembers the lunch she hasn't touched since she got here. She peels back the plastic and begins to eat slowly, picking at grains of rice as they fall, and watching the taxis come and go without consequence.

A sharp stab in her gum. The taste of blood mingles with wasabi and ginger. She reaches into her mouth and plucks something hard from the mess: it is wider than a fish bone and flat and transparent. A fragment of glass.

Chapter 6

Weeks after that first lesson, when the tents pitched at Central had shrunk in their numbers and grown in resoluteness to a permanent handful, Kallum had walked Anna to the station after one of Cheuk Yiu's classes. She had resisted, at first, but outside in the darkness, she was grateful for the company.

Cheuk Yiu's English was progressing, but Anna had felt increasingly that the eight-year-old was being stretched too thin. At first, she would be responsive, though a little nervous in her efforts, but, by the end of their lesson, she was more than distracted. It had become even worse since Christine had shifted their lessons to later in the evening, until she'd returned home from work; Anna had the feeling that Christine wanted to be present. But having Christine there made everything harder. By 7.45 p.m., Cheuk Yiu was infuriating. She would claim that she was thirsty or dig the table with her pencil until the lead snapped and she was forced to go and sharpen it. She was the miniature of Claudi; Anna recognized the stubbornness and the shape of her nail beds. She would answer Anna's questions in deliberate Cantonese, smirking, and pretending not to realize the problem; that way, Anna couldn't accuse her of not speaking, but also couldn't challenge her answers. But Anna couldn't blame her, the child must have been exhausted, bored of knowing everything she needed to and nothing that she didn't.

It was a relief to be out of the vacuum of their apartment.

'My little sister's quite stupid, isn't she?' Kallum smirks. 'You think my English is better?'

As they move under a streetlight, Anna sees that he is smiling.

The village is poorly lit, and the February air is cool. They move through the alley between blocks towards the pond. At the edge of the eastern path, they reach the triad houses, two figures on a porch fall silent as they pass. Kallum bristles, and Anna keeps her eyes on the track. They say nothing until the corner, until the houses are well behind them. When the path forks, the route to the station is blocked by construction works, but Kallum lifts up the barrier and ushers her under it, and she follows his direction, hoping the other end is open.

She is right to trust him. They reach the intersection before the station. Tonight, there's no traffic, they could make it across, but they wait at the lights. He doesn't seem to be in any hurry. Anna keeps talking, filling the silence, something tells her he wants to speak, but she's too afraid to let him. She asks him if he knows about the new Sha Tin—Central line, and how much quicker it will be, and says Hong Kong will feel smaller. Kallum listens as she rambles, laughing politely in the gaps. But his thoughts are somewhere else.

When he notices a break in her monologue, he asks, 'What can you say in Cantonese?'

She's embarrassed by the question. She isn't sure if there's a subtext.

'Um . . . I can tell the taxi "lido!" and the bus "par-cee-djam".'

Kallum laughs. 'You say, "Li-do!"' He imitates her accent.

The escalator glows with the warm light of the station. They stand to the side at awkward heights and wait for it to deliver them.

'And at the school, I ask the children, "djo-mae-ahh?"' She hears herself bragging and wishes he would stop her. But he laughs again and says it properly. She's glad she doesn't copy.

'Your Chinese is just a little, but it doesn't matter; you'll never need it.'

As they weave across the atrium, she says that might be true, but that it's arrogant and lazy, that they're too ready to excuse it. Kallum doesn't comment, but Anna is aware of him nodding cautiously beside her, unsure if he agrees or if she wants him to. A vague tension begins to settle, and so she keeps her eyes fixed on the ticket gates ahead and starts to talk about the children at the school: Patrick Phillipe's English and the French from his father, the Filipino accent he's picked up from his mother, Jenny. There's a silence, and she asks Kallum if his helper taught him any.

He doesn't answer.

She glances sideways. Kallum is no longer beside her. She swivels and scans the hall. For a second, he's vanished. Then she spots him behind a cart selling pocket knives. She turns back to join him, and, when he notices, he leaves the cart and starts back towards her. They meet in the middle.

'What are you doing?'

His whole manner is altered. He is shifty and nervous. He looks past her, towards the platforms.

'I think our train is here almost.'

'"Our train"? You're coming with me?'

He glances back towards the stairwell. He shoves her shoulder: 'We have to run.'

They force their way to the turnstiles. Anna fumbles for her card. Kallum has his own card ready, and he hurries her to find it. Once they're through, he rushes forwards, Anna trailing after, and doesn't slow until they reach the end of the platform.

'Too many people.' His voice is strange still, thin with panic.

'It's fine. It isn't even here yet.'

When the train arrives a moment later, the doors slide open, and he relaxes. They sit together on the bench as the station shrinks behind them.

'I thought you were going home again? It will only be girls . . . '

He laughs, 'I have a friend. I go to meet him. We meet in Mong Kok.'

'Is that why Christine is annoyed at you?'

'She doesn't know I'm going.'

They sit in silence until Tai Po Market, where bodies shift to make space. Over the shoulder of a helper, a child resists sleep. The woman's grip is familiar, and, as the carriage rocks, she is sturdy on her feet. With her other hand she grips the pole, balancing their weight over her shopping bags. At University Station, the carriage gradually fills, and a group with bulky instruments crush into the space between the woman and the seats. She shuffles backwards to accommodate the group, as a guitar case nudges into her shopping.

'I didn't see your maid tonight.'

Kallum shrugs.

'Is she on holiday?'

He shakes his head.

'And her day off is Sunday?'

'Can we drop it?'

She says okay.

The carriage bumps as they enter a tunnel, and the neck of the guitar case swings into the maid's shin. The child wriggles on her chest, but stays sleeping.

'She should tell us where she is going.'

'Your maid? Is that why your mother—'

'She wasn't angry! Why do you always think that?'

'The way she snaps. And ignores me.'

'Now, really, let's drop it.'

They rattle through the tunnel, each replaying the conversation and adding their own subtext, resenting the tension, but both too proud to break it. *Anna rechecks the route map above the doors, though she knows every station and every ripple in the rails.*

As they get closer to Mong Kok, Kallum's attitude changes. The agitation returns. His legs start to bounce on the balls of his feet.

'Who were you looking for?'

'When?'

'In the station.'

'You are sounding like my mother.'

They face the TV screen. Kallum reads it. Anna watches. When the news loop ends, the screen fills with adverts.

'You were hiding though. I know you were.'

He snorts, 'I was hiding?'

'From who?'

A ping announces the station, and Kallum nods towards the door; 'Kowloon Tong, you have to change here.'

'Yes, I know.' She stands to leave.

He replaces an earphone and settles back into a sulk, staring at his messages. As the train slows, she grabs the phone.

'What the . . . ?'

'I'm giving you my number. Just in case.'

'For what?'

She doesn't know either, but she hopes he will save it.

Chapter 7

On the morning of National Day 2017, the streets are crammed with bodies. Guest houses are full, queues for elevators twice as long, and red taxis clog junctions with conflicted directions as their passengers bicker. Europeans and Americans kill minutes in coffee shops, Chinese families taking pictures of their peeved Western faces. Loud, nasal chatter annoys her, though she knows that it shouldn't. She tries to make herself patient, and calm, and accepting. It is three years exactly since the protests; teenage locals speak loudly about dates and a pattern, a future in which they have no say and a restricted right to say it. At Tsim Sha Tsui and across the water, people are waiting for fireworks. Anna spends the morning wondering where will be best to watch from. She is still undecided as she waits for the train.

She's staring at the map, weighing Hung Hom against Causeway Bay, when an English voice sounds from behind her in the queue.

'Do you remember that Umbrella Thing? Apparently, there's another—an anniversary march.'

The word jams like a pickaxe in the three-year-wide dam. All morning, she's overlooked the signs, thought nothing of the traffic police gathered at corners.

Admiralty. If anywhere, that's where they'll be.

Anna slips out of the queue and heads back across the platform, back towards the stairs, Carnarvon Road, Exit D. Outside in the drizzle, she crosses back towards the waterfront and follows blue collars to the Star Ferry pier.

Thunder clouds rally. Her father messages 'stay safe' but doesn't tell her not to go.

On the ferry, she sits away from the side with the best views of Central and has the row to herself—a rare moment of breathing space. A thin afternoon sun breaks through a cloud. The light refracts off the surface and choppy waves brighten. It is hotter on her skin than she expects it to be. She closes her eyes and forgets about the rain and the IFC tower that is creeping towards them.

But as the ferry speed dwindles, on cue, the rain starts again. Anna watches fat droplets splash into the ocean, grey and oblivious. If her mother were here now, she'd try to hide her disappointment, counting backwards from the departure date, days of sun before the end. As she waits for the ferry to dock, Anna stands by the railings, and she counts decades in layers of paint on the railings. The '87 rush-out, a fresh coat for '97. But the gloss hasn't taken and is rippled and cracked. She had taught herself the history; omens outside the Great Hall of the People, Basic Law and Declarations, Wong's nattering on Netflix, but she senses something deeper between these layers of enamel. The more Anna read and watched, the less she understood. She runs her thumb across the ridges and picks at a flake. The shard drives itself beneath her nail, and the blood pools.

Her memories of the riots blur into a tapestry of articles and images, a scattering of nylon. An umbrella canopy between bridges that she isn't sure now if she saw. Tessellating octagons cropped, skewed, and brightened, until the pictures in the blog posts replaced the images in her mind.

Despite the brief showers, the sky is still heavy with cloud. She wonders if China will disperse it for the fireworks; she has heard that they can.

She passes the spot where she and Lottie and the others had posed for the picture but decided not to smile. In the photograph, their faces are conflicted, contorted.

The pavement ends and Anna crosses. She remembers this spot.

The girl's eyelids are like slithers of tuna belly. Inverted and spongy, they glisten with pus. Tear tracks are etched in the smudges of her cheeks. Her lips, too, are swollen, and the corners ooze gunge. Speaking seems painful as she peers up from the curb. The boy she is directing is also dressed in black, but his clothes are much fresher. He wears them like armour, self-conscious but proud. But the girl's passion has long since deflated. Though her shoulders are broader than his, they droop forwards. His naivety is draining. Like Anna, he is yet to witness any action.

The rest of his group have dropped their bags beside the girl, but the boy stays standing, bouncing on his trainers, staring after the crowds he is eager to follow as they flock towards Admiralty. It isn't yet clear how much their numbers will thicken; soon, it might be too late to find a spot further in. Anna catches a question repeated over and over. Who attacked first? But the injured girl shakes her head. A dark graze on her forearm creeps out of the bandages and the shadows of footprints are edged on her flesh. Anna winces at a deep gash across her knuckles. But the boy's father remembers Tiananmen, and his son does not want to miss out.

Anna reads the sign that looms over the highway. She
remembers how those letters flashed like white flares. Now, only
drivers take note of them.

Lottie had powered forwards, a 7-Eleven umbrella poking out
of her rucksack. Anna followed, already doubting their resolve.
Lottie was used to getting her way here; it was all she'd ever
known, but Anna suspected that tear gas wouldn't differentiate.
In the end, they would barely even stick out the night.

Anna continues alongside the highway, this time, slick with
traffic. Bumpers plough into spaces where bodies had swarmed.
Anna hears the crunch of gravel too loudly in her ears.

She pauses across from the Bank of America. She takes
out her phone and locates herself on the map. She's exactly
where she'd thought she was, but the space around her is
unfamiliar. On the screen, she hits Street View and watches
her surroundings spring up in miniature, a virtual city of
misaligned still frames.

She strides another few metres, and the map catches up.
Again, she sees the skyscrapers rise as she approaches. She
wanders through the map, watching frames overlap, incongruous
angles captured by a car-cam, stitched together to make the
whole.

Another step, and the screen goes dark. She thinks the
phone has locked itself. But when she tries to unlock it, she
finds the app is still open. Sunlight pollutes the screen. She
shields it with her hand. The Street View map still shows the
road, but in this still frame, it is night-time. It's not an automated
capture, distorted by the fisheye of the driverless streetcar, but
an uploaded photograph, slipped into the sequence. A memory
captured by someone who'd really been here. Someone who
cared about how people saw it, the way he or she remembered
it: tents line the highway in the orange glow of streetlamps,

protesters squat in clusters, 'Occupy' slogans painted on umbrellas. Anna remembers it too. The faces in the image are too grainy to identify. But Anna knows that she is amongst them, still waiting for the morning. It is the highway she always pictures, materialized on the screen, more familiar than the present, and equally as real.

Anna steps backwards and the map becomes daylight. Forwards, and the night scene returns. She isn't imagining it; the map is day-time stitched to night-time, present stitched to past. It is as though she has deposited a tiny piece of her history for anyone to stumble unknowingly into.

In the recess of a wall beside the government complex, she closes the map and opens the search engine: Hong Kong Protests on Street View. The night-time still-frame, complete with coordinates, is mentioned in 26 academic journals.

When she looks up from her phone, the towers around her seem counterfeit. Anna crosses over and wanders the stretch where the protesters had camped, between Hong Kong station and Admiralty. Droplets in the air have begun to whisper to each other, rumours of dissent from the sky. The air has turned violet. It is quiet; people have already scattered to find shelter from the rain.

Towards the IFC tower, she hears shouting in the air; ahead there is a barricade, and she knows the march is nearing. This time will be so much smaller. Three years have curbed their numbers. She will watch from the footbridge, looking down over the highway.

It is here that umbrellas had shielded against tear gas, where, at the whisper of bullets, the crowds became twitchy. Today there will be no masks snapped defiantly over faces, and they'll discuss long-term arrangements where they'd declared last resorts. Now, the space is bisected by oblivious cars, chalk dust still juddering in the cracks.

A curved stairwell leads up to the footbridge that had overlooked the campsite. She remembers its walls lined with tributes on post-its. Anna and Lottie had left messages too, gestures that made them feel welcome and wanted. But, today, the wall is bare but for a stainless steel warning demanding no posting, no graffiti, no hope. The words they spelled out in black tape have peeled away. Grey concrete glows with their absence.

She positions herself in the middle of the footbridge. It is here that the Occupy journalists had been stationed, Canons pointed and impatient for the tension to rupture. In the background of their footage, global banks had glimmered, razor blade giants reflecting the sky. Today, the bridge is almost empty, though the barriers that had divided them from the media remain, pushed back to the edges of the walkway. Anna squeezes through a gap for a better view of the road, and the cold steel makes her shiver. It might be this piece of fencing they carried across a slip road. Or the one they'd flipped over to bridge the central reservation. Two men had helped her cross it. She remembers the sureness of their grip on her wrists, but she can't picture their faces.

Lottie drags her towards the circle of students before she can object, while Lauren and Hope watch from the pavement.

'Admiralty is full. Please go back to Central.' The students and Lottie practice in unison.

Anna glances across at Hope and forces herself to join the students' rehearsal. They receive their instructions and spread themselves across the four lanes, fingertips touching to form a barricade. The crowds are too concentrated. Gas might be used to disperse them.

'Admiralty is full! Please go back to Central!'

Then, she and Lottie stay quiet while the students repeat the message in Cantonese.

'Admiralty is full! Please go back to Central!'

The Cantonese sounds less clunky, surer of its message. Soon, Anna can repeat the syllables. She remembers thinking she'd never forget them.

Each time they repeat it, their plea is more earnest, and soon the crowds begin to dawdle and turn back. Their blockade is working. Signs of success fuel their effort.

'Admiralty is full! Please go back to Central!'

'Admiralty is full! Please go back to Central!'

A sprawling group of expats push through their line. As Anna and the others scramble to fix the breach, she glances sideways. On the side of the highway, Hope is looking smug. The others still seem determined.

Lottie counts down from three in Cantonese.

'Admiralty is full! Please go back to Central!'

But they have fallen out of sync and their message comes out garbled. Now, other small groups who had first listened to their appeal begin to turn back around. Lottie's arms close around a woman like a flytrap.

'Admiralty-is-full!' She yells in her face.

The woman is startled. They stare at one another; each suddenly confronted by the strangeness of the encounter. But then the woman's husband starts to laugh and pulls her free from Lottie's embrace. Lottie deflates. The damage is irreparable.

Anna wanders over.

'No, we should keep going! A little longer at least?' Lottie's voice is hoarse with shouting.

They wait again for their cue.

'Admiralty is full! Please go back to Central!'

But Lottie misses the 'please', so is forced to add an extra syllable to 'Central', and the message gets jumbled.

Their defence is dissolving. From the sound of distant chanting, a larger crowd is descending, and Anna knows they'll never hold them.

The local students know it too and regroup into a circle. She and Lottie hover at the edge, useless without translations.

Their recruiter wanders over. 'You've done a great job. Our message is working. But our friend is saying that now that maybe Central *is full . . . ' Behind her, the leader speaks into a phone. The girl leans closer to share the receiver. '. . . okay, maybe . . . ' she trails off. As they wait for her to listen and translate the message, Anna notices tiny daisies along the wings of her glasses. She couldn't have been more than twelve or thirteen.*

'. . . maybe Central *is full. Now we shout, "Go to Admiralty!"'*

'But we're in Admiralty.'

They drift away into the crowds.

Anna looks down towards the spot where they'd gathered. It is unremarkable as ever, a fraction of a kilometre, measured only by speedometers. The girl had called after them. *Thank you for supporting.* Anna remembers feeling like she'd meant it.

They had tried to sleep in shifts, but damp clothes made it difficult, and journalists had trudged between their pitches throughout the night.

'So, what're we going to say—to defend why we're here.'

But, in the end, no one had asked them, pretending to buff a smear on the lens as they passed.

Chapter 8

Around 10 p.m., they'd begun to gravitate towards the station.

Seated on the curb behind a Circle K, they mull over the weight of the next seven hours. They try not to think about Hope and Lauren, already back in Tai Po. Lottie skims oil from the surface of her instant ramen, and Anna watches the grease weave a track through the gutter, each waiting for the other to admit they've had their fun.

By 11 p.m., they know they've waited too long. Anna checks the time on her phone one last time, then buries it in her rucksack. Between then and the morning, she would rather not know. They trudge back into the open, just in time for the rain.

Many have stayed, and for a while, at least, Anna is reassured by their numbers. Lottie seems to be too. Though the tourists and the expats with lager cans have gone, dependent on the last train, their absence has only strengthened the resolve of those remaining. Their departure has reaffirmed what the rest are beginning to doubt: they are more than merely curious; they have survived that first test: Please stand back from the doors.

They huddle together beneath a canopy of umbrellas and ten-dollar rain macs. She and Lottie hug the group's perimeter, craving the shelter and morale of the centre. Drips from spokes make their backpacks stiff and heavy, soaking through the fabric, spoiling their supplies. Anna stares at her feet.

A sudden pulse of energy. A shoe scuffs Anna's ankle as a surge forces her sideways. She scrambles to keep her footing as the girl she'd crashed into crumples with the collision. She grabs Lottie, who yanks her hand and points up at the multistorey car park that overlooks the highway. The building is in darkness, except for one level, second from the top, now flooded with light. In a second, it is dark again, but the silhouettes linger: a row of figures watching over them, uniformed and ready.

The click of a switch seems to resonate through the night. There is a moment of stillness, the flash still clouding their vision. Then, panic swells.

The figures weren't armed, and then someone else contradicts them. But armed with what it wasn't clear. Only cameras, for sure, though someone else swears to rifles. In this new, thicker darkness, they compare what they saw. As the ripples grow to riptides, disagreements begin to sprout amongst the most convinced and the least convincing. Rumours catch and spread, creeping like the rain through their thin, canvas shoes. When it settles to a drizzle, the group gradually disband, taking their truths to transcribe in damp tents.

She and Lottie say nothing, tuning out the snippets of English the speakers meant for them to overhear. They drift further up the highway, where it rises to a bridge, and find a spot on the slope. They lay polythene first, then sheets of damp cardboard, noting its thinness. Nestled in the curve of an exit lane, they settle, backs against the barrier, just in time for the night.

On the ground to Anna's left, a boy is already asleep, face exposed to the sky. He looks comfortable and peaceful, as though back at home in his bed, confident in his belief there is no need to hide. The blanket tucked around his body is pulled just up to his chest. Hands resting on his stomach, his expression is patient. Anna stares at his face, envious of his commitment, understated and real.

The gym bag beside him lays open to the drizzle. He is stocked up with cookies and milkshakes and corn-snacks and everything his mother has made him promise not to buy. She won't sleep tonight either; her son can't be any older than twelve. If Lottie has noticed that he is a child and is alone, she pretends not to have seen, keeping her attention on the tents down the slope. While she rearranges her polythene, Anna reaches over towards the child and flips his bag shut, shielding his supplies. But nothing about the boy says he needed protecting. Maybe Lottie thinks so too.

Anna remembers wondering if that made her more or less afraid.

The anniversary march is now circling below her. In parallel streams on either side of Harcourt Road, people carry banners. This time, Anna can't read a single slogan; they're pre-printed, high quality, no sign of torn cardboard, but the use of Cantonese is telling; this time they don't anticipate global interest. The international media has tired of Hong Kong's struggle. She watches for several minutes, contemplating joining, remembering the first time.

The second downpour had hit around 11.45 p.m., more purposeful than the first. Hong Kong was used to rain, but, up there on the highway, she and Lottie, and the child had rediscovered its intensity. There was nothing to do but resign themselves to it. The damp had spread quickly.

She remembers feeling envious of the cluster of tents underneath the footbridge, back down the highway. Although, while tents might have sheltered them from drizzle, from their own pitch on the exit lane, they could always make a quick escape. Up there, they'd have been able to get away if they needed to, and they could watch from a distance if the threat became worse than rain.

From there, she could still see the multistorey carpark, the memory of gunmen poised above the highway. The carpark had remained in darkness since the incident, the illuminated gunmen quickly fading into fiction, forgotten too easily by those on the ground. But Anna never doubted that the figures were still up there. As she'd struggled to doze, her thoughts had begun to drift to the officer or soldier who had leaned on the switch.

She thinks of him now, as the march passes below her. For a moment, she feels something like empathy for him, the gravity of his mistake, quickly fixed yet unretractable. The feeling is terror. But then, something much worse begins to seep through her skin, the idea that the reveal might not have been an accident.

Anna sits up, resigning herself to the morning. On the tarmac beside her, Lottie is still pretending she'll get another half an hour, though they both know they haven't slept for that long all night. They knew that they wouldn't, before they'd even tried. Anna could pinpoint the moment of realization, that final announcement. Please stand back from the doors.

In the 5 a.m. light, Anna peers back towards the campers. Their stronghold has endured through the rainstorms and rumours. Over Lottie's dozing figure, her attention is drawn by a gathering at the edge of the highway, protesters peering down at the street below. Last night was chaotic, their movements disorienting, but she has the vague idea that the crowd is staring towards the government building. Others move to join them. Some look weary, some fresh, only just arriving, but whatever is unfolding below the slip road has each of them transfixed. They make her nervous again, and she nudges Lottie awake, so she can feel less alone. Around her, sprawling figures also begin to stir, roused by the feeling that something is about to happen.

By the government building, the police force has assembled. Rows of pale blue shirts at odds with the sky. The officers stare forwards, perpendicular to the road. Later, in close-ups, they'll lick their dry lips and try not to look nervous, though each is aware of the assembly on the highway, their numbers, once again, beginning to rival their own.

There is a tension she has never felt before: a balance between the feeling of duty and consequence, a suspension that neither side is eager to disturb. They'd be content to remain there, frozen like a photograph in a history book, poised above the caption they're writing in their heads. But the pause won't last. In Hong Kong, nothing does. They are hurtling towards a moment, always and knowingly, the almost-mega-city, resentful of timelines.

But this time, the crowd is older, pragmatic, subdued. The anniversary march is steady, monotonous, disappointed. The march heads towards the roundabout and loops back on itself, but each side ignores the other, in denial of the predetermined route.

Poised on the sidelines, a single policeman is watching her peer down from the footbridge. She squeezes back through the barriers and takes the stairs down to the street. She'll watch from the roadside. But Kallum won't be amongst them, that is already clear. At the edge of the crowd, a woman walks alone underneath a black umbrella. As the march reaches the roundabout, the woman dips out of the stream and stands watching, now just a curious observer, as though she hadn't been amongst them only moments before. Her demeanour is reticent. Anna wanders over.

The woman tells her that the march plans to finish at the offices. And that they started at the park. But she offers little else, and Anna has to work harder. Yes, the woman fears for the future, but her voice is empty of emotion. She isn't wholly dismissive, just uninspired by Anna's question, bored with the saturation. Yes, she is hopeful that the young people will solve it. But it's plain to them both that this majority aren't students.

'And will many here oppose the marches? Beijing loyalists?'

'Are you a journalist?'

Anna shakes her head, but this admission only pushes the woman further away.

'Oppose? Only government. Hong Kong government.'

'And at Mong Kok?'

'Perhaps Mong Kok.'

'So, what's the purpose of today? Looking back or moving forwards?'

The woman nods; she has no energy to give her answer to Anna. The demonstration will end soon. Anna's questioning is tedious; it's too late in the day to go back to the beginning.

'I was here at the start of this—in twenty fourteen.'

The woman's expression stays impassive; that wasn't the beginning.

A girl screams. They jump and turn towards the steps. Four officers rush forwards. But the girl has only slipped on the waterlogged tiles. The officers stay close, eager to feel they have a purpose, but the girl's friends dismiss them. The brief excitement fades, and Anna realizes the woman has moved away.

A volunteer distributes leaflets amongst the onlookers, but he leaves Anna out. When he steps back into the march, she follows him. At the other side of the tape, she slips into a character and sidles up to a couple, 'Can I walk with you for a while?' When the man nods, she asks him, 'So, why are you here?'

'We support democracy.'

His accent is international; she feels suddenly underprepared with her questions.

'But what specifically is the message? The outcome of this march.'

'No, message. Perhaps, only change the legislation.'

'They've imprisoned those students,' his wife cuts in, accusingly, 'and the British government acts passively. What are *you* doing here?'

'Just supporting. I was here in 2014.'

An officer makes them wait before they enter the roundabout. There's no resistance from the crowd, they are resigned to this staggering, and the clustering lets journalists exaggerate their numbers. A camera screen picks out a blue umbrella. He snaps and then deletes it, wishing it were yellow. Anna shuffles away from the couple, from the woman's interrogative eyes.

Her attention is drawn to a colonial flag. The long-haired protester who carries it looks crazed. His broad shoulders are strong but still struggle under its weight, weaving a little to keep it upright. As the crowd starts to move again, Anna works her way closer.

'Can I ask you why you carry this flag today?'

His eyes flare: 'Independence! Hong Kong, all!'

Crowds turn and stare. His volatility is out of place, his message counterproductive. Anna has no reply and slinks away. Watching him, now, from the barriers, she notices that other demonstrators give him a wide berth. She feels foolish for choosing him. She is playing at being someone she never was and never could be.

Mong Kok is the real place. Central is for kids.

By the government offices, two amplifiers drown each other out with mixed messages. One calls for resignations, another for the end of authoritarian rule, and both, for the right to be listened to. Most don't. Organizers perch on steps, swapping assurances, estimates of numbers, uploading pictures of their progress and inflating successes. A media crew comes and moves quickly away again.

Anna completes her loop and ends up back at the footbridge, where she climbs the steps and watches from above. On the left of a stage that is waiting for a speaker, yellow messages are chalked. *The Hong Kong spirit will never be imprisoned.* She reads the message through the railings.

A heavy-set man in plain black clothing emerges, underdressed but important. She might have recognized his face from a YouTube documentary, the one she'd shown to her mother around 2014. The man's opening lines are short and punchy, and a chanting proceeds. For just a second, Anna feels it might escalate. But their voices are thin and too few to sustain it, and the chants swell and shrink after two repetitions. The man next to her laughs when Anna joins in the chorus.

'You are doing a study? Did you get what you are looking for?'

'Not quite, but I'm getting closer. Though I don't think I'll find it here.'

'And how *do* you find it—Hong Kong?'

'This time? That's what I'm trying to figure out. Actually, I used to live here . . . ' But the ranting from the platform resumes and the man draws back to listen to it. Umbrellas begin to open as though the speaker has called for it. The lethargic mass blossoms. Then, she notices the rain. Behind her, across the water, dark clouds hang over the Tsim Sha Tsui skyline. The steps of the cultural centre will be filling up with tourists, waving red flags with a cluster of stars. Anna weighs her options on each side of the water. Her phone screen is already flecked with wet rainbows.

The fireworks, that evening, will be more spectacular than ever.

Chapter 9

"Without a country, there is no home." Some people say like this: "China is my country. Hong Kong is my home."'

Anna repeats the phrase in her head. But the translation has dulled the poetry.

'But you don't believe that?' she asks.

'I think they forget to say, "Without a home, you have no country."' He leans forwards against the railings, staring out across the skyline. The visibility is good tonight. 'I agree that Hong Kong is no country just alone. If we believe that, we are ineffective—only noise. We must learning the art of persuasion. To communicate—that is politics. But how can I love a country that try to take away my home?'

He isn't asking, and Anna has even less of an answer.

The ferry slides across the water, dragging her back to Tsim Sha Tsui. The place where they had talked is now a crush of bodies.

Back then, home, to Anna, was a faraway location. Something she only noticed when she resented or missed it.

But still, she could never have made herself a new one, knowing she had another, no matter how distant it felt. Home was something permanent. It came back to her in moments, in the habits she couldn't shake, reflections in shop windows, the way Westerners ignored one another on buses. Hong Kong was a distraction, but it was also a reminder – of the best and the worst of it, of everything she missed. She'd never say she loved her country but only because she'd never had to wonder if she did, or how much she would sacrifice to defend what it represented. Home was still there and still would be when she was ready to accept it. But his question made her wonder.

'How about your maid? Does she call Hong Kong her home now?'

Kallum stiffens.

'We don't talk about politics.'

'Not at all?'

'It won't be good.'

'You think she doesn't agree with you?'

'I tell you already, I never talk to her about it! Why do everyone keep asking?'

He grips the railing and pushes back against it. He's reluctant to leave, but he will, if she makes him. Anna doesn't want to end the evening on another argument.

'Okay, I was only wondering. It's a perspective I never hear . . . '

Kallum looks up. A final warning. She turns the topic back to him and the protests. 'Claudi says you've stopped going.'

'The road is open. You know it.'

'So, it's over?'

'Not over,' he snaps. 'Mong Kok—that is the place now.'

'Does Claudi know? And your mum?'

'She can just say what she wants. And she doesn't know, only suspecting. She try to stop me, but I'm careful. She can't understand it.

She says we can already get what we want, for education and for business, have everything for our future, so better not to change it.'

'You can't really blame her for wanting you safe.'

'We are safe then? For now, right? "Safest place on the planet." Is that what you think? Just let them control it?'

'I never said that. I'm asking.'

'Always asking.'

'I'm trying to listen. I thought that's what you wanted.'

'Who wanted? Me?' He starts to smile, and for a second she feels patronized, but then his face acquires a shyness. 'You really listen—to me?'

She nods. His smile widens, then he decides to be serious. 'Yes. That's what we want. For people to listen.'

'So, will you tell me how it's going then, honestly?' she asks.

He looks back across the water. 'Honestly, we are hopeful, but— actually . . . No, I have said it's very good. Wait, you mean me or the arguments we are doing?'

'Both. You.'

'I am fine.'

'Because I was reading . . . '

'Is a little bit . . . Some people don't like us to protest. They are so skinny-minded . . . And the police don't do a thing. Actually, they are worse than it!'

'Yes, I was reading . . . '

'But it will be worse if . . . We need the business—yes, it's obvious, I can see it—but . . . We need to . . . for the future . . . These people!'

'I get it.' But she can't. 'It's just, did you ever—do you think they will work?' Her question is clumsy. He sneers, as though the answer is obvious.

'Not Central. That whole thing —for kids and for journalists. Mong Kok is the real place. Central is for foreigners.'

The ferry docks. Anna gets off and joins the crowds at the waterfront. It is busy for this time of evening. As the horn sounds its departure, she looks back across the channel; the air is thick with mist and sinking smoke that shrouds the IFC. She jostles with the crowd and moves no further down the queue. Mainlanders ignore it, and so does everybody else. Along the water's edge, the crowds are vast and faceless. No one comes here to be present, just to view the other side.

'Oh, I need to tell you—you forget to take the payment.'

'What?'

'The payment for the lesson.'

Kallum digs in his pocket and hands her four rolled up notes. She takes the money awkwardly, damp where he's been holding it, and she buries it in her jeans without counting.

'400,' he tells her. 'My maid says you just ignore it.'

'No, I just forgot.'

But she hadn't forgotten; Christine hadn't left it.

'So, you are rich then,' he decides. 'I guess you didn't need the money.'

'I was just in a rush.'

He smirks as though he knows otherwise but has decided not to argue, a promise not to tell his mother.

'Other families pay more, right? But you stay to teach my sister—'

'It's convenient, less hassle. And it depends on what you ask for.'

'No hassle. Right, I got it.' But his smile says something extra, like she's just shared a secret.

'I mean it's close to my house.'

His smile fades. 'Close?'

'So, I can walk there.'

She sees a twinge of disappointment. He draws back and tells the pavement, 'So, that's it then. That's the reason. That's only why you still come over.'

She never thought to say, *'It isn't.'*

Mong Kok's magic at night-time is anonymity and chaos. It is a soothing discordance. She moves silently through it. For a while, she is distracted. A puzzle of pavements line

Temple Street Markets with dai pai dongs, hot plates, and gecko flecked strip-lights. Red canvases are stretched over rusty concertinas, tangled with wires, and outdated grimy lettering. The pavements bathe in a hue of turquoise tarpaulin, and, when the food ends, there's the fluorescence of yellow-gold dealerships. In their windows, the statues of Buddhas appear molten, draped in strings of pale jade, laughing at nothing. Tiny workshops, dwarfed by tech shops and exchanges, are squeezed tighter every decade as inflation rates ignore them. Outside a restaurant on the corner, a collapsed fold-out table and three bickering vendors spill into the road. There's a scattering of sui mai and crushed polystyrene, and an overturned kick stool that forecasts a fight.

Anna loses herself in the sweat and commotion, the smell of boiled pork bones, and the rubbery magenta of market-stall dragon fruits. She remembers the first time she'd been here and seen one, and how she'd wondered how to peel it and if it all would be like this. She recalls how, back then, her contentment felt dangerous, a feeling that would linger once the images had faded, something tangible and heavy, a conspicuous presence, like the $400 buried in her pocket. She'd stuffed them in deep, so they wouldn't work themselves free, but her hand still moved to check, after each hasty crossing and every time she turned a corner, that the notes were still there. They had their own gravity, she felt them drawing attention, every gaze she imagined drawn instinctively towards them. She'd curled her fist around the money, as though the city itself might discover and decide that she hadn't the right to have earned it. She didn't care what it could buy her, just the time it represented, a record of the hours, the days she had collected. She had visions of the notes disappearing down a manhole or into a palm around the back of Chung King Mansions. Any minute, she'd reach down and find no evidence she'd been here, beyond the scars of mosquito bites and tan lines. She'd be no different than her mother.

But, this time, she feels the opposite: a presence much darker. It is an absence of attention apart from her own. The feeling is ugly, but it stalks her even closer. She is overlooked and angry at herself as much as at others, ashamed to be craving the attention she once complained about. This time, it feels like she's one step from disappearing, from the present and the past. She can feel her edges fading like mountains into smog.

The stairwell down to the station is swimming-pool blue. The steps are wet from the storm, and she takes the first few steps slowly, fearful of slipping. There's a beeping on the platform; the train doors are closing. She glances ahead of her feet to gauge the distance to the bottom of the stairs as a figure disappears onto the platform just before her. She knows its him in an instant.

Anna bolts down the remaining stairs and pushes through the crowd as they surge towards the carriage, until it's crammed and they slide shut, trapping the remainder on the platform. He couldn't have made it either; he was only just ahead. She begins to push through queues of passengers impatient to board the next one.

She weaves between a couple and a wide collared dress, gains a few metres, then gets stuck behind a pushchair. She squeezes behind a girl into a space that isn't there, crushing someone's cake box against a thigh and afraid to look behind her. Anna swerves around the next line into a crowd below the escalator, scanning faces as she passes, but recognizing no one. Her shoulder jerks. She swings around. The buckle of her bag has snagged on someone's sweatshirt. They both fumble to get free. But by then, the space ahead is blocked entirely. She scans the anonymous faces crushed together from the glass barriers to the wall.

Cantonese, Mandarin, then the English voice sounds over the heads of the crowd: 'The train is arriving. Please stand back from the doors.' It arrives a second later, and they move into the carriage. Anna shifts around the pole. The mass of bodies is impenetrable, crammed up to the window.

A schoolgirl grips the pole just below where she is holding. As Anna cranes her neck for a clearer view, her hand slides down and their fingers gently touch. Both jolt at the contact, a magnetic repulsion, and re-establish the gap, a little wider than before. The girl reddens, and Anna lets her believe it was her fault. Though the girl turns away, the strange intimacy lingers. Anna resents the connection because the girl isn't Kallum, and her stare seems to hold her back as Kallum slips away.

They are approaching the next station. The momentum is draining. She can't guess where he will be heading. Panic rises, she can't lose him. She drops the pole and forces her body into a space. 'Mm-goi. Mm-goi. Excuse me.' Most ignore or don't hear her. She struggles further down the carriage. *The train is arriving. Doors will open on the left.* Though the air inside is stifling, she longs to seal them shut.

The carriage jerks. Bodies shift, and the crowd spills out onto the platform. It is just as busy and just as vacant. His absence fills the spaces.

Chapter 10

A phone alarm sounds from the bookcase beside them. Anna jumps. Cheuk Yiu freezes. Together, they stare at the shelf, where a tent-shape of hardbacks is hiding the device. Its screen pulses, intermittently lighting a blurb. For a moment, the child pretends not to hear it, but she can't keep up the charade, and smirks like she does when Anna knows she is lying. She springs from her chair, scattering pencils that clatter as she scrambles to retrieve them, panic in her fingers. Then, she changes her mind and lurches instead for the phone. It is still vibrating. She holds it flat on her palm, staring at Anna, assessing her reaction, then rushes to the kitchen, flings open the door and slams it behind her. Anna watches through the glass panels.

Cheuk Yiu finds her maid preparing dinner; Christine is working even later than usual. Anna hears the word teacher and a gasp when she sees the phone in Cheuk Yiu's fist. The maid snatches it from her, scrambling to silence the alarm. At that moment, Christine's greeting sounds from the front door. Cheuk Yiu and the maid call back together. Saying nothing to Anna, Christine moves into the kitchen. There's another gasp, a short silence, and a rapid cascade of syllables. Though her words are Cantonese, Anna pieces their meaning together.

On the occasions that Christine wasn't home in time for the lessons, there'd been a longer delay between Anna ringing the doorbell and being let into to the house. She'd assumed that the maid was just caught up in housework and felt sorry to disturb her, to make her come to the door. But now the truth is obvious. Anna should have seen it sooner. While she'd waited outside, the maid was setting up a recorder.

The phone is still flashing. Christine grabs it, jabs a button, and slams it down onto the worktop. Why was the alarm set? But no one can tell her. Cheuk Yiu starts to cry. It isn't hers to play with; now everything is ruined. The maid nudges her towards the door, back to Anna and the lesson. It isn't Cheuk Yiu's fault. She didn't know what she was doing. The maid tells Christine that she's sorry; next time, she'll check carefully. Though they all know it's too late now; Teacher knows they don't trust her. The secret is ringing in their ears: every lesson has been monitored.

Cheuk Yiu returns, a little redder in the face, and sits down cautiously at the table. But Miss Anna is already on her way to the door.

Anna catches herself staring at reflections in a puddle, more vivid than the present. Around her, Wan Chai is bracing itself for the night.

It is always early evening in memories of Wan Chai, the rest fades into darkness and neon-lit smoke. The smoke of tired DJ booths, imported cigarettes and cigars too expensive for the bars they are smoked in. There are bars they only went to between 5 p.m. and 7. And bars they never went to and no one asked why. Bars that reek of stale mop heads and spilled margaritas and happy hours that punters didn't notice had ended, neon names promising no more than they offer. It is busy from 7 in the spaces they could see, and as soon as it is dark in the spaces that stay hidden. They might once have caught a peek as a curtain flapped open, a dull pinkish glow that made them scared to look further. Expats under thirty come for the fun of it, fifty-plus bachelors for anonymity and convenience. Wan Chai is built on reclaimed land but reeks of stability. The punters are impermanent, so nothing ever changes. She laps the block three times in search of somewhere better. Each time she takes a different turn and ends up back where she started.

Dusk 'til Dawn is still quiet. The windows are dark and smeared. Inside, the bar stools are pulled back into the shadows where single men wait for no one in particular. Anna finds a table outside and sends Claudi the address again, half-hoping she won't find it.

As she waits, Anna watches an English banker tell two women *how it is* and pull a waist onto his lap behind the pillar by the doorway. The gutter makes him happy, because when he smells it, he remembers where he isn't. He has a Chang in Carnegie's and another in Typhoon, and saves his waitress's number as 'jessie hongkong'. A bouncer watches his hands.

At the table opposite, a sandalled Australian introduces his wife to a school friend's new woman—*from Manila*. They brag about old times, while the women make slow conversation about the jade markets. The Australian woman tells the story of her morning, about forgetting the exchange rate and offering the vendor $10 for a tea set. She'd spent the rest of the morning wondering exactly how she'd caused offence, until her husband reminded her that she should have offered $100. *Isn't it just like her to forget?* She makes the husband confirm it. It is embarrassing, really, but just too funny not to share. As the Australian woman talks, the other nods at intervals, warmth draining from her smile. The men call the waitress and order two more Tsing Tao's.

' . . . no chance, absolutely no chance,' the husband is saying, '—not in our lifetime. I don't think in *any*.' He sees

Anna looking and lowers his voice. 'Think about it—no point. Military, economy, trade . . . Jinping could invade tomorrow, and by the afternoon, we'd be in China.'

'Oh, I did *adore* Shanghai.' His wife adds, proudly.

'No, I've had many conversations with many friends— local guys, you know—many conversations—over many beers, I might add. Hah. It will flare up again of course, of course it will, there's a taste for it, now. But I can't see it sticking.'

The waitress waits for him to finish and points at the women's empty glasses. The women both shake their heads. When the friend grabs an arse-cheek, the wife looks away.

'Last night, we watched the fireworks,' she suddenly announces, miming explosions. 'The national celebration . . . '

'China day. China day,' her husband interjects.

His friend, who, until now, has been nodding silently at his beer, slurs a jibe about the lightshow and they realize how drunk he is. When the others don't respond, he repeats it louder. The women smile politely at one another.

'Have you been to Shanghai?'

'Shanghai?!' says her husband. 'More like Hong Kong than Hong Kong is, and just think . . . '

'Yes,' says the girlfriend, 'I thought it was beautiful.'

'If you're asking me,' says the drunk man, 'that's what all this is about,' and smiles at the girlfriend, like he's made his point completely. The conversation fades into silence, and no one rushes to fill it. He reaches around the woman's waist and fumbles with the line of her underwear through her dress. Anna hears the elastic snap against her skin.

There's a tap on Anna's shoulder.

'I hope can help you. My English so bad now. What is it I can tell you?'

When Claudi sits down, the Australians look over. Anna orders two beers and makes a comment about how long it's been since they did this.

'We never camed here,' says Claudi.

'I just mean—since I saw you . . . I saw Josephine, yesterday. She says they've moved to Tsuen Wan.'

'Everyone move.'

'You too?'

'Yes. Go to Tsing Yi. Call it Villa Esplanade.'

'Oh wow, to Tsing Yi? That's really far from Cheuk Yiu's school.'

'Mm. Quite.'

'How's she doing?'

They talk for a while about nothing—only students they remember, Miss Lottie, and Lauren, the time Anna's mother came to class. Anna sips her beer too quickly and has to order another when the waitress comes over. The interruption kills the small talk and Claudi's expression alters.

'So, what is it I can tell you?'

But when Anna opens her mouth to speak, Claudi cuts her off.

'I get fat. Do you think it? And what do you want in Hong Kong? Want to buy the trainers? The moon cake? Because I can show you in the place, the best place, if you want it.' Her talk is suddenly rapid. She seems nervous.

'I just wanted to see you,' says Anna, but the lie comes out thin.

'Why?'

'I thought it might be nice.'

'Nice—okay. What are you asking?' Claudi leans across the table. Her smile is still polite, but there's a hint of confrontation.

When Anna shrugs, Claudi sips her beer and puts the bottle in between them. The base screeches on the glass tabletop.

'There is something. But I don't really want to ask it.'

'What? Just say it.'

'What is it you think I did?' Anna tries.

'When?'

'Your sister's lessons. Christine. And your maid.'

'No-thing!' She half sings it.

'Right.'

Claudi smiles as though it's settled and looks around for the waitress being lectured by the Australian. When the new drinks arrive, Anna takes hers and shifts on her stool to face the street. Claudi leaves hers untouched and sits drawing lines in the condensation with her finger, watching the drips pool around its base. Two men cross the street and approach the table next to theirs but hesitate on the threshold, trying to see into the bar. The more hesitant of the two utters something in German and gestures further down the road, but his friend glances at Claudi and they settle.

They might be regulars or tourists—it's impossible to tell. It doesn't matter that they wear tracksuits. They buy a vodka for the waitress who has watched them come in, and Anna sees her deposit the drink behind the bar. When two women arrive to join them, they switch naturally to English. Anna wonders if Claudi can understand their thick accents. The closer of the two tells the other that all Thai women look the same. The other disagrees, though he prefers Indonesians, and waits for the Indonesian girl who just joined them to giggle. She says *yes* to another, and *yes*, for her friend, and *yes*, *it's true Wan Chai is the best of Hong Kong.*

'Is your mum come back this time? Or only in England.' Claudi asks.

'No, it's just me this time. She hated Hong Kong.'

'Yes, I know it.'

'How do you know it?'

Claudi shrugs. 'Only thinking. Very crazy place for the tourists. Very busy, maybe, they don't like the foods.'

'It wasn't that.'

'Not?'

Anna shakes her head.

'So, who replaced me at the school?'

Claudi flinches; she hadn't planned to bring that up.

'Another NET.'

'From the UK?'

'I think it's Poland. You know, I have to tell all the childrens. Very crazy to change it. Why you stop working there?'

Anna looks at her, 'You know why! I couldn't be around your family.'

'My family? Me also?'

'All of you.' There's a silence. 'What was it then? Are you going to tell me?'

'What?'

'Christine. With your sister. What did she think I was teaching her?'

The Australians glance over. Claudi frowns. 'Why you think it?'

'If she didn't trust me, she shouldn't have hired me. I never asked for this, it was your idea! I only taught her what she gave me.' Anna takes another drink, and there's the clink of teeth on glass. 'Did you even check the audio?' Claudi almost says no, her face conflicted between a desire to keep up the lie, to deny the recordings altogether, and the obvious truth. But part of Anna is intrigued by the idea of the family all gathered around the phone, trying to decode the dialogue, Cheuk Yiu cringing at the sound of her own voice in the speaker. Or perhaps they took turns, a week at a time, each responsible for a lesson. 'You were always out, but I worked hard in those lessons, ask your sister. Listen to the audio. Is that it? She thinks I'm lazy?'

'She don't think it! It's just the maid . . . '

'So, you did know then?'

'About nothing! Only thinking.'

'For how long?' But it's no longer a question to which she cares to have the answer. She stands to leave. 'Claudi, you should have told me.'

'No, Anna, *you* should have told *me*.'

Chapter 11

It must have been a few weeks before the 2014 protests. To Anna, Hong Kong was still new, sealed inside its shrink wrap that she longed to peel away. She'd begun to pick at the edges, and once that cover was lifted, there'd be no sticking it back down. Claudi had seemed excited all afternoon and followed Anna to the MTR, though she usually took the bus. As they'd waited on the platform, Anna found out why.

'Ah, Miss Anna? Is it that you do the tutoring?'

Other passengers turn, surprised to see them talking.

'I'm thinking about it. Possibly.'

'Teehee, very naugh-ty. My mummy is asking me.'

'Your mum?'

'For my sister.'

The train arrives, and when the doors slide open, the neat queues either side dissolve into the laissez-faire rush for a seat. They stand together by the doors and brace for departure.

'But can't you teach her English? Or don't you have a brother?'

'Both can. But our mummy want a Ne-et!' She sings the word NET *and the other local teachers giggle. Anna is already used to Claudi's signals, the way she sings the words that really mean something else. 'She want the accent—native accent. English accent—very tricky.'*

Behind her, through the window, Anna spots the lime-white statue who commands the northern bank. The statue guards a monastery that she imagines they'll visit one day. They never do.

'But my sister—she's really is clever. Just needing some help about the speaking.' She giggles, 'so, just thinking maybe you. Our mummy will be very hap-py!'

Doors will open on the left.

Tsing Yi seemed a place for tall secrets. She'd been there only once before, in her first year, accidentally mistaking the station plaza for the outlets at Tung Chung. As her train crosses the bridge, she looks over the teal water, almost luminous wherever patches of industry aren't. The train reaches the island, and they slip into the plaza. *Doors are opening. Please stand back from the doors.*

Out on the platform, she replays Claudi's words—*Call it Villa Esplanade*—and checks the list by the exit. She sees Cheung On Estate, Ching Nga Court, Tierra Verde, Maritime Square, but no Villa Esplanade. Anna begins to wonder if Claudi had pronounced it incorrectly, her plan to find their new apartment feeling increasingly impossible.

She types 'Villa Esplanade?' into the notes in her phone and shows it at the info point.

'Take elevator. First Floor.' He directs her out into the mall.

As Anna passes each shopfront, she imagines the imminent futures of sneakers, of sweatshirts and watches, and the time they will keep.

Claudi said they'd moved here. But Anna can't imagine her and the family here, amongst this. They don't fit with this feeling. Everything is too present and too aware of its newness. On the first floor, she sees another sign for Ville Esplanade that points towards the glass doors and the elevators behind them. And as the signs lead her closer, the whole thing suddenly feels too easy, too simple. She disobeys the sign and heads instead for the waterfront promenade.

Outside, Tsing Yi is a coral reef rising from the ocean, bleached in the sun light. Sand-coloured tower-blocks, looming over shopping malls, are studded with balconies and ten thousand wide windows overlooking the port. Breakfast is backdropped by imports and exports. School photographs on windowsills are framed by slow freight. Though the angle of every window is a fraction different from the next, the same sunlight refracts through the stormproof triple glazing, casting each apartment in the same turquoise hue. As fathers read the news, they watch the same ferrying, wondering, occasionally, what will happen if it ends.

Anna stares up at the storeys of parallel lives, lives that cross on escalators then disentangle behind closed doors, unloading their secrets on dining-room tables. She tries to transplant the family into a shiny new apartment, but they cling to Tai Wo and familiar furniture. Cheuk Yiu's fingers pick the tabletop, as the maid runs a rag over faded mahogany, stirring dust that will resettle in minutes. *No Anna, you should have told me.* She should have asked what Claudi meant, but she was scared to know the answer.

To her left is the bridge that her train had just crossed over, and below it, huge shipping containers are piled in tens, and tens in the thousands. Bright stencils brand their ridges. Evergreen. ShenYang. Evergreen. Capital. Names Anna doesn't recognize but knows she relies upon. Together, their colours form a bright patchwork blanket, stitched together by cranes weaving steel cables. The damp air vibrates with the clatter of cargo ships. In between docks, sandy boulders fringe the border. Fishermen doze, undisturbed by the clangs. Anna traces their fishing lines into the water.

She perches on the steps between two concrete bridges, one for trains, one for traffic. And there's a third in the distance. They remind her of options she knows she won't take. Opposite, a cemetery is chopped into the hillside. Ancestors feast and mock the insatiable living. The afternoon is draining. She is done with dead ends.

Villa Esplanade. She turns her back on the promenade and re-enters the mall. To access the complex, she is directed to an elevator with only one button. A mysterious floor 6. But when the doors swing open, she sees it isn't a floor but a whole outdoor complex, six levels above the water. A short, tunnelled walkway leads towards the tower blocks. When Anna reaches the end of the tunnel, a security guard moves to stop her. Anna smiles as though she knows him, as though a family are expecting her, as though she sees him every day. The bluff works, and she emerges into a horseshoe of apartment blocks. From the edge, she surveys the identical lobbies, trying to settle on a feature, some indicative detail, but each is as likely as the next. She picks a number at random, imagining an attraction, some instinctive draw to the doors of Block 8.

The smell of the foyer makes her uneasy, and as she listens to her footsteps, the dizziness intensifies. She crosses the reception area and jabs the elevator button before she changes her mind. As she waits, she sees the camera blinking down from the corner. The concierge is watching. It is more curiosity than suspicion. She tries to let that knowledge calm her, but if the elevator doesn't arrive soon, she's afraid the balance will shift.

The doors ping and slide open. Inside, the pressure thickens, Anna panics and stabs 5. When the numbers stop climbing and 5 flashes above her, she braces herself to cross paths with a neighbour, but the corridor is empty. She exits left and walks slowly to where the corridor branches, scans both ways, and chooses left again, trying harder and harder to convince herself she's certain. Halfway along it, she feels herself slowing. Soon she'll have to choose a door. She counts backwards in doormats to the end of the line.

She takes a few steps. In the pale, polished tiles, she is suddenly aware of a reflection staring up at her. The face is shadowed and cautious, lurking between storeys. Hong Kong buildings have no fourth level; it is an omen of death. And Anna's faint, inverted figure is trapped inside this nowhere. Bound by superstition, she finds herself suspended, hovering between third and the fifth floor. A sound emerges from a kitchen: the soft thump of cupboard. She freezes outside the door, listening for another. The jingle of a key chain. A magnetic lock crunches. Anna doesn't breathe out until she's safe inside the elevator.

She steps back out into the middle of Ville Esplanade. She won't leave yet, there's still time; she needs somewhere she can watch from. Leaving Block 8 behind her, she searches for a corner, but every space is too exposed, and the evening is thickening. The sky is deep denim. She crosses towards a wall overlooking the harbour. The tiles are still warm; the stale heat makes her shiver. On the opposite shore, a crescent of identical towers grips the rocks. Through their far away windows, Anna counts thousands of evenings beginning.

She turns back towards Esplanade, and for a while, she keeps track of those entering the complex and disappearing into towers as the courtyard darkens. But soon, the footfall dries up.

Disappointment swells. Eventually, she stops looking for him altogether. All around her, glowing beacons hide their faces in palm leaves; her skin and fringed flora are bathed in soft, amber light. But the stillness isn't soothing. Dark clouds and the crickets fill the air with static.

'Teacher!' The woman's shout bounces across the terrace. Anna turns to see Jenny striding towards her. 'Teacher! I thought you leave Hong Kong by now?'

'No, no. Still here!'

'Visiting? Here?' Jenny looks around as though the complex is alien.

'My friend . . . Claudi. My co-teacher at the school. Do you remember her? She's left now.'

Jenny shows no recollection but smiles as though she does. 'Miss Claudi living here? Which building?'

'Actually, I don't know. It's her family really; they're the ones I want to see. I used to tutor Claudi's sister. She tells me they live here now.'

'Ah, you have the lesson?'

'No, no. It's just a visit.'

Jenny frowns. 'Claudi . . . I try to remember her.'

'I used to know their brother too, when they lived in Tai Wo. Actually, they lived near Josephine.'

'Josephine family moved.'

'Yes, she told me.'

'So, she told you?'

'The other day in Fanling.'

'Ah yes, it's too dangerous. That village is bad news.'

Jenny misreads Anna's reticence and nods as though it's old gossip. 'But I never see your Claudi here. You are sure that they move?'

The doors to the block behind them slide open and they both turn, as if expecting her to materialize. Instead, a small child leads a grandfather out onto the tiles. Jenny smiles as the child hops from one square to the next, his grandfather lifting him higher with each jump. A sickly sensation writhes in Anna's stomach, she wants to ask so many questions, but the moment slips away.

'So, you are waiting. She will meet you?'

'We didn't really plan to meet.'

Jenny frowns again, then laughs, placing a hand on Anna's cheek. 'Ay ah, but it is dark now. Maybe you can call?'

'I lost her number, or she changed it. I was just about to leave.'

Jenny looks sad for a moment, then her face suddenly lifts. 'Ah, but no problem—we will search it!'

Before Anna can object, Jenny takes her by the wrist and drags her towards the nearest tower, Block 5, where the concierge is already surveying them from his podium. He leans back as Jenny speaks to him in rapid Cantonese, staring at his computer, unimpressed by Jenny's appeal. Anna picks out *lao si* and sees his eyes flick towards her and resettle on his screen, but she understands nothing more of what Jenny is saying. She is about to suggest they leave it, when, reluctantly, he nods and opens up a database.

'Teacher, Miss Claudi—her name in Chinese?'

'Cheung. But I'm not certain . . . '

'And the full name?'

'I'm not sure.'

Jenny looks disappointed. Then she jumps for her handbag. 'Ah, I have it! Wait a moment.' She takes out her phone and opens Facebook. Panic rises in Anna's chest.

When the concierge types in the name, it returns several results. They scan them together. Yiu-ming. CHEUNG: Block 6. Kwok Lam, CHEUNG: Block 3. Ada, CHEUNG: Block 8. Anna shakes her head at each. Jenny rechecks the spelling on Claudi's profile page.

'She is living with her family? And you know the mother's name?'

'I don't remember,' she lies again.

The concierge jabs irritably at his list. Jenny seizes the mouse and hits search again. They wait, but nothing shifts. The man grunts and Jenny asks him, 'For all the buildings, or only here?'

'All,' he replies in English. Jenny sighs and smacks her lips.

She turns to Anna, 'And you are sure it is here? She said it? *Es-plan-add?*'

'Yes. I should have asked which building. I didn't know it was so big.'

As they move back onto the terrace, Jenny ignores the concierge, making a point not to thank him as he holds open the door. He doesn't respond to Anna's smile as she follows behind. Outside, Jenny looks worriedly at the darkness. 'Do you know where to take the train from?'

But she insists on escorting Anna to the platform anyway.

Chapter 12

The schedule says eight minutes. It is late, the trains infrequent. Without Jenny, she'd have walked faster. She missed the last one by a minute. And she's also managed to commit herself to a trip to Shenzhen. A whole Saturday with Jenny. Anna's mother would have said Jenny was *only being friendly*; that it was *lovely* of her to offer; that perhaps she was *lonely*. But Anna knows how it will go. She doesn't want to spend a weekend gossiping about Josephine and other helpers she's forgotten, rekindling a friendship that never existed. The trip is two days from now; she hopes Jenny will forget.

As Anna listens for the train, she replays the evening, still hanging open where she'd left it, and tries to settle on a meaning. *Ah yes, it's too dangerous.* But something is missing. Her thoughts refuse to convalesce, as though she's writing in a journal she is no longer keeping.

Six minutes. She begins to play out a conversation. She doesn't realize she's doing it until she catches her reflection.

In the barriers by the train tracks, she sees herself frowning, acting out a scene, like she's caught inside fiction.

I'm walking round in circles.

You went to find him?

He isn't here.

But as she listens to the dialogue, she has a feeling she remembers it.

You're giving up? You're going home now?

The familiar words unnerve her, but she can't keep from repeating them, over and over. Three minutes. She replays the soundtrack and feels herself disappearing into the memory. By the time the train arrives, she is going home to the village. She hopes Lottie has forgotten to turn the light off in the stairwell.

In the almost empty carriage, the tunnel darkens the window.

The black screen of a laptop. Anna waits for a connection.

Her mother's face appears suddenly, filling the monitor. She hasn't tested the volume, and a familiar greeting rattles through the speakers. It is something like 'Baby!' Anna wishes she wouldn't. The second word is fragmented, the voice grating and robotic.

Anna's own video appears in the corner. She adjusts her position to show more of the breezeblock. She won't give her mother what she knows she wants to see: sunshine and a balcony, the exotic backdrop she's expecting, even a glimpse of her bedroom. Anna lives here, now. She is content with banality and wants her mother to know it; she needs to show she doesn't need to show off her surroundings.

Another second of blackness, Anna's pale reflection, then her mother appears again, clearer now, and central. She is sorry she missed her earlier; they were in the back garden. It's been gorgeous! *She holds up the laptop to the patio doors. Yes, Anna can see it. And she's got* such colour *on her shoulders. Yes, Anna can tell. Her mother glances down at her chest, tanned*

skin above the vest top, proud of her effort. 'How is it there? Is it sunny?'
She sees her squint at Anna's video.

'I guess so. I've been working.'

'There's this show we've been watching, actually. All about Hong Kong. Well, not about it, but set there. I don't suppose you'll have seen it.'
'No.'

'It's this thriller, CSI thing, but we're not far into the plot. It's really got me so excited!' She counts on her fingers: 'What are we—about three weeks away? It might just finish before I fly. Don't know how truthful it is, though. I might be totally surprised. You're quite far from the city part, aren't you?'

'Mm-hm.'

'On an island? I'm quite glad of that, really.' There's a nervousness in her voice, now. 'It will feel much cooler. Are the streets really like that?'

'Like what? I haven't seen it.' She doesn't correct her about the island.
'I just don't know what to think. I am excited, though. Is it crowded?' But she is bored of the answer before Anna has a chance to speak. 'I suppose it must be. And noisy. Did you say it's sunny there at the moment?'

'Yes—the protest days were glorious.'

'Oh good. That's nice to hear. And can you swim in the sea?'

As they burst from the tunnel, the memory is dwarfed by mountains, black teeth against the navy sky, Anna traces their edges through the light-polluted window, wishing she were beyond them. Other passengers keep their focus inside the train, scrolling through news feeds and featured products they won't buy. She remembers how she'd noticed him, the only person in the carriage staring out at the hillside, like there was nothing he could find on a screen that would content him. It was daylight then, but the MTR was quiet, as quiet as this one. Though, he hadn't seemed to see her. They hadn't spoken for several weeks, and Cheuk Yiu would only shrug when she asked what he was up to.

'Kallum!' She taps his shoulder.

'Oh, hi.' But the surprise in his voice is false. And as she slides up on the seat beside him, he turns further towards the window, shuffling inside the high collar of his jacket.

'How's it going?'

'Fine. Thank you.' He sounds different somehow, thicker, like something is stuck in his throat.

'It's been ages.'

He nods once but still refuses to look at her. She leans forwards to meet his eyeline, and the reason is quickly clear.

'What happened to your face?'

'There's nothing.' He tugs the collar higher.

'Show me! Were you in a fight? We told you to stop.'

He turns suddenly from the window, forcing his face in front of hers. She draws back instinctively.

'Here, can you see it?'

The bridge of his nose is swollen around a gash in the skin. It must have been deep; the wound is healing, clogged with black, but the scab still looks shallow. The bruising has faded to yellow, but the corner of his eye is still bloodshot. When he blinks, the lid is spider-webbed with ruptured capillaries. He grins, baring a cut on the inside of the lip, pierced by a tooth. The split has closed and reopened many times. It widens when he speaks.

'Last weekend.'

'The police . . . ?'

She means has he reported it, but he misunderstands her.

'Nope. Fucking gangster.'

She had read about the clashes. But the stories had ended when she'd folded down the screen.

'We are doing peaceful work. They are not Hong Kong people. We never start the fighting. They only start it. We are peaceful.'

'At Mong Kok?'

He shakes his head, but doesn't correct her.

She remembers how an old man had stared at them across the carriage and how she'd watched his eyes flicker from her face to Kallum's trainers. They were jutting out into the aisle so other passengers had to step around them. She remembers wondering what the old man thought of them, and whether he spoke English. Kallum shifted in his jacket, exposing scratches on his neck. She thought she saw the old man notice, and she wondered if he thought of them as justice.

He slides down lower on the bench, so that a woman on her phone almost trips as she passes. Anna wants to tell him he should move his feet, but he's immune, now, to their glances. The old man listens to Anna's questions and Kallum's mumbled responses: he thought the photographs were fake, too bloody to be trusted. As he talks, Anna notices that one of his front teeth is whiter than the rest, and his tongue keeps sweeping over it like he isn't yet used to the new feeling in his mouth.

She can't say he is a child or that he has no perspective. Anna's knowledge of China comes from skimmed introductions to literature anthologies. But Kallum has grown up inside a footnote. When his parents talk of the future over breakfast, the China Question has a full stop at the end. Instead, she tells him he should stop, that there are more productive ways to get what they want, but when he asks her what they are, Anna finds she can't answer.

'What did your mum say?'

Kallum shrugs. Then he suddenly stops sulking. 'I can tell you something?' He looks intently at her. Anna nods.

'She thinks that we . . . She says we can't . . . ' He waves a finger between them. 'You get my meaning?'

'What?'

But he refuses to explain and slips back into a sulk that lasts all the way to the house.

When they arrive, Christine isn't home. The maid isn't shocked by Kallum's face, so Anna figures she is already used to the sight of it. He pushes past her and goes straight to his room, closing the door behind him. The maid ushers her to the table where Cheuk Yiu is waiting. When Christine returns home from work, she kisses her daughter briefly on the head, barely glancing at Anna, and moves into the kitchen where the maid is cooking dinner.

The maid speaks first, in a soft Cantonese, and then louder when Christine snaps at her, telling her to repeat it. Before she finishes, Christine gasps. She strides from the kitchen to Kallum's door and bangs her palm several times on the panel. His reply is lazy.

She bangs again and shouts something. This time, he doesn't answer. The next thing she shouts makes Cheuk Yiu swivel and stare up at Anna. She smiles nervously and taps the worksheet, but Cheuk Yiu goes on staring.

Christine rattles the door handle. Footsteps bound across the bedroom. A lock clicks. Christine gasps. He yells at her in English to leave him. She hammers on the wall. But whatever she yells next is answered with silence.

She bangs the wall a final time and stalks into her office.

Anna remembers, now, that dull ache in her stomach—like she was equally in trouble. She had felt it again tonight in Tsing Yi when she'd learned that Claudi had lied to her about the address.

That evening, Christine had left the payment on top of the piano.

Chapter 13

In the corner of the carriage, a TV screen natters silently. There is a montage of chaos, shots of aftermath juxtaposed with clashes from the night before. The contrast is stark—flares of orange and a sobering grey. In the evening footage, protesters are divided into two distinct groups: black T-shirts and collars. Police struggle to divide them. She thinks for a minute that the story is breaking, but then a scrolling banner tells her the footage is three years old.

Gloved fists drag umbrellas from the grip of their owners, and stragglers get caught up in the ripples of struggle. Amongst the crowd, a yellow T-shirt snags on a baton, and as he crashes into the barricade, the scarf slips from his mouth, revealing how young he is. She recognizes the film clip from the first time around. Two other men close in, they aren't police—that much is clear. They obscure the boy from the camera, but the cameraman stays focused; a narrative is developing. Back then, Anna couldn't figure it out: what the sides were and whose side she was supposed to be on—the men or the boy's. Anna wonders, three years later, if his resolve has been broken.

She remembers asking Lottie about it on the walk to Mr Wang's. She couldn't do it on the train, surrounded by Lottie's *home friends*, drowning out the audio with their acquired American accents. They were different from Anna and from Hope and from Lauren; Lottie's home friends had grown up here. They understood things about Hong Kong without knowing they understood. Anna watched their confidence as they moved through Hong Kong spaces, half jealous and half fearful that she was more like them than she knew.

At Mr Wang's, they are rude to the lady who serves them, acknowledging her only when beers need fetching and when the plate that she is carrying drips condensation on someone's phone. She is settling the bill for the table next to them, when the skinny girl named Clara calls her over.

'Excuse me!'

Lottie laughs, prematurely.

'Wai?'

'What is this?'

'This chicken.'

Clara pulls a face. The other girls laugh again. As the conversation resumes, Anna watches the waitress's eyes linger on the dish.

Anna wonders if the same waitress will be there tonight and hopes she won't remember, and that the waitress forgot them before she'd cleared away their dishes.

Though it is already dark, Anna isn't ready for dinner yet, and so halfway between Tsim Sha Tsui station and Jordan, she finds the slope that will lead her inside Kowloon Park. It is less of a park and more of a fortress, a stronghold against the madness of the streets. It is a maze of curled pathways and ill-matched imported trees. She finds her feet leading her deeper into the garden. It is a strange time to be here. The paths are eerily quiet, an uneasy interregnum between the evening and the night-time. Beside a few torn up trees, she's surprised to see that the damage from the typhoon is minimal, as though it wouldn't waste its efforts on such a disregarded place.

Somewhere close to the centre, Anna perches on the edge of a low, lit-up flowerbed, listening to cicadas and the buzz of the floodlights overhead. The light in the flowerbed casts a dull yellow monochrome, and she imagines the shadows it will draw from her features. After a minute, a maid passes with a pram. The infant must be sleeping. She steers the child into the dimness, towards the aviary and the ponds. As they disappear, it dawns on her—the woman is the only person in the world who knows she's here. She wonders, if questioned, could she describe Anna's appearance? She glances down at her clothing, envisaging a statement: loose pants, a plain T-shirt; nothing worth noting. Perhaps it would be safer to dress more distinctively.

A rapid clicking makes her jump quickly from the wall. She turns back towards the flowerbed for the source of the sound. It stops abruptly. She listens. It stays quiet. But the silence does little to persuade her to sit down again. She's about to move away when the sound recommences. This time, the light flickers, and the shadows of leaves make the bushes seem to shiver.

A cricket or cicada is writhing on the bulb. It thrashes for a moment, then lies still for another, recovering its strength for the next fruitless struggle. Anna stares at the insect drowning in yellow, like a pupil at the centre of a great, glowing eye.

Another seizure takes over its body. Anna steps back in case it leaps. But the creature can't upright itself, and she can't bring herself to help it. Against the harsh glare, it's spiny body is ghastly, but she can't tear herself away. Something about its helplessness has her transfixed. She's heard somewhere that such insects no longer follow the light; they've grown resistant to the fatal allure of our cities. These artificial moonbeams. But the luck of selection has left this one behind.

Three more quick spasms. The clatter of its wings against the glass makes her shudder. The surface must be scorching, without the mercy of a flame.

Another convulsion, but its strength and will are draining. As she watches, its thrashing steadies to a gentle, rhythmic pulsing. Slowly, it succumbs to the floodlamp's hypnosis.

Anna leans closer. It is almost still now, merely twitching, limbs slowly gyrating as it dies on its back. Her face is inches from its body, the light-gorged silhouette.

A loud pop, and the insect vanishes. She jerks back from the lamp. She snatches her bag from beneath the flowerbed and shakes out the canvas to dislodge any stowaways that might be hiding in the folds.

She moves further through the park, through the network of bridges over shallow green waters, swerving wide to avoid the low hanging branches. She follows the stench of chlorine towards the open-air pools, a vague idea of Austin Road and what she hopes will be an exit. For once, her instinct is correct. But as she turns onto Parkes Street, the yellow light from the park lingers; it clings to her clothing and irritates her skin. All the way to Yau Ma Tei, Anna hears the insect clicking, its fragile wings trying to free themselves, like it is tangled in her hair.

Temple Street is crowded. She slips between two stalls towards the quieter pavement and feels a spiderweb stretch over her face and her body. She recoils, but the web sticks. She thrashes her arms to snap the threads wrapped around her, rubbing at her face, her neck, and her forearms.

But the stickiness won't leave her. The whole length of Shanghai Street, every itch on her skin is the itch of a spider. The scratch of a label makes her skin twitch and prickle.

It was here she'd asked Lottie.

'Those riots at Mong Kok, are they still about the election?'

'Kind of. They're worse though.'

'How do you mean?'

'Triads,' Hope interjects.

'Well, obviously not all of them,' Lottie corrects her. *'They're like business owners, and taxi drivers.'*

'Protesting?' asks Anna.

'Against the protesters.'

'So, these locals are pro-China?'

'Or the government's paying them.'

'Why would they pay triads?'

'Well, it's not confirmed, but it's pretty obvious.'

'It was on the news,' Hope adds, *'something like eight of the people arrested had triad backgrounds. And did you notice that when it kicked off, the police presence was nowhere? They could have shut it down so quickly. Remember Tiananmen?'*

'Why, do you?' Lottie cuts in. Hope stiffens.

'I guess it makes sense,' says Anna, *'the road's been closed for ages. But the protestors—they're students.'*

Lottie nods and slips back into a conversation with her home friends.

Anna reaches the far edge of the markets, where she can't tell if the stalls are opening or just about to close. The Kowloon Government Offices looks unkempt and unforgiving, webbed cameras and white lights on the stark, steel railings. She is looking for Jieshu street, but takes one right turn too many, and ends up back near Nathan Road. Here, she is forced to slow down and weaves impatiently behind sluggish couples who don't notice her on their heels but seem to second guess her movements, drifting to the left and the right to block her path. A space opens up and she surges forwards, but as she does so she realizes that the group in front have only moved to avoid a poster on the pavement. And a banner just beyond it stretched around a table, and other posters on the tabletop, scattered for sale. As Anna steps back behind the group, she glances down at the artwork: the skeleton umbrella she remembers from the footbridge. Yellow tape on black canvas, strung up with guyline. *Did she hear the people sing?* Red guards reimagined: faces of angry boys beneath a red scattered sun. A melting yellow city. Another metre and she is past it.

She has memorized Pitt Street, just after Waterloo Road, but, by Soy Street, she starts to doubt herself again. It's different than before. Perhaps she's missed another turning.

The road ahead is blocked by a truck piled high with scrap metal: scaffold poles and jagged street signs, rusted cages of swing fans, wires coils and dented shutters, fragments of the city ravaged by the storm. This can't be the place: no restaurants, only workshops, the stink of welding and acetone, a paint spillage on the road. *Hong Kong's the safest place on earth.* Lottie's voice reassures her, but another voice she half-remembers reminds her not to trust it.

She ducks into a garage to check the map and re-memorize the street names as quickly as she can. Anna feels a tickle, something crawling between her shoulder blades, but she tells herself she's imagining it; a single bead of sweat or the tip of her ponytail. She looks behind her into the darkness of the garage. A shirtless man is stirring a bucket of emulsion. His presence startles her. He stops stirring and looks up, frowning at the disturbance, as if the pattern of day and night have no bearing on his workhours. She darts out from the awning.

When she's a few shops away, she glances back towards the garage, but the man has gone back to stirring his paint.

Anna walks faster, now, in search of busier streets, and is relieved to see the glow of a 7-Eleven ahead. She steps aside under the awning to reassess her options. When the door is swung open, she feels the blast of the aircon. It chills the sweat on her back, and for a second she relaxes.

The sensation of crawling at the top of her spine; sustained and horizontal.

She reaches back to swat it, and her palm strikes something solid.

There's a crack as the insect's body collides with the pavement. It scuttles back towards her sandal. She's too alarmed to stop the instinct to stamp on its shell.

Chapter 14

From the outside, Mr Wang's looks like any other restaurant. This far out from Mong Kok centre, there is no need for English shopfronts. And no one finds Wang-man's accidentally. Anna knows she is nearing the place when the street-stink of diesel begins to mingle with sesame oil, then fish sauce, then ginger.

Inside, she sits away from the window and is trying to catch the waitress's attention when a figure blocks her view.

'Here agai'?'

Wang-man's face hasn't altered.

'Of course!'

'How lon' stay hah?'

'Two weeks.'

'Two wee' hah? To drin'?'

'Huh?'

'Drin'.' He makes a tipping motion with his hand.

'Ah. Beer. Please.' He laughs at her, then disappears into the back of the restaurant. While she waits, she finds herself watching the street, looking out for the man she wishes she'd forgotten. He'd been there that evening, that night out with Lottie's home friends, though Lottie hadn't seen him and neither had the others.

A shirtless man loitering just outside the doorway. The glow from the awning casts his features in shadow, but Anna fills in the darkness. She recognizes him immediately; the porch and the path, the dim light of Kallum's village. An oily vest is slung over his shoulder and thick burns cover the left side of his torso, from navel to ribcage. As he moves to tuck the vest into the waist band of his shorts, the pale furrows twist and stretch. He puts a cigarette between his lips and leaves it there unlit. His hand is burned too, the knuckles like tight purple knots. A motorbike strapped with boxes mounts the curb behind him. As the driver dismounts, they exchange a single syllable. Hostility seeps through the glass. The shirtless man turns, shooed away by the driver, Anna notices a network of slashes on his back. Above them, a crudely inked octopus climbs the flesh. He starts to leave, but when the delivery disappears into the shop, he looks back at the window, lights the cigarette in his mouth, and a thin string of smoke rises like the dead.

'Bad man,' says a voice. Anna looks up and finds Mr Wang beaming down at her, a beer in each hand. He smacks them down on the table. When she looks back at the window, the figure has vanished.

'Where stay hah?'

'Chungking Mansion.'

He feigns hysterics and grips the table for support.

'Why hah? No hotel?'

'I didn't know it was so bad. I hadn't heard all the stories.' She ignores his performance and orders noodles with black bean.

'More?'

She shakes her head.

'Order more!'

'It's okay, I just come here on my own, this time.

He tuts.

'Hon' Kon' ha? Eng-a-lish. Seeing me hah? Meeting friend?'

'I hope so.'

'Who friend?'

'From Hong Kong when I lived here before—'

'English friend hah?'

'No, he's from Hong Kong. He's someone that I knew when . . . '

But he wanders away before she finishes speaking. He returns with the first of the several dishes she hasn't ordered but knows he will bring: half-steamed, half-fried broccoli, too wet, too much raw garlic, just as she remembers it. He snaps open her Tsing Tao, and Anna chooses a way in.

'Mr Wang, can I ask you . . . on my way here, I walked through these posters—a small group with Occupy . . . you know—with the umbrellas. I went to the anniversary march the other day. But I thought all the rest was over.'

'Yellow umb'ella! You see it? Many studen', p'otesting?'

'Yes, I remember. So, that's all still going?'

'Still going!' He nods rigorously. 'Mong Kok you will see them.'

'You support them?' She hadn't really planned to ask and hopes it isn't an intrusion.

'Suppo't it, suppo't it! Suppo' it. I tell them, "Second floor", when police come, *second floor*! "Here!" I tell, "Second floor, can stay here!" Hiding the s'udent. Can stay hah! Hiding, hiding.'

'But I thought that all ended?—opposition from locals. The roadblocks and everything . . . '

'Support ha! Support! All supporting. Supporting.' His lips are wet with excitement. 'Why?! You asking why, huh?' He scrapes his lips between his teeth. 'Becau' . . . you know China?

Know China is biggest, you know it? On'y following. You know what is China? Can follow. You un'stan' my meaning?'

He doesn't wait for her to answer.

'But Hon' Kon' is people is diff'ren.'

She smiles and nods that she knows it.

'Hah, you know it, you know it. Okay la? You un'stan' my meaning? Can not only follow. Fighting! Fighting!'

'Okay,' she says quickly. But Mr Wang shakes his head. There is something she is missing.

'My speaking not foreign—not En'lis', okay. Can't saying. Not En'lis'. You un'stan' my meaning?' He waves at his throat, 'Not foreign, can' say it.'

Watching his anger turns inwards, Anna suddenly feels guilty, finds him scrambling with the language she has forced him to use. She feels his Cantonese words bubbling, quashed by his knowledge that, if he uses it, Anna won't understand a single word. His cheekbulbs glisten with frustration that makes her wish she'd never spoken.

'When I was here three years ago, I go to the protests.'

'You are? At four thousa' . . . '

'2014?'

A steaming orange dish is placed on her table, and Anna recognizes the waitress who Clara was rude to.

'Did you go? To the protests'

'I here.' He jabs at his feet. 'Only tell them *come here la. Second floor, la.* Cannot only following.'

Anna nods sympathetically, patronizingly, and stops. A minute later, she catches her expression in the mirrored wall. She looks dumb and obliging. She looks like her mother.

There's yellow ahead, a cluster too concentrated to be anything else. Wang-man was right. She'd never realized a colour, so placid and commonplace, could fill her with such distinctive agitation. It was the colour of memories dulled by traffic and apathy. She sees black lettering stamped vertically on fabric, bold and abrasive.

As she nears, Anna thinks she might recognize characters, but she knows that out of context the strokes will be meaningless. She's familiar only with the contrast, dark hieroglyphics that she pretends to understand. Some are translated. The English slogans are cliché, but Anna believes the translators believe them. They are fighting for freedom with kick-stools and chipboard. This cluster is much bigger and angrier than the poster sellers.

Their tables line the pavement, facing the road and shielding shopfronts from the throng of pedestrians. A middle-aged petitioner confronts them; in his dark uniform, he clings like a shadow, catching their heels as they drift between shops. Anna steps from the curb to join the crowd in the road.

She still can't believe she hadn't noticed them sooner. She'd even used the adjacent street-sign to navigate. But she'd missed them entirely, even though the banners block the sign from her view. She tells herself it's because such scenes have ceased to surprise her. She won't let herself admit that she no longer sees the city.

Posters are plastered on the tarmac; cartoons and photographs, tarnished by footprints. She recognizes one, but there's no one here who doesn't. The image is grainy, but those shapes are unmistakable: the man who wouldn't move. Blown-up and repurposed, it's too easy, too obvious. She wonders at the nuance scrawled beneath it in chalk. Kallum would tell her, and he'd tell her the names of the shamed politicians, their pictures bedizened with collars and leashes. She would nod and take care not to linger over mugshots in case he asked her opinion of the latest detainment. He never did.

A man catches her looking at the posters. She switches her gaze to a photograph of an elderly woman in handcuffs. She has the jowls of a grandmother but a politician's poise. Proud but dishevelled, she looks assertive and present, even in chains. Anna isn't sure if the poster is deploring the woman's imprisonment, or a doctored campaign poster imploring her arrest.

Anna glances at the man who is watching her study the photo, wondering at her interest. Her expression feels clumsy as she tries to look neutral. His high backpack says tourist, and he nods like she's one too, like they're in this together. She shrinks from the image he has of her; a Hong Kong first-timer, too late to the rally.

Chapter 15

The transfer at Kowloon Tong is unusually quiet. The shops are empty, ready for closing, their customers already on the final train home, or else in taxis from the station, their faces flecked with grey from the raindrops on windscreens. Anna envies their knowledge that the day is almost over; it will be several hours before she can join them.

Before she'd met Kallum, Anna drifted like paper, looping, directionless, caught in the present. Hong Kong was a single point on a timeline that would pause when she left it, and she never thought about the past. Snippets of history were the temples she photographed and shared to remind others where they were and where she wasn't. But Kallum's Hong Kong was bigger. It went backwards and forwards and was always changing around him. The future he spoke about was outside Anna's framework. When he talked about leaving if Hong Kong became unsafe, there was a sadness she knew was genuine and that showed the shallowness of her own when she said she'd miss the rooftop and the TST skyline.

Anna's future, here, meant counting down to public holidays, visa applications, and visitors from home.

She found her mother wandering panic stricken out of the Arrivals gate; bright curls flattened by the flight.

Anna shuttles her to Crystal Jade, though she says she isn't hungry, and they sit opposite one another, flicking through skinny menus, struggling to compute the third dimension of their faces. Her mother laughs when the waiter misunderstands her English order, a corn soup she barely touches, and again when they go to pay and they've lost her suitcase amongst the stack. Anna helps them to locate it. Her mother is nervous. She doesn't need to be, Anna reassures her. As they leave, she thanks the manager in Cantonese to show her mother that she can.

They drag the case across the Arrivals hall and down the slope towards the buses. At the farthest bus stand from the exit, they wait indefinitely for the one that will take them across the water. She'll be here for three weeks, with a trip to the Philippines to punctuate the third. Anna has left it to her to choose the island—somewhere quiet though, not Manila—and to book their hotel. She'd booked it for the name: The White Chocolate Hills, picturing ripe mangoes, tequila cocktails, soft sand. Hong Kong might be Anna's thing, skyscrapers and street-maps, but her mother knows proper holidays, the kind with loungers and tan lines. She'd been to Turkey in her twenties, and, more recently, Greece, and would spend the next three weeks abiding by her rules for those places; misremembered customs, wondering why they didn't work.

The queue for the bus is littered with luggage, sleep deprived faces, and signs of elsewhere. A young girl clutches a violin case, and the girl's mother looks drained; she despised Guangxi province. And all that wasted tuition.

'They think you're from the mainland if you cut in the line.'

Anna gives her mother the window seat, and as they rattle between the tower blocks of a Lantau estate, her mother announces that she recognizes them from the plane. It was definitely those ones; *she remembers the layout.*

She is too tired to narrate, but her mother has questions. She gives simple answers and watches them expand. No, this is Lantau. It depends on the traffic. No, Lantau isn't China. Yes, Lantau is Hong Kong. *The answers pacify, for a while, until they see a flag in the back window of a car.* Hong Kong is autonomous; One Country, Two Systems. *And her mother says,* 'That's right, yes,' *like she knows but had just forgotten.*

They're silent for a while and Anna becomes aware of a little girl twisting her body on the seat behind them. When their small talk rekindles, Anna realizes that the child is parroting her answers. They turn around and grin at her, and the girl ducks behind her backpack.

'I'm a bit nervous about visiting you at work.'

'Why?'

'Wai?' *the little girl copies.*

'Well, I've met lots of Chinese students through my work but I've never . . . I've always wondered . . . They're always lovely and pleasant but I've just never . . . will they mind my being there? Will you tell me if they say anything after I'm gone?'

'Gone!' *the girl echoes.*

'Like what?'

'I don't know. It's complicated, isn't it. I remembered what you said about being blonde in your interview.' *She points to her hair,* 'I've just dyed it again, actually.'

'Seriously? Just to come here.'

'No, not really.' *But Anna knows it's no coincidence.*

Her mother turns to say 'hello' *to the little girl behind them. The fourth time she says it, she gets a reply.*

'How gorgeous!' *She turns to Anna, still beaming,* 'So, your lessons, do you follow a curriculum?'

'Of course, there's a curriculum—British council, I think.'

'So, China isn't in control, then?'

'What?'

'Control,' *the girl drawls. Their laughter ends the conversation. And they don't speak again until it's time to change buses.*

In the queue for the final bus, her mother watches an old woman filing her nails.

'Mainland?' *Her mother mouths.*

Anna shakes her head.

She watches her mother study the woman's handbag, squinting for the detail that Anna isn't sure exists.

'How do you know, though?' *Her mother will ask later, in private.* 'We never heard her speak.'

Anna just knows; she can't explain it.

But increasingly, she found herself believing in that difference, frowning at suitcases, shoeprints on toilet seats. She knows it is reductive, but feels a pressure to believe it. She might have learned it from what Claudi called the student from Shenzhen.

Outside the entrance to the station, an old man selling lychees and Fuji apples yells, 'Gwai poh.'

'How lovely,' *smiles her mother,* 'he's saying goodbye.'

Her mother had celebrated her arrival in her own way, chewing over the topography. It was a voiceless *Anna look!* or it was *vast* or *amazing*. She even coined a few of her own. *Joss-sticky* meant heavy incense, and *shrine-type-things*: any structures with enamelling. Several were dotted around Anna's village. But amidst the superlatives, the encompassing favourite was *unreal*, which meant simply:, '*I have never been anywhere like here before.*'

At the entrance to Anna's village, drain water gurgled over rubble from the roadworks, gathering in gutters, leaking foul smelling puddles. As they skirted the overflow, Anna studied her mother's expression that kept shifting to match her own. If something caught Anna's eye, her mother mirrored her intrigue. If Anna looked drained, she was allowed to be too.

Their heels crunch dried concrete on the temporary drain cover, as she leads her past the hatch where the Doberman keeps watch and where his owner reclined in the deckchair until dusk. By now it is dark, and mosquitos rule the stillness. By the end, her mother will find them unbearable.

'It's all owned by triads,' says Anna, as they pass the empty deckchair.

'Like the mafia?'

'But they won't cause a problem if you don't.'

Hope had told her that. Everyone knows. Most properties are. The red minibus drivers—that's why they only take change.

But soon she had settled, and her mother's fascination became irritating. Peals of delight made Anna snappy and resentful of the details that had ceased to excite her. And more than that, Anna was starting to feel like the tourist, having features pointed out to her, like she otherwise wouldn't have noticed them. The everyday litter that Anna had been drowning in, her mother acknowledged to existence. She spoke it to life. It was as though, before she came here, Anna's life had been flat, a trickle through rubble. *Aren't the train maps a mystery?*

'On-ly change, lah!'

Her mother is trying to jam notes into the coin box.

She mutters, 'Why didn't you tell me?' as they pull out into the road. Anna sees her eyeballing the figurines on his dashboard and sees more words forming like quaint *and* authentic. *She will file them in her mind to be shared amongst colleagues once she is safely back in a world she understands.*

She doesn't like the rattling and the noisy suspension and that the doors bang open before they have even stopped. Anna knows this because she hadn't either. With each clang her mother forces a laugh. So funny, so different from home. *And she doesn't like the speed. Sliding to the edge of the grey plastic, she asks silently* is he allowed to go this fast? *When they emerge from the station into the middle of the Tai Po Market, her mother's mouth opens wider.*

'This place is bizarre!'

Anna feigns ignorance. 'We can go somewhere else—if you think it's too much.'

'No! I want to see these markets . . . '

She follows Anna across a junction.

'So, is this where these protests were?'

'No.'

'Where were you then, Tai Pow?'

'Tai Po,' she corrects her, 'and this is Tai Po Market. And no, we were on the Island, at Central—well, Admiralty.'

'Ah, that's right,' says her mother, like she understands the distinction. 'So, were these ones about something different? I was reading something about the people from across the border coming here, bringing suitcases and exporting goods—something about taxes. And local people were quite rude to them. I think they really were quite violent . . . *'*

Anna yanks her mother out of the way of a wheelbarrow, piled high with oil drums strapped precariously together, and the vendor who pushes it clucks in anger.

'Woops!' she calls after him. 'Sorry!'

'No, there weren't any protests here. Don't know where you've heard that from.'

'. . . I would have moved if he'd said excuse me.*'*

Anna leads her, taking the long way, avoiding The King's Belly, where the girls sometimes go for imported British cider, and sees her mother double-glance at a brown-robed figure sitting cross legged on the pavement. A wooden bowl is resting in his lap, out of the way of clumsy pedestrians. Soon, they will walk past him, and Anna knows that her mother will stop to give him something, and not yet familiar with the currency, will give more than she intends. Then realizing that, yes, it was more than she had thought, she will shrug and say 'Ah well' to convince herself that she won't miss it, and only later, peer nervously into her purse. That would have been more than Anna could bear.

'Real monks don't beg,' Anna intervenes.

How does she know that?

She thinks for a second. Someone had told her.

But in the space that followed, Anna too begins to question. She had believed it straight away, without challenge, committing it to memory for future use. Repeated out loud, it sounded ridiculous.

Real monks don't beg. *And Anna had lapped it up. Though it might have been true, she is ashamed to have dispensed it without first checking her facts. But she insists, her mother listens, and she insists on it again. She cannot lose on this detail; it is such an insight.*

Anna realizes now that she still has not checked and probably never will. She can only hope it is true because, in the end, she gave him nothing and, on her advice, neither did her mother.

As Anna retraces Lam Kam Road, the Tupperware and fan shops, chiropractitioners, and glistening ducks hanging from their necks above counters, she remembers how her mother had surveyed a dispensary, dried medicines in screw-jars.

Enticed by the prickle of aniseed and ginseng, she peers over a tray of what look like dried apricots.

'It's not fruit, mum, it's medicine.'

'I know. I'm just looking.' She pokes a tray of dried fish maw. 'Could almost be human.'

'Might be.'

'Anna, don't take the piss.'

The shade is too hot, and the sunlight is searing. Exhaust fumes make it hotter. The air smells like steamed dough, cigarettes, and warm litter, then a stench like hot tar where a worker re-paints yellow markings on the road. A circular saw hiss merges with chatter. They cross the street to a public square with a garden in the middle, raised on a platform with benches around the edges and a fountain that teases them with its splashes. They find a bench below a banyan tree. Through the railings behind them, an old woman stacks cardboard and shouts across to another, who sweeps leaves into a bag.

'That's what will stick in my mind,' says her mother, 'old people working so hard for so little. Can you imagine? You'd never get that at home.'

'That's what you get without social security.' Hope had said that once, and Anna liked the way it sounded. Her mother likes it too, and will repeat it later as though the words are her own.

Domestic maids tuck their legs up on benches in the shade of a pagoda, staring sleepily at phones until 3:25 p.m. Her mother tries to copy their position but can't make herself comfortable. An old man sitting opposite is watching her struggle.

'I wonder why they find us so fascinating,' she says aloud. Anna wants to tell her that they don't, that no one is looking, that she's imagining their interest, but knows her mother will only try harder to catch someone's eye.

The old woman sweeping leaves is losing her battle. Two builders drink cans of lager and point to a bundle that she's missed. When the breeze dies, they realize the heat of the sun. Anna is about to suggest they move on, when a figure on the street at the far side of the square catches her eye. He is moving through the crowds, much faster than those around him, his body fixed with purpose. He's not close enough yet for Anna to pick out his features, but something about him holds her attention. He passes behind a cluster of trees and she loses him. Her mother hasn't noticed and is eyeballing a grandmother. 'I do wonder what they're thinking.' *But then the figure re-emerges. Anna picks out the grey vest, smeared with dark oil.*

He sidesteps a cart piled high with trash bags and rounds the corner, navigating the crowded pavement faster than seems possible from up here in the garden. He is moving in their direction, and something about his speed sets a nervousness in Anna's stomach, like he exists in a separate dimension, a tape on fast-forward. He is closer now. Sharp cheekbones and a cigarette between his lips. There is something familiar, but Anna can't place it.

Their eyes meet across the garden. An instant later, she knows him.

Anna grabs their bags and sets off in the opposite direction, her mother trailing after her.

When they reach the other side, they duck into a fruit shop. Anna glances back towards the corner beyond the bench where they were sitting before; the leaf-sweepers are still there, but the man has vanished. Anna checks her app; they're almost at Heung Sze Wui Street. They can rest again there, she promises. It will be cooler inside.

They move faster now, her mother spurred by the prospect of shade. She follows Anna's sudden turnings and impulsive redirections, unsettled by her constant backwards glances. They aren't lost, Anna reassures her, and she's too disoriented to argue. Finally, they run out of back streets and are forced to re-join the main road. It really isn't much further. At the crossing, Anna nudges to the front of the waiting crowd. She turns and scans the pavements. They seem to have lost him. But still, she doesn't settle until they're deep inside the market.

Three years later, she approaches the entrance to the market, but this time something keeps her from going inside. Something more than the stench of warm butchery and fish guts. No one pays her any attention, but that same apprehension seems to emanate from the dimness. She glances back once towards the crossing as she had done then, the feeling of being followed lurking in the crowd.

At the far side of the entrance, on the steps by the interchange, a group of drivers eat from Styrofoam: char sui and scallions and something Lottie had called *syun*. Anna scans their fingers as they manipulate the chopsticks, searching for scars. The figure who had followed her that day isn't amongst them. She can't picture his face but would know him on sight.

Anna watches their habits, their purpose-built perches—
stacks of cardboard and oil drums—their indifference to their
surroundings indicates routine. The idea unsettles her; maybe
some things *haven't* changed. It is misty and overcast, the
landscape sketchy and pastel. It is almost midday. Had it been
midday then? Any second, he might emerge from the market
hall behind her, a hand over her mouth, twisted flesh against
her lips. Instinctively, she turns. She is suddenly exposed.
The market is a labyrinth of possibilities and traps.

She moves quickly from the entrance, past the huddle of
drivers and the smell of charred pork, and doubles back towards
the station. Until that day with her mother, he'd only seen her
once before, in the porch light that evening as Kallum walked
her through the village. But no, that isn't right, that night outside
Wang-man's, he had known her then too. She is sure of it,
now. He'd recognized her, as she had him, and she feels he'd
know her still. She'd been away for three years, but time here is
different, a familiar lagging, faces have a way of sticking. While
Hong Kong Island remembers, Tai Po had never changed. He'd
remember her now because he'd never forgotten, because no
time had really passed.

As she approaches the station, a woman in an oversized
T-shirt emerges from the underpass, watching her feet and
chatting into a phone. Her pace is lazy, and her flip-flops scrape
the ground as she strides, an overstuffed carrier bag hanging
from her elbow. When she gets closer, Anna recognizes a
Filipino accent.

'Ahh, haha, yes! Sun-day! No, no. You can show me . . . Aha,
you can, you can.' She trills into the phone.

A few paces away, she still hasn't looked up and drifts
unconsciously towards her. Anna moves to the side, but the
woman still hasn't noticed. They get closer and closer, Anna

swerving to stop their paths from converging. Just before they collide, the maid suddenly looks up. Their gazes meet for just a second, but there's no mistaking her face.

Anna pulls away quickly and concentrates on the tunnel ahead, but behind her, the scraping of flip-flops has paused.

Claudi hadn't just lied about the new address at Tsing Yi. The family had never moved. They are still here in Tai Po.

Chapter 16

Her mother wanted adventure. She just didn't want to walk. She had *told her that earlier. Anna promises it isn't far.*

Bride's Pool was just a bus ride from the front of Anna's village, which was good, because her mother asked for a rest from the MTR. It is a series of shallow ponds, linked together by waterfalls, and undulating paths that trace loops around boulders.

The gateway to the Bride's Pool is up the hill from where the bus stopped. It is short but very steep, and already her mother is too hot and getting flustered.

This is nothing—Anna tells her—with the girls, they hike much further, but Anna says that she is sorry; she hadn't realized how much her mother would struggle.

On the rocks beside a shallow pool, a family spend their afternoon in the shade of umbrellas. The women wear long sleeves and headscarves and shield their skin from the rays. Anna sees her mother see them and braces for a question about their religion, but this time she says nothing. She knows her daughter is already planning her reply, already twisting her words into things she didn't say. So this time, she won't say them. Instead, she asks, 'It almost feels like a waste of this weather, don't you think?'

Anna knows what she means but frowns as though she doesn't.

'I mean, to stay all covered up.'

'Not really,' says Anna. 'You're obsessed with the sun. And besides, it's the one day of the week they get to wear them.'

She drops the comment casually, like she herself hadn't only heard it the week before, when Hope told them some employers ban their maids from wearing veils. Anna thought it sounded cruel, but perhaps there was a reason. Though she couldn't think of one herself.

'Really?' Asks her mother, surprised but willing to believe it. 'I hadn't even thought. But I can see them being like that.'

'Who being like what?'

'I didn't mean it that way. You said . . . I'm just repeating.'

Her mother was craving an *honest conversation*, the kind she'd call *real-world*, filled with *the-things-you-shouldn't-say*. But Anna wouldn't let her; she couldn't breathe without a backlash, every observation questioned, sometimes before she'd even registered what she'd seen. It wasn't that Anna thought it would make any real difference, but because language was a game that she was becoming used to playing. They all were: Hope and Lottie, even Lauren. Sometimes, she played against herself. And it felt good, for once, to know she had the better chance of winning. At the time, Anna believed it was her mother she was critiquing, but now she hears herself deride the thoughts that she was scared of having.

Her phrasing was contrived, the silences deliberate. Her voice sounded lofty and her accent unnatural. It was the voice she used in interviews for jobs she resented needing, with strangers at boarding gates, and in exchanges with Wang-man to help him understand her. She used it with herself when she rationalized being here, in her thoughts about the helpers, and with Kallum on the bad days. She didn't use it among the girls because they shared the same subtext: the swamp, wide classroom windows, sideway glances at bus stops. But around her mother, she couldn't help it. It was a way to show their difference. They were not the same as one another; she was no longer her old self. Anna had grown a new surface, and she was careful to show it: a barrier between them, a skin-deep resistance.

Her mother has exhausted all the questions she can think of. Another springs to mind, but she'll save that one for later.

Soon, Anna gets a feeling that her mother is waiting for the adventure to be over. A little under two hours, but she is ready for an ending. They take the shortest circuit through the remainder of the pools: an escape route for the heat-sick and the over-ambitious. Anna feigns annoyance and says it's fine *to show it isn't. Though, in truth, she craves the same relief from the humidity and silence.*

Her mother points at a ribbon tied to one of the branches; it is yellow, and Anna tells her it is left here from the protests. That surprises her; she'd assumed it was just to mark the direction. But Anna shakes her head, the path is obvious; they don't need them.

She'd told her mother about hikes that ended at beaches, private coves that no one knew about, deserted in the winter, where the owner of the barbeques would be happy to host them. Her mother pretended to consider it, then said she'd leave it to the girls.

There was one where Hope had told them about a boat that they could call for, to take them back towards the taxis. But they'd arrived at the bay too late, and the boat was locked-up out of season.

The girls gaze longingly towards the dinghy. Their calves are still twitching from the rocky descent. Lauren blames Lottie, and Lottie blames the boatman. And Hope insists she never promised that the boat place would be open.

Down here on the sand, the mountains look even steeper, and the dimness is already gnawing at their edges. But they can do it, they will make it—Anna tells them over and over—they can't stay here and turning back will take longer, they'll be home in two hours. But the owner of the barbeques says nothing—he doesn't need to—they have forty-five minutes until the path will be entirely in darkness.

They choose forwards, and this time they don't stop to take pictures, barely glancing at the landscape through gaps in the foliage. To the right of the road, the hillside is lined with plastic, holding back the rubble. The left is bordered by trees, sheer cliffs just beyond them. The slate sea is unremarkable, deep greens turned to black, and the pale, anaemic sand would feel cold if she could touch it. They climb steadily around the hillside, Lottie up ahead, scouting for the signposts that will only confuse them, and Lauren trailing behind.

They aren't lost; Hong Kong trails are finite and numbered, the routes all connected, every junction plotted. The island won't lose them, but it won't guide them, either. They just need to keep walking; it doesn't matter if they trust it.

Lottie seems to have abandoned them and wants them to know it, but before long, she'll get bored and double back to remind them. Anna rests at a milestone to give Lauren a chance to catch up, listening to the breakers and Lauren's steady footfall. There is a gap in the barrier by the trees and beyond it a clearing, where a boulder buried deep into the hillside forms a platform. Anna wants to see the sea again before they lose the light completely. She squeezes through the gap, and edges out onto the boulder. She peers down into the crevice.

Scattered amongst the rocks, there are patches of colour, yellows and reds in surprise little clusters. At first she thinks they are seaweed, torn up and tossed together, but their shapes are too regular. Then she puts on her sunglasses and they come into focus: a tideline of litter. Bottle top blues glow like washed pebbles and pearls of polystyrene mix with the shingle. Tucked away from the breakers that claw at the border, they cling to the island, refusing to be taken; they have a right to belong here.

'Has Lottie gone ahead?'

'She'll wait.'

Lauren joins her on the edge. 'Do you know how far?' *She scans the sky.*

'Lottie or the taxis? It won't take long to catch her.'

But Lauren shrugs and stays put. All day she has kept her distance. Now, Anna suddenly understands. She wants to talk to her alone.

They stare out across the bay together, watching the night thicken. There is a feeling of connection, neither of them eager to break it.

'You'd never picture this, would you? Before we came here?'

Anna guesses not.

'Like, I'd only think of China.'

'I never really thought of much.'

It's not the answer Lauren hoped for. She goes quiet again, thinking. But as the quiet stretches longer, and Anna can't bear the itch.

'But yeah, I guess you're right. I didn't picture coast.'

'It's like a secret.'

'Besides this,' *she points down towards the litter, but Lauren's mind is somewhere else.*

'Do you think Lottie takes it all for granted? Like she doesn't notice where she lives.'

'I guess no one does completely.'

'True, but here, I think, it's worse.'

Lauren tells her how she wishes she'd stayed longer at the protests. In a way. Now they're over. And now she knows it's too late. It's just— didn't Anna feel weird being there? Like they were getting in the way. Like it wasn't their place. It isn't fair what they are doing, trying to take all this away. And she knows it will still be here, but it won't be the same. She says she feels like a hypocrite, sometimes, always saying that she loves it, but kind of taking advantage, and doing nothing to defend it. She thinks part of it is knowing that she'll be home before it changes. It would be different if here was *home. She doesn't know how Lottie can stand it. 'I mean, she couldn't at the start, right? But then she seemed to lose interest.'*

'No. She was really only playing.' We both were, *she wants to add. 'I think she just got bored of going.'*

Lauren starts to speak and then changes her mind. Instead, she waves towards the path and asks, 'Is that what this is all about?'

'What's "this"?'

'You and Lottie.'

'I mean, I think she's just impatient. You know she doesn't like waiting.' But they both know that this isn't what Lauren is asking. She doesn't mean today. There's been a tension between Lottie and Anna for weeks, but she is hesitant to go there. Together, they stare down at the cove of sun-bleached plastic, nets relieved of fishes, and the rusted rods that snagged them.

'There's no hostility on my part,' says Anna.

'But why would there be?'

'Exactly.'

'I think Lottie thinks there is, though.'

'No, she doesn't. She just likes drama.'

'So, she's wrong?

'You're really asking that? He's Claudi's little brother.'

'I know,' says Lauren.

'Good, I'm glad.'

'Because whatever you're doing—it can only end in disaster.'

Chapter 17

A cry outside the window, too raw to be human. Anna freezes. It ends abruptly, but she hasn't imagined it.

The second cry is louder. Clearly feline, now. A youngster. Its voice is shrill and urgent. There is danger, it can feel it. From the centre of the room, Anna looks over at the window, but her feet won't take her closer. She stands fixed between boxes, arms stacked with linen. In the next room, Anna hears an empty suitcase unzipping. Lottie will have heard it too, but pretends to ignore it.

The third cry drains to a howl, gentle and uncertain, a low undulation. Then silence trails after. It is watching now, waiting. The pack assess the kitten's movements; they must be cautious now and patient. Any rashness and it will scarper.

But Anna knows that it doesn't. She's learned already what is coming; any second now, she'll hear it.

The fourth cry is more aggressive; an articulated warning, learned from its mother. The kitten is nervous. Anna can hear it. The dogs can hear it too. For now, they keep their distance. They are patient. Anna feels complicit, knowing soon they'll come to claim it.

Next door, the shuffling stops; Lottie is listening for a snarl. Together, they wait for sounds that they are terrified of hearing. The walls are thin in the summer heat; they can keep nothing from them. Anna listens as the stalemate. She only wants it to be over.

A snarl like fractured plastic. A throat fills with saliva. The cat replies, and there's a whining sound that could have come from either. A hiss and a snap. This time, teeth make contact. Yellowed canines graze a shoulder blade as it grips below the armpit. The cry is rapid now, frantic. Too startled still for agony. It will come though, Anna knows. She wants to speed up time and end it.

The second dog approaches and the alpha growls a warning. The threat mingles with the shrill meows. Then strong jaws begin to shake it. They drag the kitten to the wall, and Anna hears the screams come closer. The snout digs into the rib cage, pinning the body in the gutter. There's a chattering as the dog adjusts its grip around a sternum. The cat is calmer now, whimpering. She hopes its mother can't hear it, that she's far away, hunting.

The dogs scarper. Something has spooked them. Dew claws click against the tiling. Anna traces them to the open gate. Then Lottie is behind her. From the doorway, she looks around at Anna's boxes of bedding and piles of clothing that she will never get around to packing. Her eyes find the sleeve of a sweater she'd once loaned her, but she doesn't really see it. A different scene is replaying. Avoiding the window, she crosses the threshold, something she hasn't done for weeks. It is like she has forgotten. Anna watches from the corner as Lottie moves to the bed, to a space between two cases, and perches on the edge. Her lips are parted like she wants to speak, but in the end she says nothing.

It's quiet outside now. Anna moves to the window, afraid to look through it. Lottie doesn't tell her not to. She peers through the fly screen. The dogs have gone. It seems safe. Though she knows that it's too late and going out there will confirm it. There's no sign of any kitten.

Perhaps they have dragged it. Her heart stops as she realizes they might not have killed it.

They dawdle in Anna's bedroom, half hoping that someone else will find it, a neighbour home early, so they won't have to face it. But no one comes, so they force themselves out of the apartment. She follows Lottie down the stairwell, and they hover outside the building. It isn't clear who left the gate unlocked, and Anna's glad they don't debate it. Blame and speculation won't make them feel better. Anna waits by their front door while Lottie goes to shut the gate. It clangs, and Lottie turns and strides back towards her. Still not meeting Anna's eye, she storms past towards the corner, pauses, then disappears around the side of the building. Anna hesitates, debating whether Lottie means for her to follow.

At first, she doesn't see it; Lottie is crouching on the patio, a few metres from Anna's window. She moves slowly towards them, wishing she didn't have to.

Its fur is pale like the tiles, off-white, almost yellow, and it lies on its side, paws stretched forwards together. It is facing away, and from this side there's no damage, though its body looks weary, like it knows it is broken. Its soft tail is curled around its hind legs, the tip peeping in between them. Lottie reaches to touch it and immediately recoils. A stomach or a liver—she can't tell from the colour, but the shapes are familiar, perfect, and painful. Like secrets, they spill out onto the tiles, their glossy sheen already drying, the membranes brown and crusted. Their lustre is fading, turning waxy in the dust. The flies will soon find it, and while it's wounds will never heal, Anna knows they need to move it.

Lottie's eyes don't linger on the wound. She can't look or chooses not to. She catches Anna's gaze but can't bring herself to hold it. Instead, she begins to search the patio for something to contain it, something they can close it in and lock it away forever. They see the cardboard crate together. Anna goes to retrieve it, cautious, expecting spiders, hesitant to touch it, but

Lottie is braver. She reaches inside the layers and folds down the bottom, testing the weight it will hold with her palm.

They squat down and Lottie lines up the box beside the body, slides a palm beneath its ribs and takes its hind legs in the other. Her hands are steady, as though she's used to this. Her face is stoic and unflinching as she lowers the body into the coffin. Anna can't stand it. How can she be so unfeeling?

Will they bury it? Anna wonders. Should they ask for permission? They don't know who owns the land or what they'll say if someone sees them. Or how deep to dig the pit, or if the cat has an owner. She looks briefly for a shovel and is relieved when she doesn't find one.

At the same time, they stand up and draw back from the bushes, then wander vaguely towards the path to put the village behind them. It isn't right to keep it here, two feet below its place of suffering, disturbed by burst drainpipes and shovels that will uncover them. No, they need somewhere quiet, somewhere out of the sun.

The fence beside the path is still torn as Anna passes, the hole is stretched a little wider. She's heard reports of wild boars here, though the girls had never seen one.

If the box was getting heavy, Lottie didn't show it. She let Anna lead the way, though they both knew where they were heading.

When Anna glances at Kallum's house as they cross the carpark of his village, Lottie keeps her eyes forward, but makes it clear that she has seen it. Lottie strides beside her, cradling the sodden casket, her nose wrinkling at the sourness rising from the cardboard.

Once inside the fence, she puts down the box too heavily, and Anna feels the thud like a punch to the chest. Lottie wants her to feel it. She shakes her arms to loosen the ache in her muscles and starts scouting for something hard and sharp to dig with. As Anna begins to help, Lottie triples her effort, and they scour the ground without speaking, as though the words to break the silence are buried somewhere in the shrubbery. Anna loiters near the box, clearing the earth of dead leaves with the side of her foot. The feel of damp leaves on bare skin makes her shiver, and she jumps when a beetle gets caught in the lip of her sandal.

Lottie reappears with the broken-off corner of a signboard, dismissing the piece of fencing that Anna has discovered. Lottie crouches and immediately gouges at the earth, dragging the corrugated plastic across the dirt. Anna marks out a rough rectangle for her to follow, but Lottie disregards the boundary. It needs to be wider; *she's surprised Anna can't see that.*

As they work, Lottie scatters loose earth over Anna's knuckles; all accidents, it is clear, but Lottie silently claims them. The plastic sign begins to bend, then it catches on a sewage pipe, splitting down the middle, but Lottie is persistent.

*Soon, she has scraped a shallow channel in the dirt. For a moment they are proud, but when they pick up the box to test it, it is clear they'll need to dig deeper. And they'll need a new tool to dig with. Anna scans around them. Lottie sees her looking and slams the plastic onto the ground. Anna glances towards the village—*there is someone we can ask. *But Lottie shows no recognition, and stares stubbornly at the ground. If Anna wants to invite him, she can say it out loud.*

*Instead, Anna frowns to tell her—*it's over; we did our best. *But Lottie is determined and is studying the box. They can't leave it so open. She suddenly takes the piece of fencing that Anna had used to mark the grave and pulls at the diamond, stretching the links. It is stronger than she expected, but she manages to break it, pulling it apart into three crinkled wires. She shuffles closer to the casket, takes one of the wires, and pokes a small hole into each flap of the lid. Next, she bends the wire and threads it into one hole and out of the other. Anna watches as she takes the two ends to secure them, but the wire is too rigid, and the eyelet tears as she twists them. She leaves it unfastened and repeats the process with* *the other two pieces of wire, bending them into hooks and piercing the soft cardboard. They stand to survey her work: three clumsy stitches. Pointless but important; an offer of protection.*

When they return to the village, the man with the rottweiler notes their damp knees and watches them up the path. Lauren never asks where they've been, and there is nothing to tell her.

Chapter 18

Anna is awake long into the morning: Villa Esplanade, Claudi's easy lie, the maid at Tai Po Market, her face looming inside Anna's mosquito net. She realizes then that she had never asked for her name; she was just, and still is, the family's helper. *Our maid hates you.* Kallum's words resurface. And in that moment by the underpass, the maid's eyes had confirmed it.

After she'd dragged her mother through the crowds, she'd dropped her at a hotel and gone back home, to the swamp, to pack their bags. In the days they spent together, her mother became an object that she'd begun to study with equal quantities of fascination and revulsion. Like a spider in the bath, struggling at its slippery sides, she was flailing, determined, and a foil to Anna's cruelty. It was something about the way she moved through the space, the vastness. *Anna could feel the meanness churning, an instinctive aversion, because the spider was also crawling inside herself.*

When she stepped inside through the door of her apartment, her phone pulsed twice. The first was from her mother saying the hotel was wonderful, just what she needed to relax before tomorrow. The second message was from a number that wasn't saved in her phone.

'Can we meet'

She ignored it, tossing the phone onto the sofa–probably the friend of Lottie's she'd given her number to in Lan Kwai Fong. She was packing in her bedroom when the phone pinged again.

'It's Kallum Cheung.'

On the bus she reads the message, over and over. The other passenger gets off, and then she is alone. In the black screen of the window, she imagines dark faces, fingerprint smears clawing out at the night. She reads the smudged markings and tries to guess at their meaning.

There's a blockage at the junction. Anna knows it's closed before they reach it. A sign suggests they make a U-turn, but the driver is determined to defy it. He nudges between the traffic cones, barely wide enough to fit them, and by the time they reach the torn-up road, it's too late for him to backtrack. They crawl to a stop. Anna peers through the window. Plastic piping is scattered all around a wide chasm. Work has stopped for the evening, but there's no way around it.

The driver curses at the windscreen, but only Anna is there to hear it. She wants to yell that this is his fault, the signs were there, he should have listened. They sit for a moment, waiting for nothing, and Anna watches the minutes, deciding how long she can stand it.

The gearstick churns, and they reverse, inching back towards the impasse. Anna checks Kallum's message: half an hour since she received it. The driver locks the wheel, and they swing back into the junction, he crunches the clutch, and they lurch back towards the turning.

As they speed between roadworks and streaks of amber light, she peers out through greasy glass and hopes this new road is a short one. Temporary traffic lights ahead. Anna swears they can't be working. There's no one here; the road is empty, but they stay red for several minutes. Impatience turns to anger, and anger turns to panic. Why aren't they changing? She checks the message again; it's been thirty-seven minutes.

They switch to green. The driver swings around them, but still, he seems uncertain. At every turning, he hesitates, unsure of the direction. Anna tries to check the map and finds the route is unfamiliar. They are moving closer, she can see that, but she has no way to gauge the distance.

Kallum hadn't answered when she asked him why. Just a cryptic 'Fanling Station'. She'd tried to call but it just kept ringing; something was keeping him from answering.

By the time they reach the interchange by the footbridge, she is frantic. She is waiting at the bus doors when the driver flings them open.

As she crosses the highway, she peers down at the traffic. She thinks of Christine and Claudi and knows that Kallum would have too.

She slips between commuters. The crowd scintillates like static. She searches their faces, but their eyes stare straight through her and only turn when she's behind them. She doesn't know if she's eager or hesitant to reach him. She doesn't know what she'll find or if she'll even find him. The soles of her trainers stick to the floor. She needs to keep going but can't make herself want to. The air is close and sickly with bodies.

She gets caught up in a bottleneck. Now would be the moment to turn back. She whips her head around instinctively, telling herself she's looking for no one in particular. She clears the bridge and heads to where she hopes he will be—the same table as always, or the bench when it is busy. She scans the tables. It's too late; he isn't here.

Then she sees a round face grinning at her from the corner.

He is stirring a pot of ice cream and doesn't look up when she reaches him.

'You're fine?'

'Um, yes. I'm fine.' He grins again.

Anna sits down in silence, searching his body for bruises.

'How are you?' he asks, as though their meeting is an accident.

'Kallum, why did you message me?' Her voice cracks unexpectedly.

He shrugs. 'To hang out?' He continues with his ice cream. He looks hurt that she would ask, but she can't find any sympathy. They both stare at his spoon as it scrapes soft cream from the edges, mixing it back into the middle, leaking stripes of sickly colouring. 'We can just say it's like a lesson—like after my sister's lesson.'

'I came to help you. I thought something had happened.'

'Happen?' He can't hide the smirk. 'You really think that you can save me?' He looks down at the table, now openly grinning, and Anna notices he's put too much product on his hair. Longer strands from the top have got stuck in the gunk at the sides.

'I was worried.'

'I'm sorry.' He stabs his spoon in the mixture. 'We can just talk. I will talk. You take a holiday, right? With your mother?'

She is surprised he remembered. 'Yeah, tomorrow actually,' she glances down at their bags. 'I brought them with me. We fly early.' She means to remind him of the disruption to her plans, but she finds her anger waning.

He laughs. 'I already say I'm sorry! I will help you to carry them.'

'It's fine. They aren't heavy.'

'By the way,' he says brightly, 'my maid hates you.'

'What? Why?'

He shrugs and sucks the spoon.

'What do you mean? Why should she?' It is suddenly hot inside her sweatshirt. A waft of hot grease is expelled from the kitchen and mingles with the sharpness of Kallum's aftershave. She feels sick.

'What has she said?'

'Not—nothing.'

'Not nothing or nothing?'

He shrugs again.

'Well, which is it? How do you know she hates me?'

'Just know it.'

'What about your mother?'

'Well . . . she's thinking you encourage me, like it's you that make me go. Well . . . not really make me go. More like you give me some ideas.

Like I will get some from you. It's so crazy. She's *so crazy. Nobody makes me go.'*

Anna's mind suddenly fills with the image of his parents bickering in a bedroom as they get ready for work. It's a phase. *He's getting worse!* His whole peer group are into it. The tutor is fine; *she's only being dramatic.*

'And what does your dad think?'

'Doesn't care. Always working. He's a shithead.'

'No. It's just your culture to work those hours.'

'Not *my* culture to be shithead.'

'So, you're still involved then? Even after . . . ?' She points at his tooth, and he covers it. 'But I'm the one that told you not to. I tried to stop you. Did you tell your mum that? I'm the one looking out for you. Like tonight—I came to help you. What is it she thinks I've said?'

'She's an idiot . . . Help me, what?'

'Today, in Tai Po Market, I saw that triad guy from your village—'

Kallum's face shifts a fraction.

'—He followed me.'

'No, he didn't. Don't always need to panic. He doesn't care about you. Anyway, you're leaving soon.' He kicks her bag. 'How long you'll be away for?'

'As long as I can bear it.'

But he doesn't catch her meaning. Sometimes she thinks he gets it, her relationship with her mother, but he is still Christine's dependent and is yet to feel the frustration that comes after that detachment. So when Anna tries to explain it, her frustration often doubles: what her mother had said or done, and when Kallum doesn't understand it.

Lately, her mother has been acting like she knows that Anna is watching, every word, every action, each exaggerated gesture: the way she echoes the phrases of cashiers over counters, repeating them under her breath on the train; the way she flicks through the trays of jade pendants on Antique Street, fussing over their uniqueness, their cracks *and imperfections; the way she picks at her pad thai, nibbling at the tofu, stirs a rage inside Anna that she can barely keep from exploding. Anna is filled with an inexplicable venom that only the pages of the journal can contain. It is as if her mother has peeked between the pages and committed herself to bringing the character to life. If she can own it entirely, Anna can't take the credit, so every comment is deliberate, no matter if she means it.*

When Anna next checks her phone, she's surprised to see how late it is. But as she gathers her bags to leave, the unease comes creeping back.

'What are you looking about?' asks Kallum.

'Nothing. Are you getting the train somewhere or going home? I'm going straight to the hotel.'

Kallum shakes his head just enough to be an answer.

A hiss from a cistern sounds somewhere overhead. Anna shifts in her bed, twisting to face the wall, tangled in the net. There's a mosquito on the inside, but she tells herself there isn't. An itch on her eyelid; she can already feel the swelling. The central rooms at Chungking look out onto others; the road is far from her window. But she imagines she hears the soft rush of tires on tarmac. The cistern fades. Last night she fell asleep dreaming of fountains, but tonight she dreams of highways and feels utterly alone.

Chapter 19

Towards the top of the building, a man is cleaning windows, leaning back over the street as though the height, to him, is nothing. Anna traces his safety rope, tied to the railings that line Mong Kok streets. The knot appears loose: a quick double loop and the end tucked under in a figure-of-eight, but friction holds it in place.

The idea enters her mind before she has time to shut it out: for a second, Anna wonders what it would feel like to untie it. To look up and see the man kick back from the window and fall out into nothing. She imagines stark concrete widening below him, and for a second she shares that sickly feeling of sinking. It is not, she reflects, out of any desire to harm him, but just to feel for a moment that she has some impact on the world. As she stares at the knot, the potential fills her, but then gravity hits, and she is suddenly afraid. Afraid of the fall, and the knowledge that the thought was entirely her own. No one else had made her think it—not her mother, nor Kallum. It was hers and hers alone, right here, in the present. She feels an urge to tie it tighter, to save him from herself.

Her mother's time in Hong Kong went quicker than she'd expected. In a four-hour layover in a stormy Manila, they'd waited for a reconnection: between themselves, and their flight to Dumaguete. The turbulence would be bearable, but small talk was becoming noticeably smaller, silences stretching behind them like contrails. As they landed, their sighs had mingled with the engines. Her mother had chosen well; Negros Island was sunny.

In the taxi, she catches a mosquito against the window and crushes it on the glass. Staring at the smear, they share the tiny triumph. Her mother hopes that they have bug spray and those diffusers at the villa. Jerry, the driver, winds them closer, dipping in and out of sunlight that reveals them in flashes. Their faces share the frame, clammy white and peering through the dull tinted glass.

Through the dust of the road, they taste the moisture of fridges selling 'rhum' and fresh mangoes to no one. From the shade of the shop, the owner tracks them along the road, peering beneath his NYC baseball cap.

Turning inwards, her mother lowers her head, raises her eyes to meet Anna's. 'Lot of poverty,' she mouths, so Jerry won't hear. Her mother's face is fixed with a deliberate expression; between interest and concern that she hoped Anna would see and believe was authentic. Really, *her mother supposes,* they are selling what they have: *bamboo and spare parts. She guesses that is all, really, anyone can do. Anna stays quiet.*

Their eyes scan further, to the corn drying out on wide sheets, each hungry for something that isn't Hong Kong. The corn is gathered into bundles that look like lotus leaf dim sums that an aunty had given her. It starts to rain. The locals had known it was coming. Anna had not, though her mother said she could feel it. She takes out her camera and captures a man in a faded, red T-shirt, who glances up at the lens as they pass. She wants to remember the nothing she knows about him, but the lens can't focus through the rain-splattered glass. And neither can she.

The dust turns to mud and small streams begin to wind around the rectangular corn mounds. They turn brown and look to Anna like newly covered graves.

Her mother leans forwards between the headrests and asks Jerry a question.

'Yes ma'am, it's safe,' he answers. Anna feels the tire treads drag deeper into the dirt. He might as well have said nothing. Her mother predicted his answer and established her own before she'd even asked. Already she was planning her escape route.

They pass through a gate in the glossy white fence, their own sunlit sanctuary. Here, they will be the brightest of ghosts. They are met by a heavyset Austrian named Gunther, who, like Anna's mother, liked to sunbathe. She remembers the relief in the sheen of her face. But still her mother asks again as they are being shown around their room—the maid this time.

'Is it safe, here?'

'Yes, ma'am,' the maid answers. Her glossy ponytail reminded Anna of Josephine's.

'. . . and outside the gates?'

The maid looks puzzled. Her mother pauses, then tugs at a strand of bleached hair.

'. . . ?'

'. . . oh yes, ma'am,' she nods.

Anna glares at her mother, hoping the girl will see that she doesn't share the question.

'Don't worry. It's very safe.'

Her mother never wondered how her question really sounded, though Anna would remind her of it again and again, in the weeks and months that followed, and always get the same response. *Yes, but, in Turkey* . . . They had been at The White Chocolate Hills for a whole two days before her mother let Anna lead her out beyond the gate. She turns to cross the road and remembers the panic. And how she promised her mother they wouldn't go far.

An anchor of motorbikes closes-up around them, but their engines don't drown out the hum in their ears. Her mother's hand flaps in protest, but the insect is persistent. She will never get used to their thirst. It is bad in Hong Kong, but here it is worse. The bikes are persistent too. Worn sneakers bounce on footrests, impatient for custom. Their own feet are filthy, a sweaty, dusty paste inside the straps of their sandals, as they shuffle to avoid the drivers. No thank you. *She flaps her hand again and her foot slips off the curb, scuffing her toes in the dirt. Tiny red beads swell. Her mother kicks the sandal loose to inspect the graze and to remind Anna she can't run fast in these shoes.* If this gets infected . . .

'Hey, missy, where going?'

'Hey missy, want a ride?'

But she doesn't. She never did. Heat ripples from the metal. Her sunburned skin is already stinging. She was happy inside the villa.

'Hey missy!'

A shrill driver in a gilet gestures directly at them and walks his bike closer. Anna has told her it is best to ignore them, but her mother just *isn't like that.* A smile costs nothing.

'No, thank you. Maybe later!'

Her acknowledgment encourages them. There is a flurry of responses, and she grips Anna's arm tighter.

'Later, har? Now. Where you going? Where your hotel?'

'No, thank you. Later. Later.' She is panicking now. She grips Anna's forearm until her nails imprint tiny crescents in the flesh.

A petrol tanker thunders towards them. The driver pounds his horn. The bikers don't move. They know he won't hit them. But her mother does not. Angry tears burst from her eyes. The bikers laugh harder.

A driver reaches out and catches her mother's wrist. Anna bats the arm away. Then she realizes he is only stopping them from stepping out into the traffic.

For the first time, her mother wishes they were back in Hong Kong.

Back inside the villa, her mother had tried her best to forget about the motorbikes. Across the table by the bar, she kept glancing at Anna, hoping to catch her eye, then scanning the gardens, the pool, and the palms to say *isn't this enough?* But it wasn't a question. And she knew Anna's answer. She still wasn't sure where Anna had wanted them to go.

So, they had sat there, at the poolside, as if they'd never tried to leave. Anna had watched her mother track the barmaids across the flagstones and lower her book politely as they came by to check her drink. Her mother soaked in every smile and mirrored each with the privilege of her own. A spiralling regression of politeness. She'd begun to blind herself with her own shiny brightness.

Later, the two waitresses tell her that she and her daughter are beautiful. Her mother smiles and says, 'Thank you,' and that the maids in Hong Kong are very cute, always smiling. *She giggles shyly, trying to mimic what seemed, to her, theirs.*

On the morning of their departure, her mother tips them after breakfast; just enough that she'll remember, when she's forgotten their faces, that they are living better lives now with the last of her currency.

After the maids take their photographs and Anna's mother takes theirs, she goes to buy a packet of cigarettes from The Lady in the Shack.

'I gave her that blue cardigan,' she says, when she returns, 'it looked horrible on me.'

'Feel better now?' Anna asks.

'If you'd seen her face, Ann. She was so happy.'

She and her mother had taken a final stroll on the beach and watched bats swoop and flicker across a sky of honeyed magma. It was beautiful, she'd had to admit.

The image blinks up at her now from her phone screen. She removes her sunglasses to see the colours, filtered by the lens. She opens Maps and lets the compass recalibrate. It finds her; she is heading in entirely the wrong direction.

Chapter 20

Lauren groans at the TV screen, 'That still isn't over?'

'Nah, there's going to be riot or something in Wan Chai.'

Lottie speaks casually, but at the mention of the word, Anna scans the carriage; no one seems to have heard her. Two women return her gaze. Anna continues to look vaguely in their direction for a moment, pretending to be interested in the map above their heads. But her intentions are obvious; she doesn't want to be listened to, and now she's caught their attention, they can't not listen if they tried.

Anna and Lauren speak faster, in accents, when they don't want to be understood. They return to the old habits they don't notice they've lost until they talk with their families on video calls and they resurface. Now, they do it on purpose; flat vowels and glottal stops, the lazy sounds of a language they can't disappear into.

Anna turns back to Lottie. 'What riot at Wan Chai?'

'No, actually, I think it's Mong Kok. Yeah, it's Mong Kok—on Friday.'

'I'm pretty sure there isn't. Where did you hear that?'

'My dad,' replies Lottie, '—his boss hacked a group chat.'

'What group chat?'

Lottie shrugs. Then adds, 'They always do it.'

Though the women have turned back towards each other, Anna can feel them listening, and when they think she isn't looking, they glance over again.

Unlike Anna and Lauren, Lottie never bothered to disguise what she was saying. She'd never learned to be ashamed of who she was or why she was here, the language she used, her plans to drink until she vomited. Her home was Hong Kong, and her life was part of it.

'What group though?' Anna presses her, 'There are so many fake ones. And the ones that are real, apparently, they aren't even run by the same people anymore. Like, the admins have left because of people posting shit . . . '

'Can you do that?' Lauren cuts her off, 'I didn't know admins could leave.'

'Yeah, that's why you can't trust them. It's a rumour for sure.'

'Yeah, you can. But I don't know, though,' says Lottie, 'My dad seemed like it's happening. He's going to cover it, anyway, so I kinda hope that it's happening.'

Shadows stripe across the window and the memory flickers for an instant. Then the sunlight breaks through and the hologram fades. They slip into a tunnel.

In the darkness of the tunnel walls, Anna sees herself floating. Not one detail is inaccurate; she recounts Lottie's words like she is sitting here beside her. She longs for the tunnel ahead to burst open. But the tunnel extends. The air is thinning around her. Their velocity increases and the temperature swells. The window in front of her is warm and rigid and Anna knows she is fixed fast behind it. Her chest aches and her temples are bursting. Then the tunnel expels her. Breathing deeply in the daylight, her reflection slips back into the white expanse of sky.

'But has he actually checked that group though? Like, has he found out who's planning it, who the organizers are? I really don't think it's happening.'

'No idea,' says Lottie.

'Guess we're not going to Wang-man's on Friday, then,' says Lauren, and takes out her phone to tell the others.

'I guess not,' Lottie shrugs. 'Yeah, I've remembered—it's definitely Mong Kok.'

'Are you sure though? You just said you weren't.'

'If it's happening,' Lauren adds, 'then I'm not going near it.'

'It isn't.' Anna shakes her head. Kallum would have told her.

Anna stares through glass as green hills rise to mountains, and cranes reach out their limbs, clawing for air. Against the backdrop of the harbour, she replays fading sound bites. Fence posts flick past like stripes in a film reel. The train slows and then pauses, and she steps off into the set.

West of Nathan Road, Anna wanders through the streets. At a crossroads, she pauses. Balancing on the comma between a pair of coordinates, she finds herself unable to choose a direction. The night of Lottie's riots, Anna had wandered blindly, letting impulses guide her, trailing after groups that looked vaguely conspicuous. But here, in the daylight, she scans for a familiar detail, determined not to have to take her phone out for directions. Every time she turns a corner, the colours of the buildings surprise her; every time, she realizes she's forgotten their shades. Though she can feel it in flashes on the backs of her shoulders, it's as though the sun has chosen to stay away from these backstreets, as dense as they are inscrutable. The atmosphere feels guarded. No one asks each other's business because they already know it and are concerned more with their own.

All around her, evidence of the typhoon is scattered. White branches are strewn, stripped of bark, along the backstreets, where slabs of grey concrete are snapped like polystyrene. Grandmothers pick through the debris in alleyways. Access routes must be cleared; mobility is everything.

A newspaper seller is perching on a tree root torn up from the pavement, engrossed in the stories she has given up selling. Anna glimpses pictures of devastation and Tai O stilt houses, sad before-and-afters. As Anna weaves around the stall, the woman ignores her, just as she ignores the anonymous others. She might be the woman who had pointed back towards the station that night she'd come to find him, looping desperately through the streets. Or the one who shook her head.

Anna shivers at the air-conditioned blast from a shop front and crosses towards the corner. All the way, she thinks of Kallum, the questions she never asked him, and scarred thumbs pressing into the hollow between his collar bones.

Anna emerges into the dirt-dulled geometry of a public square. Under the cover of the banyan trees, Tin Hau crouches at the edge. She'd heard of a temple tucked away in Yau Ma Tei; travel sites referred to it, an advert for the contrasts and the shades of the city. It might have been this place her mother told her about, the time Anna had lost her in a crowd and found her forty minutes later on a parallel road. While Anna bought her a sim-card, her mother had told her about an old woman who had offered her an orange on a bench beside a shrine. Anna had doubted the truth of that detail, but the image feels real now. She can finally see it.

At the entrance to the square, three old men are playing Go. The scene is too obvious. She almost doesn't believe them. A polo shirt drowns the figure sitting closest. He squints up as she passes, then goes back to his turn. The other two keep their eyes on the move he is considering.

The temple is quiet, discreet, and understated. There is none of the fuss of Po Lin or Man Mo. Anna feels that Hong Kong was hiding this one from her, withholding its secrets, not afraid she won't keep them, only knowing that she won't do them justice when she tells. And now she has discovered it, she can feel the words surfacing. She forces them away and moves towards the centre. She ducks to avoid the spindles of branches that hang low over the square, remembering Bride's Pool and the spider that got tangled in Lottie's hair. She sits back against a marble stool and watches the temple. Sparrows and dragons play chase along its rafters.

Soon, her thoughts begin to drift. As she stares at the crumbling brick pillar beside the steps, the impressions of faces emerge from the pattern. She studies the pale etchings and rectangular shadows, until mouths gawp and grin from the dull terracotta. A guttural sound rouses her. The man in the polo shirt spits beneath a sign: *Offender Will Be Prosecuted*; he rubs his bald head and doesn't care or believe it. That kind of thing doesn't matter here. The shade is thick with the feeling, a self-regulating balance of crime and correction. The police, Kallum told her, are rude and irrational, and this place didn't fit with that pace of regulation.

She hadn't asked him what he thought of them, but he'd felt the need to tell her. *They are political tools*. He liked the sound of the metaphor. *They should keep their minds calm instead of using the weapons*. She might have asked him what he meant by *a peaceful way of talking*. But if he answered, she hadn't listened, and neither would the CE.

The tiles all around her are flecked with the white ash that drifts out from the roof and across the courtyard towards her.

Anna watches a tiny speck settle on her forearm and wonders how long it would take to cover her entirely.

She dusts off her jeans and wanders towards the temple, peering through the bars in the perimeter wall. The walls are studded with turquoise, imitation bamboo, glossy and grimy from tree sap and the seasons.

She hesitates at the threshold; the darkness of the temple is the respite she craves from the labyrinth of jewellers and shady exchange booths. But it feels like giving up, the search already stagnating. If she goes in, knowing he won't be there, her sense of purpose will suffer. She has tried to deny it, but her footsteps have been slowing and she's been finding it harder to feel like she's still looking. It's a familiar stasis, the dull ache before failure, an echo of that evening when she'd come looking for the riot. *They aren't riots.* She shouldn't call them that. *We are peaceful, you know this.* Either way, she'd scanned the drizzle for whispers of tear gas.

Inside, the floor drops away to the square in the middle, where joss sticks and candles illuminate pots. The extractor fan growls and does little else. The air is spicy with coils of incense. Their glowing heads crumble into trays of dirty brass. They hang from the ceiling at the centre of the temple. Anna looks up at their undersides and fifty warped reflections. The reflections blink down at her, warning her to keep silent and stay back against the walls, where stacks of red packets promise fortune for $50 and an emperor is dissatisfied with a dry, dumpling offering. He follows her with his eyes and says she shouldn't have come here.

Another pair of eyes are watching her from the shadows in the corner. The smoke obscures his features, but his gaze is unmistakable. Anna pretends not to notice and shifts to the back. Between dark wooden beams, she watches him through the haze. His hair is cropped to bristles, his face looks thin and unhealthy, but when he leans back on the chair, she sees his torso is sturdy. It is the first time she has noticed him. She is sure he hasn't moved since she entered the temple. He hasn't followed her, though it seems he knew she would come here.

The extractor fan swings, and the smoke shifts a little. His expression isn't curious, but steadfast and certain. It's like he knows all her movements before she even makes them. She steps right, and the man disappears behind a post. But the temple is filled with a thousand other painted gazes. She leans back into the light and, without checking, feels his eyes rediscover her and follow her down the steps as she moves closer to the barrier. She's afraid to look up and keeps her own eyes on a midpoint, a cauldron of brass overflowing with ashes. She tells herself to be calm; she's been here before. But as she grips the wooden bar, the man's focus intensifies.

The air is getting thicker. Maybe, this time, her fear is justified. She scans the haze, counting witnesses, and wondering who would guide her to some safe, secret exit.

A light touch on her shoulder. She turns to see a man gently ushering her to the side, while, behind him, a robed figure shifts a coil of burning incense. The thin pole quivers under the weight, swaying dangerously above them, and he concentrates hard on maintaining his balance. Anna moves to make way. He nods curtly to thank her, eyes fixed on the coil as he raises it higher.

She suddenly remembers the guard. She glances back in his direction and realizes, now, he was just staring at the burner. This time, when she steps away, he doesn't track her to the shadows, and she slips out of his notice just as swiftly as she had entered it. She puts the sound of shuffling sandals and muted clanging behind her and heads back towards the entrance. Nobody stops her.

Outside, the three pensioners have progressed no further with their game. Not one of them looks eager to speed up the outcome.

Anna drifts back into the tangle of Yau Ma Tei backstreets and, beyond them, Mong Kok. And for a moment, she can almost forgive Lottie's error; if she'd had to guess a place for trouble, she'd have picked this one too.

Chapter 21

On a slab beneath a footbridge, a group of women have spread their picnic. Their tight skirts and trainers remind Anna of the barmaids at their resort in Negros. Her mother's favourite feature: their sunny, neon uniforms. She hadn't been able take her eyes off them, her face fixed with intrigue as she watched them at work, airing towels over balconies, skimming leaves from the pool.

'They're not at all like you said,' her mother half whispers.

Staring past Anna at the table, she studies each sweep of the palm brush across the patio, each tweak of an umbrella, every micro-adjustment of a grenadine bottle, as if every gesture is loaded with sentiment.

'What do you mean, "Like I said"?'

'The impression you gave me. Like they'd resent us for being here.'

'Who says they don't?'

Her mother still doesn't look at her, determined not to miss a single glance in her direction. Every titter, every wave, it's like she is counting.

'I had a lovely chat with them this morning—when you were in the water. They're not sisters, like we thought, but they think of each other as family.'

'I never thought they were sisters.'

'Oh, I did! They're so alike.'

It isn't curious that these soulful chats, between her mother and locals, always seem to happen when Anna is elsewhere. Perhaps she really does prevent them, perhaps her mother has begun to hold back when she's around, always fixating on her word choice and deriding her afterwards. She now openly calls Anna cynical, and there is no doubt she is. But perhaps there is another reason, a little more likely and much easier to accept: her mother's imagination; a desire to show Anna a fresh understanding. Her eyes had been opened, like she'd told herself they would.

Anna struggles to quash the jealousy when the youngest maid comes over and taps her mother on the shoulder.

'Your drink, ma'am,' she almost curtseys. 'I put a little more of the red syrup like you asked it. A little sweeter—like you.'

'Ah, you remembered!' her mother adds for Anna's benefit. 'You sure you don't want one, Ann?'

'I didn't know you'd ordered.'

'I ordered this morning. You were in the water. Why not? We're on holiday!'

'No, thanks,' Anna smiles with deliberate falseness.

'Maybe later,' her mother adds, taking her own drink from the waitress, and they giggle together, as though Anna's surliness is the subject of a joke, a private joke they'd shared earlier—when she was in the water. As the maid moves away, her mother shuffles her chair out of the shade. She closes her eyes and speaks towards the sun.

'It's no wonder the maids in Hong Kong never warmed to you.'

'What do you mean they haven't warmed to me?'

'You told me! You said the maid of that family you work for hates you.'

'No, I didn't.'

'Yes, you did! Well then, I must have made it up.'

'Yeah, you must have. Because it isn't true.'

Her mother sucks the milky scum of the pineapple wedge, over-ripened and already curling at the edges.

'Mm, that's lovely, very light.'

'Actually, I find the helpers in Hong Kong are much more genuine. You know where you stand. They're not reliant on tips.'

'Good job, really—with you around.'

This time they both know her mother has won.

Only vaguely convinced of the direction she is heading, Anna weaves her way through the crowds, replaying conversations. She isn't even sure if the script is authentic; like a vision of a story that someone once told her. A memory of a memory that isn't quite her own. And as she replays it, in moments, she feels like she's present, like the scene is still pliable, like she can alter the outcome.

Anna turns down a side street and glimpses Nathan Road, perpendicular to this one. When she reaches it, she scans left and right along the shopfronts. They're all too familiar. She can't remember which sequence will lead towards the wharf. At the corner between railings, a sign divides the road; she takes the direction of diminishing numbers.

She asks Kallum straight out if the riot is happening. She'd planned to be subtle, but the words come spilling out. She imagined he'd probe for the details, some explanation, but he shakes his head without asking, dismissing it as nothing. He doesn't care where she heard it. He tells her rumours are spreading. It doesn't matter who told her. He is cold and condescending. They watch the ferry drift closer, until faces appear at its windows.

'And they aren't riots. You shouldn't call them that. We are peaceful, you know this.'

She fights with the words, but it's the wrong time to argue.

'So, no? There's nothing planned then?'

'Those informations are fake. Anyone who is serious doesn't waste their time to listen.'

Those group chats use decoys, though he doubts that's the case, because this time he hasn't heard about a real one. There's been nothing for days. Anna feels that she trusts him, she has no reason not to. Even now, his words convince her; for just a second, she believes him.

As Kallum talks, she feels frustration rising inside him. She thinks of questions but swallows them. He is speaking to himself, now; his own thoughts already rile him. He says that now, if they don't show, it will look like they're afraid to, like they've broken a promise, even if they never made it. He says the media will be expecting them. They will seem uncommitted, like their ideas are only talk, like the movement is fading.

She asks him if it isn't. He thinks for a moment, like she's trying to trick him.

'There are wiser ways and surer ways to fight for our home.'

In the space between his words, she feels a vision unravelling, a tension she'd never thought about, fractures inside the movement. The more time she spent with Kallum, the more he'd showed her, without trying to, subtle shades and complexity she'd never guessed might exist, positions between two sides that almost felt like contradiction.

'At the start, we were stupid. It's true. I can admit it. Risking the chance of prosecution without doubt. But when I see so many Hongkonger sitting on the street, how can I stay home when they fight for the civil right? I am impressed by their courage. One more person stand with them, lesser chance of they seize us. Lesser chance they will detain us. We can all go home safely. This is what I thought. Can you blame me to think it?'

'I don't blame you,' she tells him. 'They inspired me as well. And Hong Kong's the safest place on earth. No one knew how it would spiral.'

Kallum bristles. 'I thought this too.' He is careful with his tense, now. 'I think this is why so many foreigners decide to join us. And all the media. But even when we stay, when the others are leaving, we still think the worst case to happen would be okay, might be something like the past, like they just carry us away.'

A picture is forming—in his mind and in hers. His body limp as two officers take him by the ankles and under the armpits. Roughly but steadily, they drag him out from the others, a parting in the crowd, his arms still stiff and fingers pointing, his throat raw but still shouting. Friends and acquaintances rally around him; he's the first to be arrested, but they know they're right behind him. A horizontal martyr. Anna sees him envisioning a video and sound bite, a scrolling TV screen in a crowded MTR train.

But when the cameras turn away and the crowds are behind them, Anna sees the two officers toss him into the police van. The doors muffle his shouting. It is quiet now, underwhelming. He prods a swelling below the skin and hopes by morning the bruise will have surfaced and darkened.

'No one doubts your commitment. It's just this Mong Kok thing sounded scary.'

But he misunderstands her and insists again it isn't happening. He says their gameplan has changed now. They need to be clever. The threat has mutated. It's no longer just arrest or a fine that they'll be risking. He leaves the line hanging and stares down at the waterline disturbed by the ferry. Anna has a feeling he's saying more than he'd planned to.

When the ferry docks, time resets, and the next horde gets on. Anna doesn't join them. Instead, she leans against the wall where she and Kallum had watched the breakers. More than once, she'd told her mother the story about the time they raised the fare, the five cent increase that caused commuters to set fire to buildings. Her mother had looked thoughtful and said she thinks that she remembers, but Anna said she doubts it because it happened in the 60s.

She can't remember if she read it or if Jenny had told her, but it comes back to her now, as she stares across the water. Her thoughts drift back to Kallum. How convincingly he'd spoken. The riot wasn't happening. The line had settled like an anchor. But now the questions she never asked him swell below the surface, so vivid that she's almost surprised the waiting passengers don't see them. But it was Kallum who broke the silence.

'So, who did *tell you about this riot?'*

Anna smirks, 'I thought it didn't matter?'

'It doesn't!'

But still, she sees him brace for her answer.

'Somebody saw it in a group chat. Just a friend, who overheard it.'

'Got it,' he grunts. 'I understand now. Yeah, I think I got it.'

She's about to ask him what he means but is tired of trying to argue. He has that look that means he'll twist things or deny he ever said them. When he's like this, she's learned better than to tease at the tangles that only tighten into knots. She knows, beyond this point, her every word is catastrophic. But as she struggles with the silence, she notices his expression; there's something else inside the anger, like a sadness or resentment.

'Is he like me then—Hong Kong people?'

'Who?'

'Your friend. The guy who told you.'

It suddenly makes sense. Anna knows that it is cruel, but she doesn't correct him, 'No, no. Like me—a foreigner.'

He nods, like he expected it.

She feels the three years grow between them.

The air is still wet, like it was when she left him, but this time it reeks with the sourness of the storm. The dankness feels alien. As she wanders past bao stalls and milk pudding shops she's never seen before, she finds herself missing the familiar sights of Tai Po. The pale mosaic buildings and the steep cobbled verges they had to scramble up and over when they forgot to call their stop. If Kowloon was insanity, the New Territories was mild inertia, an oldness she could reply upon and a stasis she could trust. The Island and Kowloon had the chains supposed to comfort her: the consistency of Starbucks, the accessibility of Apple. But it was Tai Po and Fanling that had grounded her mornings: the faded lanterns at the roundabout, the broken turnstile's peeling sticker. It wasn't comfortable or easy, but a moment she could cling to. And now, she longs for that time before everything had shifted.

As she waits outside Langham Place for a car back, she smiles at a yellow ribbon pinned to a backpack. She hopes its wearer will see her looking and deduce she knows its meaning, but the girl doesn't notice and flags the taxi Anna missed.

When she finally gets one, the meter clicks to thirty-two. The driver asks her where she's going and, for once, doesn't ask her to repeat it.

Chapter 22

Anna wanders through Tai Wo station. Three years of distance haven't dulled the apprehension. She crosses towards the exit and the space fills with mnemonics; things they'd laughed at, things demolished, and things she doesn't recognize. The old man in the sweet shop gurns over his melon seeds, cookies, nut candies, and a sign for the new *ParknShop* that will put him out of business. Anna doesn't miss his glare, just the version of herself who had felt this glare so harshly. This time, when she forgets him, he will disappear entirely.

She emerges from the station. Here, she pauses beside a hawker, triple checking the address that Claudi had scribbled, that she remembers by heart.

Anna passes the stand for the minibuses where the cockroaches scuttle beneath the escalator shaft. The girls used to join the queue here after work, counting the vacant seats through the window as it approached. Now, the vacant seats stand out more than ever.

Retracing Claudi's directions three years later, Anna crosses the station gardens towards the junction at the corner. By the basketball court, on a bench in the shade, a maid waves a fan over the infant in her lap and watches Anna through it as she passes. The pavement is fractured by shadows of pagodas, and she is grateful for their shade. She approaches the junction. Piles of construction sand block the pavement opposite, where a scorpion digger is deciding where to sting. As she crosses towards it, the drill tears into the concrete with a piercing shriek.

The chaos of the roadworks dissuades her from carrying on along the main road and entering through the car park, as she had the very first time. She remembers the rubble was spread across the concrete, dotted with cartons, snapped zip ties, and polystyrene. White dust covered everything, an apocalyptic monochrome, only the windows of houses stayed black. Their dead eyes blinked down as Anna crossed the pale car park. *Ah yes, it's too dangerous. That village is bad news.* But Anna couldn't ask.

The front entrance to the village is too exposed. This time she'll take the path. Though, when she gets to the first corner, she finds it is no less torn and cluttered than the road. The space pours itself into the mould in her mind and only then does she recognize its shape, remembering every twist and every turning as she takes it.

The path is bordered by chain link and trees either side. Branches stretch above it, poking spindles through the bars. They've grown thicker in her absence, though it might have been the season. From a distance, it is jungle, but up close, it resembles foliage in a zoo; roots force their way through paving slabs, swallowing fragments, ensnaring cracked traffic cones and dry concrete trolls. Their eyelids bulge as she passes. They remember her.

The path winds nearer to the houses, and Anna's feet begin to drag. She counts down the corners, the four remaining turns, and when she reaches the final bend, she stops, hovering on zero. Behind it, through the bushes, the triad porch is waiting. One more step and she'll be in sight of it. She listens for voices. The air is thick with quiet. Nothing sounds above the susurrus. Everything is still. She leans closer to the fence and listens harder. But there is only the hum of their filthy refrigerator that thrums in time with her pulse.

Between the fence and the porch, branches keep her hidden, but she still shifts her feet carefully as she crouches to see through a peephole of sunlight. Something flicks across the gap. She jumps back from the fence. But it is only a sparrow, nesting in the bushes. When it settles, the stillness returns, and Anna notices the highway churning steadily beyond it.

She takes a breath, inches forward, and peers around the corner.

The porch is deserted. She stands for a minute in case one of them appears. When no one does, she takes a step and begins slowly towards it. Her pace feels unnatural, too slow and too stiff, but to rush feels like inviting a chase she can't win. The shop is closed up, their stools pushed back into the corners, but something tells her they aren't far, and she doesn't want to test it. Memories of their faces whisper as she passes. She'd never dared to turn around, and neither had Kallum. This time, she can't either, like her attention might provoke them. Their absence watches her all the way to the pond in the middle.

The pond sits at the centre of the grid of squat housing blocks. Beyond their rooftops, she can see San Tong village up the hill. She counts the days—only a week since she'd looked down from the roof of the old house. So much had changed in her since then, and yet, so little had happened that had brought her any nearer. She can't decide whether being here only magnifies the distance. She looks over at the carpark. Though most of the rubble has been cleared, the rest of village remains eerily unchanged. The narrow alleyways are silent and trimmed with faded chūnlián, black slashes in silk mark some timeless new year. A cloud shifts, and sunlight bounces off the surface of the water. Three years concertina, and when the folds open out again, Anna feels herself split.

From the railings, she watches herself move tentatively across the drive towards the houses.

She reaches the block and jabs Christine's doorbell.

Anna remembers how she'd waited, the felt-tipped '3' behind the plastic, and how someone had traced over the faded number with a biro. The detail had made her nervous, it was somehow too intimate, a reminder of the realness of the home she was intruding. How she'd pictured the father who might not know to expect her but would pretend not to mind the disruption to his work. He would answer, maybe smiling, and stride back to his office, calling Claudi to come and meet her, and shut the door behind him. His family respected his privacy when he was working. But it wasn't the father who answered.

'Miss Anna!' A maid's face appears at the glass. She holds open the door.

Anna watches herself stick out a hand, wishing she hadn't. The maid will shake it, awkwardly, before gesturing for Anna to lead the way up the stairwell. She watches herself disappear into the memory.

Inside, she has begun up the second flight of stairs when the helper calls after her, 'Here, Miss! It's this one.'

Anna turns back and stumbles.

'It's okay, Miss, don't hurry.'

Anna struggles to tug her shoes off as the maid loiters in the doorway.

She pushes open the door to a cluttered apartment. Laminate and crystal are bathed in warm sunlight that streams in soft sheets through the turquoise-tinted window. The light catches in picture frames on top of a piano, besides stacks of new textbooks that spill over from the bookcase. Three have been selected and arranged on the dining room table.

Just inside the living room, a pair of flannel slippers are expecting her.

'Cheuk Yiu, teacher is here!'

Anna hovers by the door, deliberating over the slippers. The helper rushes to retrieve them, then reconsiders, dropping them back at her feet.

'Is okay miss, do you want?'

Anna steps politely into them. The smell of a rice cooker thickens the air, not altogether unpleasant, but it will linger on her uniform.

'Ah, Miss Anna!' A voice in the doorway behind her. Christine is home from work. Anna turns to shake her hand, but instead Christine goes to hug her. And when Anna pulls away, her bag strap catches on Christine's name badge, who fusses to detach her. When Anna turns back towards the living room, a young girl in pajamas is waiting at the table.

Another chair has been pulled out beside her but not quite far enough, and when Anna squeezes herself in, the legs make a piercing screech on the tiles. The four of them shudder.

A single grain of rice is stuck below Cheuk Yiu's collar. The whole thing feels too close, too domestic, and too familiar. She looks around at the closed doors; there's no sign of Claudi. Anna senses it's her turn to speak. Christine and the maid loiter.

'How old are you?'

'I am eleven.'

'Great . . . ' There's a silence. 'I work with your big sister. Did you know that? Is she here?'

But she isn't. Anna nods at a photograph on top of the piano.

'Your older brother?'

Cheuk Yiu nods, the conversation already over.

'So, do have a book you're reading?'

Christine signals, and Cheuk Yiu scurries to her bedroom. There's a zip sound and a clatter that suggests she is searching. Anna's eyes settle on the photo on the piano. The boy in the frame has the same shaped eyes as Christine, but he squints a little, and his expression is suffused with defiance. He looks too old for the uniform, but the crease down the sleeve gives away his dependence on the maid who does his laundry. Christine sees her looking.

'My son. He's a rascal.'

They scrunch their eyes up at the corners.

Christine leans in closer: 'You can give my daughter homework each week after the lesson. You can follow the curriculum. But I think you know what to teach her . . . '

'Here, Miss, some water,' the maid interrupts. Christine pauses mid-sentence to let the cup be delivered, but as Anna turns to thank her, Christine has already resumed speaking. The maid looks embarrassed at being thanked and backs away into the kitchen.

'Teacher, some nights I need to working late in the evenings. Sometime, I'll be in Kowloon. Sometime, here in my office,' she waves at an adjoining room, and inches tentatively towards it. Anna nods to reassure her and turns back towards the books. She knows what she is doing.

The office door softly shuts.

Waiting for Cheuk Yiu, Anna sips at the water; it is warm, and it tastes like the smell of the rice cooker.

The same sickly aroma drifts across from the houses and finds her now in the present as she stares across the village. She turns back towards the pond and leans against the railings, gripping the cool iron, and immediately recoils; they are crocheted by spiders. Rubbing web from her palms, she checks the time. 17.26. He'll be home soon. She will wait for him here. The fountain in the middle has stopped altogether. It is clogged with black slime; a carp navigates the darkness.

When a gust scuffs the surface of the water, it vanishes. Anna stares at the ripples, willing it to live again. The breeze calms, and the fish resurfaces, a blood-speckled silver.

A minibus passes along the road beyond the car park. It pulls into the bus stop. She holds her breath. The doors open. But no one gets off. When the bus pulls away, she turns back towards the path—perhaps he'd got off one stop early, he might be walking from the station. The porch is still deserted. But Kallum isn't there either. She stares for several minutes, until she can't stand it any longer. Another minibus passes without even stopping. She glances back towards the road, then down at the koi-paisleyed water. The quiet throbs against her skin.

A gurgle makes her jolt and she springs back from the railings.

As she trips on the rubble, the fountain gurgles again to spite her.

The road adjacent to the village feeds a steady stream of vehicles to the junction, the turn to Fanling highway or straight ahead to the station. This time, Anna takes it. Ahead of her, a white Toyota waits to pull out of the carpark, and Anna watches with the driver for a break in traffic. The trucks thunder along, the green buses even faster.

Anna follows the running track that floods when it rains, typhoon debris strewn across it. Though the potholes she remembers have been filled in her absence, Anna still finds herself weaving to avoid them, and sidestepping the sandbags vomiting sludge into the gutter.

At the junction, the pavement and the village path converge, Anna glances at the entrance while she waits for lights. The endless green and white cycle commands the intersecting traffic, intercepting collisions, never blinking, all-knowing. All across the city, lives stop and start to its pattern. Anna is one of them, though she feels their indifference. She moves closer to the curb, teetering on the edge, testing their authority, wrestling for control. A truck is thundering towards her. It beeps its horn, but she ignores it, refusing to step back. Toes hanging over the precipice, she sees the remnants of a head lamp, fragments of amber cloaked in black dust. She stares at the glass in the road, imagining the sound, the sickening crack, a shiver of fragments. The truck's horn is sounding wildly, unsure if she has seen it. The rush of hot air takes her breath at it passes.

She blinks up at the lights, but they refuse to give way. She's half convinced they never will. They are mocking her, like the fountain, her inability to cross, to put the afternoon behind her. It's like they knew all along she wouldn't find him at the village. Anna's chest is still thudding from the near-miss with the truck, but the echoes feel dull now, something darker is stirring.

The lights are blinking green, but she swears they never changed. Perhaps to find Kallum, she'll have to lose herself completely.

Chapter 23

Anna perches on the middle seat of a red Island taxi, expecting the driver to insist they get out. Instead, he gestures to stay put. The other man had hailed it first, but he'll give up soon, the driver knows it. They listen, and they wait, but the rival is persistent, ranting at Lottie as she hangs onto the doorframe. Behind them, a queue of other taxis is ready to take him; they beep their horns to call him over, but, no, he still wants this one.

'Close the door,' she tells Lottie, pulling her fully inside the car; it is up to the driver, and they've no need to be sorry. They'd flagged the same taxi. The girls had got there first. It happens. It's done, now. The driver is on their side.

Though his preference does surprise her—and how adamantly he is sticking to it, no hint of regret for the dispute it has led to. Usually, red taxis are reluctant to take them, many of them refuse, and the girls are left waiting, sometimes hours, for a green one. Often, even the green ones drive past without slowing, but Anna can't blame them; she's lost count of the times her Cantonese has misled them. But this driver is insistent. And the local man can't accept it. He spits insults, and Anna's glad that she doesn't understand them.

He moves in front of the taxi to stop the girls from leaving, glowing white in the headlamp. Riled and ranting, his expression is grizzly. The headlamp nuzzles his calf, but the pale man ignores it and stares at the windscreen. Though it's too dark to see through it, Anna feels his eyes find her.

He bangs on the bonnet. The driver revs the tired engine. But as the man steps aside, another taxi swings in front of them. Their exit blocked again, the man approaches Lottie's window. His fingers find the narrow opening before the girls have even noticed it. He grips the glass and tries to rattle it. Lottie shrieks and it startles him. She finds the handle but doesn't wind it. Then, suddenly, his face is calm. For several seconds they share a silence, then when he speaks his voice is measured. He's trying harder now to reach them, like there is something they're not getting.

The car in front shifts, and a gap inches open; Lottie yells at the driver, but he has already seen it. As they start to pull away, the man's grip loosens on the window, he swipes his fingers across the glass and calls after them, laughing. Anna doesn't know his words, but she senses a warning, some advice they've ignored, like he knows what is coming.

They speed away faster than Anna is prepared for, forcing a young couple to jump back at the crossroads. Lottie doesn't notice and complains she's too sober, but Anna is glad. That guy seemed serious; she was scared he might attack them. Lottie replies that it's all talk; he's just pissed that they beat him to it. Hong Kong's the safest place on earth. She's being paranoid. He wouldn't touch her.

Anna isn't drunk either; she says she's holding out for Friday. Then Lottie suddenly remembers what she's been meaning to tell her.

'Oh yeah, I checked with my dad: that protest actually is happening. He says there are multiple sources they're using.' She takes Anna's silence as indifference and adds, 'I think we'll stay at the swamp and have a roof night instead.'

Anna thinks about Kallum; he'd dismissed her questions so casually, with no hint not to trust him. She feels the sting of his deception.

'Has he told the police?'

'About the riot? I didn't ask him. They're not supposed to interfere. It's like this question of ethics.'

Anna is about to argue when she notices the meter; the driver hasn't set it running. She shows Lottie, who leans forwards to ask about the fare.

He responds with a number. Lottie translates it incorrectly, because the figure is ten times higher than they'd ever have to pay him. She asks again, in a mixture of Cantonese and English, and again she gets the number. He confirms it with his fingers. They take a moment to frown at one another, but it isn't time to panic; he's just mistaken them for tourists.

Sitting forwards, she declines and quotes the fare they were expecting, making her Cantonese sound natural and pointing at the meter. He shakes his head to say it's broken. She feigns a laugh because it isn't. Then he is silent for a minute, while Anna guesses his expression. She sees a tightening of his cheeks, but he decides against speaking. Lottie shoots her a look: Keep your mouth shut; I've got this.

But as they swing into the middle lane, the realization thickens; he won't let them out without some form of reparation. Lottie never loses, but the driver is used to winning. His routine is finely tuned; he protects, and now they pay him. Though Lottie usually does the talking, Anna is restless in her silence. She can't help feeling that Lottie is isn't doing enough to dissuade him. Traffic swells, and cars on either side block them in, as Anna stares at their windows, seeking faces that won't help them.

'Does he even know where we're going?'

'Tai Po?' says Lottie, louder.

'Tai Po, ah.' He repeats the number.

'But does he know where that is though?'

Lottie speaks in Cantonese. The phrase is short and casual. The driver grunts to say he's got it but shows no sign of recognition. The traffic begins to move again, and a gap in the right lane opens up. He forces his way in, jamming the accelerator. Anna opens the translator app, and Lottie tuts that no one trusts her. She's told him. But then *the driver snaps his own phone from the dashboard. He speaks into the microphone and passes it back to them. It takes a second to transcribe:*

'I had a fight for you,' it tells them.

'We never asked you to,' types Lottie; that isn't their problem.

He cuts the fare by half now, confirming the inflation. The sudden drop makes Lottie furious. She flings the insult she always favours. He snaps something back, and Anna doesn't ask for the translation.

They are approaching a tunnel. It's almost too late not to take it. They're losing space to turn around; their leverage is dwindling. The lanes begin to funnel. They are running out of minutes. Lottie glances at the lock, and Anna knows she is brave enough to try it. Perhaps they look at one another then, or just imagine the connection. But the locks click shut an instant before she snatches for the handle. She rattles it anyway, banging the headrest.

'Pull over!' She yells, but he won't—that is obvious.

They're approaching the final slip road before the tunnel will trap them, though they're still two lanes away with no sign that he plans on switching. He is silent now, clearly thinking, deciding if they're worth it. Lottie's aggression is unconvincing, but he's unsettled and reassessing. Anna scrambles with her phone, choosing the words that might persuade him, when Lottie grabs her arm and squeezes.

'There's a knife under the dashboard.'

They stare at one another. For several seconds, they stay frozen. Anna can think of nothing but Lottie's fingers against her skin. Her grip is hot and tight. Their next decision will be critical. Did he mean for you to see it? *Anna wants to ask her, but instead she says something like, 'Your hand is really sweaty.'*

Lottie stares at the hand like it belongs to someone else.

'Oh . . . ' When she withdraws it, the skin beneath is cold and clammy.

As their lane merges with the next, they are forced into the middle, closer to the slip road. Anna leans forward.

'Lido.' She tries, too quietly. He stares forwards at the tunnel. She grips his headrest and tries again. 'That way.' Her voice shaking. Lottie

is louder. She reaches across Anna towards the exit lane and bangs on Anna's window. The driver slams the brakes; they are only crawling, but the jolt still throws them forwards. They push into the left-hand lane. He takes his phone to write a message.

Anna interrupts and shows him, 'We can't pay you'.

Lottie tries to say, 'No money.'

But he won't listen or believe them. A car horn blares behind them. Then others, spreading like ripples. They are blocking two lanes, but he fixates on his typing. Anna rattles the handle, though she knows it is useless. Perhaps Lottie is yelling again, or this time maybe she is. There's a screeching of tires, as cars begin to swerve around them. He thrusts the phone into the backseat.

'I'll drag you back to where you came from.'

'Do it,' Lottie spits. But Anna's heart is pounding.

They hand his phone back; let him drag them. He re-reads his own message to check he typed it correctly. Lottie reaches forwards and taps the screen to confirm they've seen it. But Anna re-reads the threat over his shoulder and prays the word is a poor translation. He tosses the phone into the pot beside the gearstick, yanks the wheel, and they swerve left. Another taxi almost slams them. But then they swing into the slip road, and the tunnel is behind them.

'Happy?' Lottie snaps, 'I told you I'd tell him.'

Anna wants to argue but it's true; without Lottie, she'd have no chance.

Lottie opens up a monologue about how no one ever trusts her. Although she says she isn't drunk, her words blend together. It's been her home since she was six years old; people forget that she grew up here; she knows everything about this place; but they treat her like she's stupid. She knows how they all see her—like her dad's a dirty banker or the CEO of Cathay—he actually taught her about the history; he learned the language just to come here. The city means something to him, though she knows that Anna can't believe it.

Anna says she never said that.

It doesn't matter; she implied it. Lottie knows Anna thinks he doesn't care, but he really does support the protests. She knows she thinks he's heartless, but it's his job to tell the story . . .

'And it's better if there's violence. No police.' Anna prompts her.

Lottie says it isn't like that; 'Fine, then. I'll ask him. But I can't promise he'll call them.'

'Please.'

'Okay! I promise.'

Anna feels the driver listening.

Back outside Carnegies, the doors click, and they wrench them open, scrambling out before they've even stopped, and the car speeds off into the morning. Lottie calls something after him. Anna grabs her wrist to stop her. Is she insane? He has a knife.

Lottie shrugs, 'I was only guessing.'

Chapter 24

Signs of the storm had roused a feeling she'd forgotten. It was the feeling that she'd missed out on something important.

Too tired to prop herself up on an elbow, Anna shuffles down into the duvet and reads it horizontally. The Chungking mattress is too thin. The bedsheets smell musty; the smell reminds her of the old house, plaster dust and damp linen. The side of her face is buried in the pillow, so she has to keep one eye closed to focus on the text. The open eye stings but she can't bring herself to close it.

She scans the reports. They'd be talking about Hato long after it was over. The stories would replace the torn branches and dented road signs. When it hit, she'd been somewhere in the sky over Eastern Europe, listening to the ticking of sleeping student's headphones. And yet, she would remember it, the destruction and the debris. She would talk about the carnage, the transformation of the city, but couldn't say she'd really *been there*. If she laboured the detail, perhaps they wouldn't even ask her. If she focused her attention on a street name or even a district, they'd assume that she'd seen, not just read about the damage. Her memories would blur and she'd recall an image from an article, and believe she'd really seen it. It might even be this one. She finishes the article and searches for others.

The first few are warnings written a day or so before the storm hit, when flight cancellations were the primary disruption. Writers speak of a threat but remain vague and noncommittal when they talk about trajectories and predicted damage to property. One says *considerable*. Another says *severe*. Anna knows, as well as they do, South Asian typhoons are capricious, prone to veer off at the last possible moment.

She returns to the search results, skipping the links that look similar, and settles on one towards the bottom of the list. It shows the same map, but on this one, the black trajectory is steadfast and determined, connecting red, bloated S points with increasing conviction. Though it teeters a degree or two with each hourly update, it's the surest she's seen. Intent on its course, the line bisects the blue expanse of the South China Sea. It will strike just south of Macau, sometime just after 12.00. By 12.10, they'll know for certain. The Hong Kong observatory is marked on the map, a blue diamond that spans the channel between the Island and Kowloon. She pinches the image and tries to enlarge it, but the quality is too low and makes a pixelated blur. And the remainder of the article is standard, crammed with clichés, lazy descriptions she has no interest in reading. She wants first-person panic. She needs to feel like she was present.

She clicks back and finds a link: 'A Recent History of Hong Kong Storms'.

She reads about shacks built from tin and tar paper, and refugees on the hillsides, and feels her eyes scan ahead for injuries and death tolls. She'd read about fires but hadn't thought about typhoons. In 1971, she encounters an ominous fog bank, the most intense since Typhoon Wanda, with electrical failures and a landslide that killed four children. One of the bodies was never found.

Her scrolling lifts her through the decades, closer to the present, and soon concerns become financial, capital losses. They speak of creeping high tides and surges and stock exchange standstills. Anna starts to skim faster, pausing only when she glimpses a word that looks promising. And when the scroll bar is almost depleted, she finds it.

Only the third T10 in twenty years, Typhoon Hato struck the South China coastline on Wednesday. Streets were ravaged by flooding, evacuees seen swimming, as thousands fled to shelters. Fierce gusts brought flying debris, uprooting trees and street-signs and scaffolding, smashing windows of skyscrapers, and barricading main roads.

At noon, the storm made landfall in the mainland city of Zhuhai, bringing destruction to Hong Kong from a distance of 37 miles. Two million Guangdong households were briefly without power. Macau's casinos were forced to run on backup generators.

The writer speaks of misfortune; a rapid drop in pressure with a record high tide. Then the tone gets political: poor predictions of ferocity and bureaucratic failures.

A tiny fly lands on the corner of the news report, drawn to the glow. Too close to sleep to swipe it away, Anna watches it hover in the space between paragraphs then wander back towards the margin, torn between the action and the coolness of the frame. It braves the brightness for a moment longer, then blinded, takes flight, circling just outside the halo.

South Asian storms are getting stronger. Their violence is magnified by rising sea-surface temperatures. This represents a heightened threat to life in the region.

As Anna's eyes begin to close, she glimpses warnings of danger, sentences blur, and the reports begin to tangle.

She's mining news sites for any mention of a riot. She finds promising snippets, but when she enters the site, the reports are outdated. Flare-ups and flashes she already knows he has avoided. There is no mention of anything new. But still, she can't settle.

She'd trusted Lottie until the morning. By the afternoon, she was doubting. And by 10.00 p.m. Friday, she knew the riot vans weren't coming.

Tonight, they'll sleep easily—Lottie's father and the police. The streets are calm and complacent. No one will alert them to the nothing they are planning.

She is almost asleep when the fly stirs again, too close to her ear. She jerks awake and swats it. It loops inside the net and re-settles on the article, the grey map of Kowloon, a pale patchwork of districts. It is still for several seconds, taking in its new surroundings, then it turns from Wong Tai Sin and fords Victoria Harbour. It finds Causeway Bay and worries at the border, then it makes a choice to leave the city altogether. It ventures into the text, tracing rings around plazas, conflict zones and clashes, as though circling connections, buried leads she's overlooked. She tries to blow it away, but the fly is persistent, and re-settles like a vector pin, urging her to trust it. She closes her eyes and blue light fades to blackness.

When she opens them again, she is on the streets of Mong Kong. It's like Nathan Road—but isn't—with the shops of Tai Po Market. The atmosphere is heavy, sticky, and sluggish, thick with the knowledge of the storm that is coming.

While the city is well practiced in dealing with the danger, the ferocity of Hong Kong's typhoons should not be underrated. Luckily, the city has an easy warning system, an intensity prediction. You'll see it posted in the corner of all MTR TV screens.

Anna's phone is in her hand. She looks down at the storm tracker app open on the screen. The map is dashed with minor threats that veer away at acute angles. Their trajectories look unnatural, but she is used to this pattern. They will bring the black rain but no permanent damage.

T1 means there's a good chance it will miss Hong Kong entirely. It's primarily a notice to be aware, in case it worsens.

Anna walks a little further, scanning the names of familiar shops she's never entered, reading them out loud, like she's committing them to memory, as though if she forgets, they'll disappear entirely. She is looking for something, with a hot, redundant energy, but she can't grasp what it is and or where it might be.

T3 means winds are picking up across Victoria Harbour. Depending on severity, you should avoid coastal regions.

The feeling is growing stronger. Her feet seem to know the way, but her limbs are getting stiff and beginning to resist her efforts to move them. The storm is creeping closer; she needs to move faster.

Vendors pull carts stacked with cardboard across her path. They don't care if they obstruct her; it's like they don't see her.

She tries to ask one where he's going, speaking a language she doesn't know. He seems to understand, but she misses his reply. As he turns to leave, she sees he is the student from the plane. She tries to follow him, but her feet are glued, she begs him to repeat it, reaching out to stop him leaving, the voice inside her screaming.

Her feet come suddenly unstuck and she lunges towards him, crashing into his cart, scattering cardboard on the ground. Damp boxes break her fall, then she is sinking as they drown her, heavy with stagnant water. The student reaches but can't save her.

T8 is a 2 hr warning of winds in excess of 180 kmph. Stay away from exposed windows. Prepare for routes to be diverted.

The backdrop has shifted now. She's farther from the harbour, somewhere closer to Yau Ma Tei. And her goal has shifted with it. She has one purpose now: find shelter. She knows the place she's looking for, but can't fit it in the puzzle, and every combination of corners brings her back to this beginning. The pavements are strewn with debris, as though the storm has already hit. Steel barriers block the sideroads. The air is wet and rancid. She looks down at the tracker. Now, the minor storms have vanished. But in the corner, a circle pulses; the big one is coming.

She looks ahead down the road. A branch of low cloud is emerging between buildings, drifting across the street, and it is gathering momentum. The cloud swirls around the edges, beckoning her towards it, and with her next breath, Anna tastes the bitterness of tear gas.

Her eyes begin to sting, and when she rubs them, they burn harder. She breathes in deeply, without thinking, and a new lung-full chokes her. If she stays here, it will strangle her, but something draws her closer.

She checks the map again, though the screen is barely visible through the smoke. It is billowing around her now, hot and acidic. The map shows Kowloon Tong and the Island, studded with pulsing red circles of danger. But she can't find herself amongst them, the tiny marker keeps shifting, disappearing behind labels and sixty second updates. She walks blindly through the streets, towards a sound of distant coughing.

She looks up. Tin Hau Temple. Wang-man sits beneath a tree. He smiles up as she approaches, but his eyes are sad and bleary. The ash from his cigarette rises into the air and mingles with cinders settling in his hair. They are hot against her skin. There are scorches on his jeans, brown singe marks, still smouldering, widening into holes. The skin underneath is blistering.

She tries to tell him – he's burning - but he waves away her words. A resignation in his movements; he knows already what is coming. In the distance, there's a chanting, the steady marching of a crowd. She reads the circles in Wang-man's denim; the storm is almost upon them.

The trudge grows louder and faster; in an instant, it will swamp them. She opens her mouth to yell, and ash and smoke rush in to choke her. She tries to swallow, but her throat is raw. Trapped embers stick and burn. The chorus and the clatter of batons is deafening.

T10: a direct hit. Though the phenomenon is rare. The damage will be immense. Fatalities almost certain.

Anna jerks awake, awoken by a rattling. The early morning is still thin. Her eyes are gritty and swollen. She lays still inside the net, listening to the bickering; two women speaking Russian.

They, too, don't trust the lock, and are testing the mechanism. Though Anna's nightmare is fading, she can still taste the ashes and wishes she'd thought ahead and bought water for the morning. There's a dripping in the bathroom, but the crusted tap is unappealing; she's read too many stories of bodies floating in the cistern.

She sits up and finds her phone tangled in the bed sheet.

'Meet at Tai Wo Station.'

It is Kallum. She's found him.

Anna stares at the number. A moment later, she remembers. It isn't Kallum. It is Jenny. The trip to Shenzhen.

Anna moves to the tiny bathroom and takes a mouthful of chlorine, retrieves her passport from the pillowcase, and heads out for the border.

Chapter 25

Somewhere between here and the mainland is a border. With each bend in the road, she expects it to materialize. But as the road stretches longer, the bus ploughing onwards, Anna starts to wonder if she's already beyond it. For several minutes, she has uncovered Hong Kong's deepest secret: the dotted line is just a rumour that no one has bothered to test. But then they the cross the final crest and the new city confronts her.

Shenzhen is pale and bursting, hungry for the air that abides by the divide. Anna suddenly feels defensive of Hong Kong's landscape. She wants to cast herself over the open fields to protect them. She is angry at rectangles, that dense greedy margin. Tower blocks are crammed window-to-window. They jostle with one another to be closest to the edge. It is something like a wall, but more decisive, more definitive. Each side is envious of the other. On that side, the only space left to claim is the sky. Urban planners dream upwards; the projections command it. On this side, tired architects dream of a plan.

Jenny couldn't make it. Anna got the message before her train reached Kowloon Tong. But Anna had expected it and decided to go there alone. She was anxious, but it was easier than another second of searching.

On the bus from Tai Wo station, she checks the map for the millionth time. There is a highway and a river that she assumes marks the border, but north, beyond the station, the perimeter fades. Zoomed out, she can see the grey demarcation, a vague box around Hong Kong, but the moment she tries to look closer, it vanishes, like she's permitted to imagine the boundary from a distance but, close-up, must understand that both sides are one. There is no hard, red line, just a port and Jenny's promise that foreigners can get through it.

Lottie used to tell the story that she had fallen asleep once and crossed over. She was woken by a guard requesting documents in Mandarin. Anna knew it was unlikely, but still liked her to retell it. A reminder of just how close they lived to the real thing.

The road surface blends into the dust cloud just above it, a dust as pale as the sky, anaemic and wheezing. It stretches above the half-vacant villages. They remind her of storm drains and thick, throaty diesel. Through the window, torn-off branches punctuate the pavements, but this far from the city, they inconvenience no one. Here, at the edges, they are accustomed to barriers. She looks beyond them to the mountains, visibility is shallow; they'd used the sharpness of their edges to gauge the pollution each morning.

Anna's signal bars are empty, as though out here she'd never need it. Nothing to tell and no one eager to hear it. She remembers how she crouched in the corner of the attic; he wasn't answering her phone calls, the instant message said delivered, but he might not have data—he had to know they would be unaided.

She remembers how she'd battled through old curtains and shoe racks to the highest point in the house for a single bar of coverage. She'd leaned against the broken barbecue, shedding rust onto the floor tiles, for once not caring about the spiders.

In the memory she crouches, staring at the screen.

A single line in the corner. The glimmer of a connection. The signal holds. It starts to ring. She listens to the buzzing, fighting back the flashes of dark men in dark clothing.

The pauses are too long; between each ring she thinks he's answered. She holds her breath. The silence swells. Her heart leaps and then crashes.

But he refuses to answer. He is making her suffer. She wishes, at least, that he'd reject the call, just read the messages and trust her.

He won't pick up now, Anna knows, but she isn't ready to believe it. She isn't ready to accept that something is keeping him from answering, that somewhere there's a van with ridged steel flooring, harsh suspension, blackened windows, and overtightened plastic bindings. Somewhere in gym bag, a cell phone is pulsing. The boys pray it's one of theirs and that it means help is coming.

The bus pulls up to a railing. There is a tall fence and a check point. Beyond it is the border town, a refuge before the city. Instinctively, she hates it. There's a stillness and indifference. Anna knows she isn't welcome. She gets off the bus and stands for a minute in the sun, staring at the houses, wondering who owns them. But she can't dislodge the memory of Kallum and that evening, the dial tone, the waiting; the line had just kept ringing.

When it times out, she reconnects and turns it onto speaker. The signal holds back down the stairwell, but at the second floor, it falters. Inside her apartment, she grabs her train card and a jacket. Lauren doesn't ask where she is going.

She tries to call him from the taxi to the station. She prays the trains are on her side and that Kowloon Tong is quiet.

Once inside the train, she deliberates. She can stay onboard until Mong Kok East, but transferring might be faster. She thinks of changing at Prince Edward; the red line exits might be closer. She realizes then, she has no idea where to find them. Lottie said Mong Kok. She'd never offered any detail.

At Yau Ma Tei, she finds an exit and is lucky with her choice. It leads her onto Pitt Street and shops she recognizes. She isn't lost but doesn't know where she is heading. The dark streets seem more likely, but she is reluctant, now, to take them. Anna moves between people and street signs and railings, with the same sleep-drunk clumsiness of an early morning hotel room. She trips off curbs and follows streetlights with a vague idea of direction. She needs a system, but there isn't one, Hong Kong leads her round in circles. She traces corner after corner, and each street blends into the next one. But Anna tells herself Hong Kong is small; if he's here, she will find him.

Around the back of Langham Place, she sees a group of high school students. It's too late and they're too young to be out here without a reason. She approaches with the map screen, hoping they will help her; they'll be shy at first, like she is, but they'll decide it's fine to tell her. She plans to point and ask them, 'Djo-mae-ahh?' but her words come out in English:

'Is something happening?' She shows a girl the map. 'Just here—a demonstration?'

The girl frowns and says she doesn't know. Her friend leans in to try. 'Ah, you want a . . . what?'

'To find a place.'

'Which place? I help you search it.'

But Anna says she isn't sure, and he apologizes for his English.

As Anna walks away, she hears them arguing behind her, debating what she meant, the skyline or the station. She chokes down tears of frustration; it's all a cover; they must know something. She thinks of Lottie's vagueness; her imprecision feels deliberate. Now, the street signs make her angry, just as unhelpful and indifferent. She feels caught inside a memory but with the immediacy of a dream, that feeling of urgency and half-remembered streets.

The phone map is worse than pointless, intent on misdirection. One moment it places her and tracks her south along Canton Road, but then it jumps her to the next one, the vector spins and points her east. And when she zooms in to try to steady it, the marker disappears. It is guessing, just like she is, but her only option is to trust it.

She passes Mong Kok station and glances right down Argyle Street, then carries on towards the markets, though she can't image that's where they'll be. She scans the faces that stream past her, searching for a sign, unrest in their expressions, rumours she can trace. She checks her phone again. No message. And her battery is draining. Panic rises. She needs to save it. But if she turns it off, she's lost him. She reaches the wide triangular junction, but this space is too ambitious. She's too far out now, that much is clear. But she is running out of options. Anna crosses towards a shopping mall and steps aside under a doorframe, where she tries to load South China Morning Post *for any updates, any mentions. But the page gets stuck halfway, though the bar has finished loading. She hits refresh but doesn't see it through. She already knows it won't help her.*

She joins a crowd beside a crossing on what she thinks is Mong Kok Road, and as they wait for the lights, she spots a camera bag, too expensive to be a tourist's. The man who carries it is Western. His clothes are plain and understated. He could easily be a journalist. The more she stares, the more she knows it. His muted face makes Anna nervous, there's something off in his expression, and when the lights change, he stays put; he is waiting there for something. The crowd surges. Anna fights sideways towards him. He is waiting for a call. And when it comes, he will lead her right to them. It isn't Lottie's dad, but Anna wonders if he knows him, if they'd shared the tip off, if they'd discussed whether the sources could be trusted, if they'd rationalized their decision to keep the police in the dark. They'd give the students what they wanted: the permanence of a story.

As Anna battles through the crowd, he reaches into his jacket and checks his phone with impatience. He is anxious, just like she is. But then, a woman in a holiday dress emerges with two waters, he links an arm around her waist, and they disappear towards the skyline.

Anna feels the night get thicker. She's lost her lead and is getting desperate.

Her battery is at 6 per cent. But what if Lottie doesn't answer? No, she has to.

5 per cent, now. Anna dials her number; she can't delay it any longer.

'I'm walking round in circles.'

'You went to find him?'

'He isn't here!'

Lottie's breath in the receiver. 'Give up, then. You're going home now?'

'No one will help. They think I'm lost.'

'Okay, then, tell me. Where are you?'

'I've been walking round for hours. I'm back at the station, now. Exit . . . B.'

There's a mumbling as Lottie calculates how Anna could have missed them. A sudden silence. 'You do mean Wan Chai, right?'

Her vision blurs. 'No . . . Mong Kok East.'

Anna walks towards the border, the tiny booth that Jenny mentioned. Here, she can apply for the visa if she needs it. She has her passport open ready, though Jenny said they rarely check. But Jenny has the language and the credibility that comes with it. Somewhere in the distance is a prison on a hill. Anna moves towards the check point, the pages sweaty in her pocket.

At first, the guards ignore her, and she relaxes a little. But then she steps off the curb and they rise in unison to stop her. They carry batons at their hips and rifles strung across their shoulders. This is their territory, now. She doesn't doubt that they'll defend it. Anna keeps her pace constant, but she can see it on their faces: there's no chance of getting further. Appeals will be hopeless.

Rapid firing sounds behind her. Anna ducks and grabs the railing. Pink smoke rises from the hillock. Firecrackers.

The border guards are laughing.

The same driver takes her back again. This time all the seats are empty. So much vacant grey leather makes Anna fidgety and anxious. No one knows that she's alone here, without witnesses or purpose. Cowering at fireworks. She can feel their faces grinning. The atmosphere is thicker now. Anna swears Hong Kong felt brighter before she'd learned that she couldn't leave it.

Two stops later, an elderly couple joins them. They sit apart from one another and shout above the engine. They are courteous but familiar, a friendship of habit. Tucked away, at the back, Anna goes unnoticed. She hopes they get off before she does. She does not want to provoke them.

It is mid-morning, still early, they'll think she's come here for a daytrip. They'll say she lives in Shenzhen. They'll call her an outsider. She can't stand to let them think that Hong Kong is new to her.

On her map, the marker pulses along the line that marks her progress. Soon, she'll pass the old swamp house and the stop she won't get off at. She returns to the home screen. A red dot beside the app. Some kind of audio message. She's never seen one before now.

'*So sorry teacher. I couldn't make it. I wish you could have fun there.*' Indecipherable mumbling, something about an order. '*Anyway, teacher, if you want, I have the time now. If you want, I can still meet you.*' She is moving through a crowd. The background noise is getting thicker. '*Or did you go to Shenzhen?*' There's a disturbance in the audio. '*I'm at the Festival Walk, um—it's for shopping, do you know it? I'll be here for an hour. So, I don't know, if you can get here?*'

Jenny's message ends, but Anna stares at the symbol. She can't bring herself to replay it; Jenny's uncurated voice feels too intimate in her headphones. Another message appears below it; 7 seconds. She quickly taps it.

'*Anyway, if you know it? Or I can send you my location.*'

Anna's been there countless times. She can make it in an hour, but she hovers above the mic icon, too shy to speak in real time. Instead, she types her message, half-hoping for a drop in signal. She scans the mountains for a phone mast. A raindrop splatters against her window.

There's a screech of glass in metal. An axle smacks a tree branch. The engine cuts. There's something final in the rising stench of diesel.

Chapter 26

She pulls the jacket around her shoulders and peers out from the exit. Puddles too wide to step around pool along the walkway. The damp denim of her jacket is coarse against her sunburn as she grips it by the collar and makes a dash towards the plaza. Stretches of path are covered, and Anna sprints in between them, but the final slope up to the doors of Festival Walk is left wide open.

Inside the first set of doors, she parts the panels of plastic, pats her face dry on the lining of her jacket, and checks the fabric for mascara. The mall is cool and spacious. She knows the layout and the levels. She checks the pin that Jenny sent her, but the link has now expired.

She finds the coffee shop on level two and loiters outside it. It is almost two hours later than she'd said, but she arrives ahead of Jenny. When Jenny finally finds her, there's no apology or excuses; she seems surprised that Anna's hair is wet and offers her a tissue.

The café is dimly lit, the ambience artificial. Jenny orders coffees in English, dismissing Anna's refusal. When the waitress brings them over, Anna thanks her but doesn't touch it. It sits between them on the low table, a film forming on the surface.

She isn't sleeping as it is. The door to her hotel room rattles throughout the night, even with her suitcase wedged upright against it. She inquired about the lock, but the manager didn't get it and came to show her for the third time how to beep the sticky key card. That last time, she didn't even pretend that he'd helped her; she just told him to forget it and left him standing in the corridor. Back inside the room, she'd dragged her suitcase to block it, or at least stop it from juddering in the early hours of the morning. Strange sounds through thin walls already invade her nightmares, a terrifying quasi-sleep she can only half awake from. But she can't tell all this to Jenny without admitting where she's staying. She'll think she's cheap or naïve, and Anna can't bear to give her either.

'You go to Shenzhen?'

It's clear she didn't, but Jenny asks anyway. Anna is about to lie when Jenny's phone interrupts her. The interruption feels like a warning: Jenny is too discerning; she will see through Anna's words before she's even spoken.

'Not really,' she admits. 'I didn't have the papers.'

Jenny switches the phone to silent, but leaves it face-up on the table, and asks 'You tried though—to get through?'

'Yes, I tried. They wouldn't let me.' The truth sounds pathetic.

'Did you show them your permit?'

'Permit?'

'The ID.'

Anna nods. Jenny frowns and glances at her phone screen.

'Then they should have let you through. And you showed them? Can I see it?'

'My passport?'

Jenny pauses. 'Not the passport. The ID card.'

It all suddenly makes sense.

'Oh right, I don't have one. Just my passport and the visa. My old ID card has expired.' She adds, '. . . now I don't live here.'

She reaches for the coffee to distract from Jenny's surveillance. The surface rocks to reveal a brown rim on the ceramic. Jenny nods slowly but doesn't seem to understand, like she's piecing things together, but crucial details are missing. Anna can't blame her; she still hasn't really told her the reason she's back here, only offered vague notions about meeting old friends. It wasn't entirely deliberate. It's just that the shape of their conversations never pressed her for specifics. Hong Kong conversations have a habit of drifting.

'Ah, I didn't know you don't have it. So, I don't think they'll let you enter.'

'No, they didn't.' It comes out a little more aggressive than she intended.

'I thought maybe they'd changed the rules, that maybe, now, anyone in Hong Kong cannot enter.'

'No, I think it's just my visa.'

'Yes, with the passport, that is different.'

Jenny watches Anna sip the coffee. It is lukewarm and bitter. Kallum said the ID cards showed that Hong Kong was something different, but when she asked him what that was, he told her to forget it.

'Why did you think they'd changed the rule?'

Jenny frowns, 'When I hear they didn't let you cross.'

'But, I mean, is there a reason you can think of why they would?'

'Close the border?' Jenny shrugs, and doesn't offer the obvious, and Anna isn't sure why she's leading her towards it.

'—like a political reason?'

There's a shift in Anna's tone and, this time, Jenny feels it. But she doesn't want to go there and tries to diffuse it.

'Ah ha, yes, I guess. Should be.'

They both laugh the same laugh. The coffee leaves a sourness on her tongue.

'Do you think it's getting worse?'

Jenny shrugs, 'I hope will getting better. Or the same. Just stay like this.'

The phrase is familiar. 'Really? Do you believe that?'

She laughs again and says she hopes so.

Jenny shifts in the chair to redirect the conversation, picks her phone up from the table, and appeases its flashing. Anna suddenly becomes aware of those around her. The table adjacent is a little too close; the slim gap between them, an illusion of privacy. Though they don't seem to be listening and are staring at their screens, the couple beside her might have heard her every word. Anna stares at their faces and back across at Jenny, something close to apathy dulling their features. It's as if they're all awaiting some announcement, some update. Until then, they'll gaze patiently at bright moving boxes.

Jenny has stopped scrolling and seems to be reading. Anna is about to give up when Jenny surprises her by speaking. Jenny sighs and taps the screen.

'I really don't like the argument. I don't know if it is politics, but somehow it started and now everyone and everything get mixed up in the middle. It's not the argument even, but the number of people who get stuck on each side. Like I'm this and you're that one. So, I don't know if I believe it.'

Anna realizes now that she's still debating her question; she isn't indifferent, but disappointed and angry.

'These people,' Jenny continues, tapping the screen with her nail, 'they like to comment on everything. They say some terrible things.'

'Yes, it all gets so tangled.'

'I guess you didn't hear the news.'

Anna is suddenly embarrassed. She says something about having no data on her phone.

'Well, it happened a few years ago, but only now we see the consequence.'

She relaxes. Old news. She's less to blame for having missed it.

'Around the trouble with the students—they really do a lot of damage to the streets and to the transports, and some locals like to fix that.'

Anna's skin prickles. There are different forms of damage. She doesn't say it out loud, but she feels her expression stiffen. If Jenny notices, she ignores it, already tired of the debate.

'Anyway, there was a video. I didn't know if you have seen it. A local woman, like a grandmother—you see her picking up debris. Well, they say that she's a nationalist, that she's working for China, that she's the hypocrite and the devil, and they say it like she's a traitor. That she's the enemy of Hong Kong, but I don't know if they believe that. They'll just say it and . . . ' she taps her phone, ' . . . because of this, they all repeat it.'

Anna shifts closer. The coffee shop is filling up; it's getting harder and harder to hear her words above the chatter. A crowd spills out from the cinema next door; the movie is over, a disappointing ending.

'Well, this woman I tell you about—they find out she has a grandson. So, they connect him with the video. And they connect him with this policy about nationalist education. It doesn't matter he support it or just try to defend it or just try to be reasonable. They just decided his position. They just claim that he support it.

'So, he just take his own life.' She says it bluntly, without warning. 'All because of the video, you know, the impression.'

'That's terrible,' says Anna, but Jenny nods a dismissal. It's old news now, and she begrudges the interruption to her story.

'And now,' she taps the plastic, 'they post heartbreaking messages. Congratulations to the woman. So, how can I support them? How can I listen to their message?'

The conversation is over. She doesn't need Anna's opinion. It's like she knows that Anna isn't even sure that she has one.

On the train back to Chung King, Anna replays the moments: the morning at the border; the rainstorm; the conversation. She didn't regret going to meet Jenny, exactly. But she just couldn't stand being someone else's regret. Someone's wasted afternoon. An absence of hours. She wanted to be worth it, a valuable addition. She wishes she could have offered what Jenny couldn't think of. A nuanced perspective, a new angle to consider, but she couldn't find the questions and her responses fell flat. Instead, she listened to Jenny growing tired of talking and wondering why Anna wasn't drinking her coffee.

The video is easy to find. She reads the comments while it buffers, skipping down to those in English, scanning for a profile picture or initials in an alias.

There's a Cantonese crack as the audio loads. Anna scrolls up to the video. The old woman's voice scrapes as she drags a cone across the tarmac. As she tugs, it shifts off centre, straining the orange tape that connects it to another. The tape stretches and the knot around the head pulls tighter. Her fingers fumble as she picks at the impossible tangle. *Why tie it so tight? Don't they think even a moment ahead of their actions?*

She heaves the cone, again, and tries to steady the base, grips the tape with both hands and pulls, trying to snap it. But the tape only stretches, orange fading to white, Anna imagines the plastic getting hot inside her fingers. The old woman is conscious of the crowd that is forming. They are enjoying her struggle.

She drags the other cone now, closer to the other. The tape slackens, she unhooks it and gathers up her victory.

A laser pointer traces the contours of her body, worrying at the wrinkles of her clothing and her skin. She stoops to escape it. The beam quickly re-finds her. She's already tiring of their childish persistence. *What? They will shoot her?* She stands tall to receive the bullet. The red dot disappears. The victory makes her bolder.

Her tone becomes shrill, her diction poetic. She spreads her arms wide, welcoming the onslaught. She juts out her chin. She'll be a martyr; she can see it.

Two protestors come to help or else to hinder her efforts, still deciding if they mean to assist or to stall her. They hover at the edges, in and out of the frame. Their gloves find the cones she has already shifted and stand them upright where she dropped them. But Granny ignores their efforts, she never asked them to help her. They're ruining the image. She'd prefer them to beat her.

She gestures at the rubble, bricks, and branches torn from banyans. *Messy children, and ungrateful. Did their mothers never teach them?* She crouches down, finds a stone, and tosses it towards the curb, but she means to send it further. She thanks goodness that her own children are nothing like this rabble.

A journalist, now, takes the brunt of her anger. *Why don't they beat her? That's what they are here for.* She can't unmask the revolution if they won't even cut her. There's venom in her finger. She tries to rouse their resistance. But their retorts are calm and cautious. *Because we don't want to hurt you.*

Still, they take care to keep their faces hidden from cameras. Anna places Kallum's, half-hopefully, amongst them. In the daylight, their clothes are too personal and too distinctive: an old, repurposed hockey mask, a ski buff, a bandana. In the daylight, black uniforms are brown and navy blue, faded from re-washing, old T-shirts their helpers have got tired of folding.

This morning, they speak quietly. Some answerphone calls from home, calls they've avoided all evening. *What did they think was going to happen?* They are urged to reassess the worst case situation. But they're more determined than ever, they urge their parents to believe them. Others mill around in twos and threes, giving statements to reporters. *We called for help. It never came.* A minority show aggression.

The old woman is getting jealous, and fights to hold their interest. She's the one who'll clear the road. She's had a taste of the attention. She moves closer to a journalist and prompts another question. She doesn't answer when they ask her, *'Granny, do you have children?'*

Chapter 27

The jade markets are quiet, more traders than buyers. Inside she is 'Missy!' or else she is despised. They squat, bare-kneed, on stools and look up as Anna passes. Another tugs her shoulder and points at his trays of jade pendants. He guides her to his trinkets and tells Anna she likes them, but she doesn't, they aren't right, her mother likes the deep green ones. When she's passed, he goes back to printing date stamps in a notebook.

Inkpad, chop, inkpad, chop.

The dull thud is too familiar. She sees the stamp in Claudi's hand. The afternoon was almost over.

Anna listens to the sound as she watches the parents through the window, lining up outside the classroom. Inkpad, chop, inkpad, chop. *The glare on the window means her own face is concealed as she picks out the adults' features that she recognizes in their children, the shape of a nose, a point in an eyebrow. Raymond Lee's father is chuckling behind the glass. He has a mole in the hollow below the cheekbone with a hair that grows out of its centre. She has learned it is lucky; she will tell her mother that evening.*

'Can I help?' Anna gestures to the rest of Claudi's handbooks, more of a request than an offer. 'I can chop the rest?'

'It's okay. Nothing to do.'

But she means there is nothing she'd trust Anna to do correctly. Claudi signs her name and stamps 'MISS ANNA' in the box beside it. Anna's eyes follow the chop to the page, and when she lifts it away, she hears tiny ink tendrils snapping. She blows on the letters. Anna awes at her precision.

She remembers those capitals sitting neatly in the lines and wishes everything could be fit into snug little boxes. She liked to tell herself, in such moments, that she'd never forget the details. But remembering it now, she can't be sure of the timeline; it might be the day her mother visited Anna's school, or much earlier, before the protests, when everything still felt new. But she remembers those letters, perfectly centred, and is tied to a feeling that everything is unravelling.

By now, she has begun to crave conversation. The silence that once shielded her feels heavy and oppressive. As she flicks through the jade disks for a present for her mother, she finds herself searching for memories of connection.

That final bus ride to the airport; her mother's time to leave. The journey had passed almost too quickly and was tainted with their wondering what the trip could have been.

They speed towards mountains crowned with emerald-eyed apartments, glistening in the glow of a grey Hong Kong evening. The sky is translucent, and a tentative yellow leaks from the washout. Their eyes settle on the sun poised above Tolo Harbour. As they stare, a branch of cloud splits it in two. They accelerate towards it, and the cloud widens, disappearing one half and reducing the other to a tiny glowing stone, and when the road curves, she loses it behind a cluster of tower blocks. The freeway divides. Their bus bridges a river, where a crimson-scaled dragon snags ripples in its silk. The roads coils again, and a rock face opens wide to inhale them. The sun is left to burn itself out in the smog.

Anna has booked her an evening flight home; crossing the bridge to Lantau Island, they watch the pink sky fall to violet and purple then grey beyond the mountains. As the clouds switch their shades, the lull stretches longer, and they are at risk of becoming the types they despise, worse than uninteresting; uninterested.

The sky has turned to slate.

'You're looking brown,' says her mother, meaning: not as brown as me.

'Not as brown as you,' says Anna, and she means: you will never understand Hong Kong.

At the terminal station, Anna retrieves her mother's suitcase, points her to the smoking bay. It will be her last for 18 hours.

They say goodbye beside the check-in desk and Anna watches her mother disappear inside the panels. She is sad that they'd never found the time to make it to the jade place.

The wide departure hall is filled with lives, intersecting, twitching, and clutching at elbows, rechecking papers. The lights are too bright, which makes the outside seem darker, but Anna welcomes its cover as the crowds grow thin towards her bus stop. She doesn't miss her mother yet, though she isn't as relieved by her departure as she expected she might be. The Tai Po bus stand is the furthest from the building. The queue doubles when she joins it.

'Tai Po?'

A nod and they stand together in silence. On the bus, she sits upstairs. The woman from the queue joins her. For most of the journey, they are lost in the streetlights, then the glow of pagodas when they get closer to home. Through the reflection on the window, Anna recognizes buildings; she will have to swap buses soon, just beyond the Ka Fuk estate. She has never disembarked here. Though the outside is familiar, mild curiosity has never taken her further. She wonders if it ever will as the estate slips behind her.

When it is time to change buses, she crosses the bridge to Kwong Fuk Road and waits beyond the second bus stop because it never stops any closer. Tonight, it almost drives past her.

Anyone new might mistake Kwong Fuk for Central; but Anna had long since learned the difference. Everything is smaller. Fewer signs are trimmed with neon.

When her second bus stalls at the roadworks near the village, Anna notices that the woman from the first is seated across the aisle, a few rows behind her. Anna twists a little in her seat, leaning her shoulder against the window so she can study the woman more closely, wondering why she was at the airport and where she is going home to. At the Tolo Highway intersection, Anna realizes the woman is preparing herself to speak. Silhouetted by the pulsing amber beacons of roadworks, the woman shifts to the edge of her seat.

'I want to ask you some questions,' she frowns, leaning closer. 'Do you know where Scotland is?' She asks as though it is missing, and she's concerned about its safety.

'Yes . . . '

'Oh. Is it near England?'

'Yes, it's just above' Anna points to its position on an invisible floating map.

The woman smiles and the shadows around her eyes lift for a moment. At first Anna's answer seems enough, but then she inches even closer.

'And do the men there wear . . . ?' She runs a finger across her thigh.

'A kilt?' Anna laughs. 'Yes, some people do.' Then, worrying that it might seem like she is mocking the question, she adds in a more serious tone, 'It's usually just for special occasions, though.'

'Oh, like weddings, special parties? And ceremonies?'

'Yes, exactly like that.'

The woman smiles again and sits back in her seat, and as they round the next corner, her smile settles to a look of contentment.

Anna wonders for how long that question has troubled her, if perhaps she had debated its truth amongst friends. She hopes the woman will tell them about the girl on the bus. Anna's is the horse's mouth, and she has never even been to Scotland, but she decides not to ruin her authenticity with the truth.

There was nothing more for either of them to say, though Anna remembers feeling happy, like a thread had grown between them. The woman seemed to feel it too, but now Anna can't be sure. She doubts that the woman still remembers her face. The detail she had offered, having satisfied a niggle, will have faded once more. She wonders too if the woman ever made it to Scotland, because Anna still hasn't been there herself.

She's too tired, tonight, to walk the streets of Yau Ma Tei, so she lets herself take the bus. Between the markets and Chung King, it is just a few stops, though she isn't sure she can face going back there just yet. As she drops coins into the lockbox, a vague sadness suddenly fills her. No one here wants to know where she comes from, or anything else—about Scotland or home. The threads are all untangling, but they lead only to dead ends. *Nothing to do, Miss Anna.* Tiny ink tendrils snapping. Her connections are all broken. She is running out of options.

It's not far, but she sits upstairs; the seats are almost full. She takes the final empty double, behind a *jeje* and his grandson.

Immediately Anna knows someone has seen her. She doesn't turn around yet. The feeling is familiar. The same sensation has followed her since that night on the roof, but it is closer now, expectant.

She turns. Jenny is sitting on the seat just behind her. She grins when Anna notices, no hint of animosity, yesterday's bickering at Festival Walk forgotten.

'Did you eat yet, teacher? You look so tired.'

'Ah, sorry, I didn't see you.'

She is tired, and Jenny's comment reminds her just how much. She's barely slept for several nights. For a moment, Jenny seems to share Anna's preference for silence.

'I forgot to ask you. So, did you find your friend?'

Anna pauses.

'In Tsing Yi.'

'Oh, Claudi? Yes, I found her.'

Anna is too tired to think up an explanation. And she is no longer even sure where the truth starts or ends. Jenny nods, unconvinced.

'I'm sorry I couldn't help you. I don't know many people at Tsing Yi.'

'It's okay! It isn't your fault.'

'So, it is good that you found her.'

Anna is beginning to wish she had just said no, but it's too late now to backtrack. She can feel her lies unravelling, Jenny picking at the threads. She could stand to be pictured as alone, but not as a liar.

'Actually, she came to me. I forgot she had my number.'

There's a ticking from the windowpane. *Tiny tendrils snapping.*

A jolt. They grip the seats in front. The ticking briefly subsides. But as they accelerate, it starts again. *That village is bad news.* Ever since Tsing Yi, when Jenny spoke about a danger, the words had seemed to chase her. She played them over and over, a steady repetition, like she was teaching them to Cheuk Yiu, a drum beat in the distance, pacing to its rhythm. The words resurface now, surging with each tremor. The lights are too revealing. She can't bear it any longer.

'Jenny, when I mentioned that Josephine's family have moved, you said something about the village not being safe anymore.'

Anna hears her mother's words come spilling out into the aisle.

'Hong Kong is safe for you, teacher. You don't need to worry. I told you at the shopping mall. I really think you shouldn't worry.'

But that isn't what she means. There is a story. She knows there must be. She asks Jenny to tell her.

'Your friend Claudi didn't tell you? I'm surprised you haven't heard. It was a long time ago, in fact, you might have just missed it.' As Jenny talks, Anna senses the distance of hearsay. The scene shifts with each retelling, as she embellishes the detail.

'They chased a helper through the houses, it wasn't Josephine, but Filipino. The family was the reason though. The son got mixed up in some trouble. It's like I said before, these games don't only affect the ones who play them. Yes, they chased her to the station. A message—like, to scare him.'

Long after Jenny's stop, Anna finds herself staring at the empty seat. She is lost for several minutes, before she notices an envelope wedged below the window. Jenny might have left it. It might be important. But as Anna goes to retrieve it, she finds it is only a leaflet. She is about to discard it, when she notices the heading.

As Anna's reads, it transports her; between paragraphs, she's the helper, fleeing between the buildings.

Chapter 28

Establishing a positive relationship with your helper not only makes your life easier but prevents tensions in your household. Such tensions may have a negative effect on your children. It is better to establish clear ground rules early on.

From the balcony they call to her, just loud enough to hear. They call her bun bun and street girl and ask her for a price. They call in Cantonese, then English, and the second insult hits harder.

She thinks she knows one of the voices, but can't decide from where. They aren't neighbours; she doesn't know this house. But they seem to know her.

It's too dark to see their faces—she knows this and doesn't try, keeping her eyes fixed on the ground, just ahead of her sandals. The path is uneven, dashed with crevices and fractures. Her feet feel clumsy; they are watching, and she is conscious she will trip.

While your helper has the right to keep their whereabouts private, you may explain to her the benefits of sharing such details. You may ask her

to disclose where she is planning to go. Concern for her safety is ideal for you both. Nevertheless, outside of work hours, her time is her own.

In her head, she counts her footsteps, like she used to teach the children to help them learn their English numbers. Her sandal flicks a tiny stone against the wheel rim of a car. She prays it isn't one of theirs; they are close enough, now, to hear.

The balcony goes quiet; she thinks they've gone inside. She takes the chance to scan her surroundings. There is no one; she's alone.

Giving praise can make your helper feel house-proud and loyal. Around young children, a motivated helper is ideal. Make sure to explain clearly how you expect things to be done. Failure to do so may lead to resentment.

The ripple of a tree root in the concrete disrupts her stride. She loses count of her steps and glances up at the house. A little way ahead, she sees three figures—maybe four—under the awning.

As she nears, the men call louder, one voice clear above the rest. She hears liar, and traitor and gǎngsòng—Hong Kong filth. She tries to shrug off the words. But these names are too specific. At first, she doesn't get it; she's done nothing to offend them. Then, it hits her. It's Kallum. A warning not to upset them.

Abandoning their circle, they turn around to face her. She pretends she hasn't noticed it, but the closest saw her looking.

It is best to avoid political discussion with your helper. Heated debate is undesirable and may cause tension in your household. You can never be sure how your employee will react, and you should always be cautious if such topics arise.

Stepping out into the road, she swerves wider to avoid them, trying to make her route look natural, but they begin to move towards her. She thinks of Kallum's battered face and that no one is here to help her.

Further up the drive, a light shines down from Christine's office. She'll be impatient but distracted; she won't come to the window.

Let your helper know your standards in a supervised trial run. Make her aware of your routine and how you expect things to be done. Increase work hours slowly when you believe that she is ready. You may wish to oversee her work until you trust her entirely.

They spread themselves across the road, pretending not to see her, closing up the passage, so she'll have to step between them.

A space opens in the middle, and it seems to be the better option. But as she guides her feet towards it, the men move to close the distance. It's a game and it's too late now to decide she isn't playing. She looks beyond them, at the house, to where Christine will be waiting.

It is important you respect your helper's personal space and privacy. Remember, in most cases, she is an adult already.

She steers back towards the fence and the group drift towards her. She looks behind but won't run yet. She will not let them scare her.

The gap between the fence and closest figure is narrowing. It is impossible to ignore him now. He is looking directly at her.

She steps left and mutters, 'Sorry', but he anticipates her movement, stepping right to block her path, pressing his body up against her. She steps back to avoid his hands as he folds them around her shoulders. A latch clicks on the patio. They look to see who might be coming.

She turns and runs; she can't help it. She has a second to get ahead. At first, she thinks she hears them laughing, then, their footsteps on the gravel.

She runs back down the driveway, towards the car park and the road; she'll double back into the village and lose herself amongst the buildings.

But she can't be sure they won't be there to cut her off from the side, force her back towards the highway, back into the open.

As she runs, she looks ahead. The car park is too exposed. Then on her right, she sees the path that leads away from the houses. The path is dark and narrow, and winds between high fences. Thick trees on either side block the moonlight and streetlamps. There's just one block until the opening. It will be dangerous to take it. Once inside, there'll be no stopping until she's far away from the village. She can't risk it. They will catch her. A second later, she's passed it.

She heads towards the car park, praying someone she knows will be there. She can't hear above her breathing, but she knows they're close behind. The gravel shifts beneath her feet. She can't make them go faster.

The way ahead is suddenly blinding. The road is drenched in silver light. Two headlamps out of nowhere. He breaks hard to avoid the collision. The glare disguises the driver, but something tells her he's no friend.

She turns; the men have scattered. The car seems to have spooked them. But she doesn't trust the quiet; it's all part of their fun.

She makes a split-second decision: the path towards the station. The dark opening in the bushes. She glances up and slips between them.

Stay alert to traffic updates. They can change without warning. She may not be as familiar with Hong Kong's transport links as you are. Due to civil demonstrations, routes may be disrupted. Make sure your helper is aware of alternative options.

She runs until the rumble of the engine fades behind her. She prays she got a good head start. She doesn't think she can hear them.

The chain link is seamless and forces her onwards. It is easier to run on concrete, but the path is longer than she remembers. She runs until her eyes have readjusted to the darkness. She sees glimpses of the road and traffic through the branches.

Up ahead, the path forks; the right loops back towards the village, the left will lead her to the highway, but it is closed off for construction.

She dares to break the barrier. Beyond the tape, the way looks clear. The builders left weeks ago, maybe months. She could chance it.

She hears a shout. They are close now. She can't outrun them for much longer. She lifts the tape and ducks beneath it, praying the other side is open.

The path is littered with the tape that blocked off the entrance, wrapped around tree trunks and draped over branches. Traffic cones that once marked the edge of a pit have been abandoned. She trips once where a ditch has been lazily filled. The path curves slightly to the left, but she longs for a sharp corner, a bend she can duck behind, a chance they won't see her. She was right about the building works. She hopes the men don't think to follow.

Another shout. They aren't playing, now. There's an edge to their tone. She can't make out the words. But they are nearer than she'd hoped.

Voices behind her at the fork. They discuss which way she's chosen. She prays they don't split up, or there's no chance she'll escape them.

He calls again. Another answer. They won't stop now. She knows it. It's no longer about Kallum. She's given chase and they will take it.

Remember, your helper is entitled to her freedom. Respect her statutory rest day. Let her know a day ahead if you will her need her at the weekend.

The exit is barred. But low enough to scramble over. At the highway, she doesn't stop. She's lucky—there's no traffic. She tears across the slip road, and lurches around the barrier. When she reaches the far side, her ankle clashes with a railing. The collision throws her forwards, but she stops herself from falling.

A shout somewhere behind her, where the path meets the road. She shouldn't have left the village, but it's too late now. She thinks of home. Her ankle throbs as she ploughs onwards, towards the glow of Tai Wo station. All the restaurants will be closed now. She prays they've kept the stairwell open.

Anna closes the folds and scans the back of the leaflet. Two-thirds of it is in Chinese, only the final third is English. Perhaps the English is more concise, perhaps they've used denser language, or the writer just decided to leave some parts untranslated. Anna wonders what they left unsaid, glad she doesn't have to read it.

Chapter 29

There isn't much to gather: a few T-shirts, a pair of sandals, a box of mooncakes that Josephine had given her outside the school. She wraps the mooncakes in her T-shirts and places them in the suitcase beside the crumpled denim jacket, still damp from the rainstorm.

Lottie had given her that jacket three years ago, not a gift but a gesture to show she didn't know who owned it. Anna should take it. She didn't care. Anna remembers the time they thought the cleaner was stealing, and how the items turned up inside a drawer in Lottie's closet. She wasn't a thief, only careless with possessions. She was used to owning everything and buying more when she lost it. For several painful hours, they'd disentangled their lives, flinging tops at one another, that neither remembered ever buying, and stuffing items into boxes that refused to get full.

She sits back down on the bed and lays back against the pillow and the rising smell of dampness takes her back to the apartment. She remembers how the house felt so much cooler after the walk; the path through the village, the kitten in Lottie's arms. The silence was a burden, then, as they went on with their packing, as though nothing had happened, both too stubborn to break it.

Anna turns her face into the pillow and breathes in the stink of mould. Something squirms inside her chest. She has the memory all twisted, Lottie's movements all wrong.

Her hands are firm but gentle. As she slides them beneath its body, she doesn't even flinch. Anna's watches the fur sticking out between Lottie's fingers, she'd never seen her so tender, so careful how she moved.

Anna feels a rising sadness, like the mildew behind the headboard. Perhaps a paw twitches, still dreaming of running.

She sits up and looks around the almost empty hotel room; the yellow bedside table is suddenly depressing. She can't stand to look at it a second longer than she needs to. She slides the suitcase under the bed, making the space even emptier. One more night. She jerks the handle and moves out into the corridor.

On her way out of the guest house, a commotion is blocking the elevator on her floor. She takes the stairs down one level and calls it down from there.

She waits. The arrow flashes. The doors judder open and then close behind her too quickly as it jerks into motion. Already too late, she notices her error: she's taken the left one, which only stops at odd numbers. She watches the countdown, the familiar sinking. When it stops at level 1, the doors seem reluctant to open.

She steps out and looks around her. The shops are all closed, the space deserted. Peering between dark rows, she searches for a stairwell. Eventually, she finds a door at the back between two stalls. Instinct tells her not to take it, but it's the easiest option.

The heavy door swings shut behind her. The air inside is cold and reeks like an abattoir, she has the feeling immediately—this is not the place to be. A conspicuous bundle is tucked away into a corner, and dark stains have hardened on rags flung on top. The light streaks the walls with an icy florescence that barely reaches the steps, and halfway down them she pauses, deciding whether to turn back. The lower staircase is even dimmer. She peers down towards the door.

She takes another step towards it, then another down the first stair. On the second step, she hesitates, a voice urging her to listen: there are secrets in these shadows; this place is quiet for a reason.

The door she's just entered through bangs suddenly in its frame. Anna bolts down the remaining stairs and skids across the tiles. She reaches the door at the bottom and yanks it open. As light spills in, Anna glimpses a red drag mark in the gunge.

Here, safe inside the mall across the street, Anna shivers. In the syrupy air of a coffee shop, the memory is already fading. She smiles at the cashier, but he repeats her order with indifference. She gives her name to his pencil and fumbles with loose change, then slinks away from the counter to a seat by the window.

Want guesthouse? Need SIM card? Anna recalls the sounds of Chungking through the glass. Across the road and six floors up, she can barely see inside the entrance. She tries to keep her thoughts from straying, but the memory pulls her deeper, past the trays of rice that glow a turmeric neon, beside the pink chicken wings that have shrivelled by 10.00. Beyond the queues for the elevators, where single girls clutch their backpacks and, when the doors reopen, check that their passports are still inside them. It drags her deeper and deeper. And she knows she must resist it. She still has one more night there. She must forget about the stairwell.

Her attention is drawn by a local girl at the counter. The barista's face warms; their greeting is familiar. Her Cantonese order bounces with routine, and the barista smirks when she says something Anna can't guess. His retort sounds witty, but the girl tuts and shakes her head. She is beautiful like Claudi, soft cotton grazing her pale skin.

Anna watches as an older woman approaches the counter. She gestures at the milk and asks him something in Mandarin. The barista smiles politely as he fills it, but as the woman moves away, he and the pretty girl snigger.

The girl settles at a table with her back to Anna's bench, and unlocks her phone to a newsfeed, sipping at her drink. Anna watches over her shoulder as she skims past faces of friends, pausing periodically to inspect tags or to like them. She stops at an article. Anna can't read the Chinese headline, but when it loads, she sees the numbers '2014'. The photograph shows crowds beneath yellow pagodas, and Anna knows from the colours that they are pro-democracy campaigners.

The girl nibbles the straw of her iced coffee as she reads. Though Anna can't see her face, she senses dissatisfaction. She flicks faster and faster, hovering over links. Sometime ago, Anna would have claimed to know what kept her scrolling. But that was before she'd met Kallum and everything had changed. He'd exposed, without meaning to, shades of feeling that she'd never considered; complexities of thought that seemed like contradiction.

'Some think that we are very free—to have the freedom just to do it. They think it's better not to change—how can I say it?—don't rock the boat. Can get whatever we want, now, right? Because our parents will just

buy it. To have everything when we need it. I don't think that makes us free.'

'What does Christine—'

'Too much freedom, she say it also. She cannot see the real picture. "Get employment from the government. Don't waste the lessons on the streets." Even, I can't miss school for just one day, even she says that. But my friends, we do it anyway. It is our future. What can I say?' His jaw tightens, then relaxes, 'The combat-ivity of Hong Kong is . . . regressing. And for the future? All . . . too difficult. But we must face it either way.'

'Is she pro-China?'

He smirks. 'It isn't like that. We are China, we cannot deny it. We don't want to separate, only be . . . '

'You don't?'

'Will never be like that! Is craziness to think it. Maybe you think . . . but you don't live it.'

They stare in silence into the water, at something far away and shifting.

'Did you hear about the Lion Rock? It's this thing about the past. It means a neighbourhood flavour; we look after each other's backs. That's where you find the Hong Kong spirit. You want to find it? It's in the past.'

'So, do you think that you will win still?'

'That's not the thing—to win it.'

'Is it time to stop then? Now that your point is made.'

'Too late. I'm a like target.'

The girl finishes her coffee and slips her phone into her handbag, looking over at the barista as she walks towards the exit. Anna's own drink is almost cold. She removes the lid and sips it. *You want to find it? It's in the past.* But it is different than she remembers it.

Some places were about the *where*. The ones they looked forward most to seeing: a Great Wall or half-day Chocolate Hills; the oversold and underwhelming. Some places were a *when*:

a slow front desk; a missed appointment; a reply lost in an outbox; an end-of-era celebration. Or the time she read the date wrong; a jet-lagged bed; a brand-new time zone. Some places were defined by *what*: what they saw there; what they ate; a place distilled to several photographs; a checklist destination. Some places had a *who*, like the corner she avoided, or the place to meet a long-lost friend, arbitrary, convenient. Some places even had a *how*: a how-did-I end-up-here?; a rewound sequence of events; a slow motion re-enactment.

But in Hong Kong, the rules were different. The *where* was warped by time. The *who* kept her awake at night. And she'd stopped searching for a *why*.

Back at the flat, she hadn't planned to, but she had knocked on Lauren's door.

'I think Kallum's in some sort of trouble with a triad.'

'What? Claudi's brother? Did she tell you that?'

'No . . . he did, tonight.'

There's a silence while Lauren wonders what to ask next and how to ask it.

'Why were you together?'

'Well, he walks me to the station. Christine makes him, half the time. After Cheuk Yiu's lesson.'

'Does Claudi know?'

'About the triad?'

'That he walks you to the station.'

Anna shrugs. 'I guess. I haven't asked. Do you think that I should tell her?'

'About the walks?'

'That he's in trouble. Or he might be. Someone's following him.
Lauren frowns. 'Who'd be following him? Apart from you.'

'This guy with weird scars. He lives in Kallum's village. And I keep seeing him when we're out – like the other night outside Wang-man's. It's like he's following me as well.'

'The minibus driver?'

'What? No, just this guy out on the street.'

Lauren nods. 'He drives the minibus. I saw him too—with all the scars.'

Chapter 30

Anna takes the next red car and hopes the driver won't speak. The evening yawns, clouds twitch and roll over. Anna is restless. She leans forwards to check the route map, but the matrix means nothing. The air inside the taxi is getting thinner. She wants to check the address but doesn't trust her intonation. The radio clock is stuck at 3.50 a.m. A photograph is taped to the dashboard beside it. The infant in the picture couldn't have been older than three. She counts backwards in years to 2014: a new-born, a distant future, and seventy-seven days without pay. She presses her forehead against the cool glass and counts ridges in the road.

You kill people; set fires.

We never did; show us the ashes.

Can't they see? They're all around this place, in the gutter, in the bushes.

Anna closes her eyes and lets the momentum drag her forwards; the old woman from the video rattling in her ears.

She takes a fragment of brick and tries to fit it with another. She will show them crazy if they want it. She hopes her son will see her on the news, the anger in her madness. The crowd has grown in number; they've heard rumours of the scene. Granny beckons a reporter, and she tells her what to ask them. She doubts they'll have the answers, but she's earnest with the question. She wonders what they're building with all these broken bricks. The Great Wall? She asks them. Her hands are red and swollen. She isn't strong, she tells the camera, but she won't heed the doctor's caution. Someone needs to stop them.

She kicks a bin lid filled with rubble. This kind of bin is heavy, she tells the camera, she dragged one yesterday just like this. She makes a sound like she is aching.

If they used their time to sweep the streets, Hong Kong would be so clean. Instead, they spread their trash. What use is that? To kill people and break things.

A protestor chases her with a stick flag, arm stretched out for her to take it. She throws her hands up, she won't accept it, she knows better than to touch it. They always try to set her up. But he plants it in her pocket. And as she plucks it free, the crowd jeers, and the camera finds an angle. She knows what they are doing, but she isn't here for any Party. She only wants to let the bus get through, to liberate her city.

She plants the flag into the flowerbed of the central reservation, dusts the soil from her hands, and goes back to clearing debris. She drags iron fencing, and Anna cringes as she drops it, jumping her feet back from the impact zone at the last possible moment.

Granny has watched the weeks becoming worse—four months—she shows them on her fingers. On her calendar, she looped the day she knew their brains were broken. She doesn't know if they are demons, if their mothers weep in mourning. She doesn't claim the past was better, she's never seen the city greater. She isn't angry at the present, just the few who wish to strangle it.

It's too bad that kids were beaten, but maybe now they might see reason. They can't block the road indefinitely. Mobility is everything.

When they pause at a junction, Anna opens her eyes, a small face is watching her from a window parallel to her own. It has been watching her for a while and doesn't look away when Anna notices. Her eyes remain fixed as their car pulls away.

'Broccoli? Wan' Broccoli?' He fills a tumbler with red wine. When he brings it to Anna's table, she decides to ask him outright.

'There's this man, Mr Wang . . . ' The aircon drips into her glass. 'There's this man. I think you know him. I've seen him hanging around outside.'

'Wan beef, hah?'

'Hm?'

'Err . . . meat!'

'No, thank you.' They watch another droplet land.

'Last time I was here—no, not the last time—but before . . . '

He slaps her shoulder as if she's told a joke that he pretends to understand.

'A long time ago, when I came here, there was this man outside the door. He has these scars,' she rubs her forearm. 'You must know who I mean.'

'Hah? You have?'

'Have what?'

'Have scar?'

'No, he has. Do you know him?'

Another drip from the aircon.

'The place you stay, hah, Chun'Kin' Mansion. I know it. Whe' you feel unsafe, you come here. Many Indian, ye', many Pakistani. You know it? Feel unsa' you come here, okay?'

'Okay. I will do, thank you . . . ' but she knows he'll tell her nothing more.

A couple enters the restaurant, and he guides them to the empty seats at Anna's table. Reluctantly they take them. Anna focusses her attention on the pattern of the tabletop and notices they are printed with MTR route maps. She is tracing the Tsuen Wan line when the man beside her speaks.

'The only problem here is I don't speak Cantonese.'

His accent is Canadian. He grins at his wife who looks around for English menus. But Wang-man is already on his way over to help them. He slaps a hand on the woman's shoulder, a little harder than she's expecting. She adjusts her blouse across her chest.

'Okay, la? Order many, many order. I like a fat girl!' In a moment, Wang-man is back to the caricature.

He pulls up a chair and fills his own glass with the wine, pouring Anna another, though she hadn't asked for the first. She protests, but he ignores her, lifts both glasses in the air and roars, 'Manchester! Manchester!' to an eruption of laughter. Then he nudges the glass towards her and nods until she sips it.

When Wang-man disappears into the kitchen, the loud Canadian leans over.

'You're from Manchester?'

'Actually, no.'

Anna shrugs apologetically and they laugh at his expense. Anna watches their blurred reflections shifting in brushed steel.

The man asks, 'So, what d'ya order?'

'Whatever he brings you.'

'Bit of cat, bit of dog?'

She feels suddenly defensive. 'Actually, it's really good here.'

'And cheap!' His wife joins in. Unlike her husband, she isn't new here. And she wants Anna to know that. She used to live here.

'Oh, I did too!'

Anna's mouth is dry, but she can't bring herself to drink; she wants to show the woman she doesn't come here to take advantage of the price. The man asks for Anna's story, and as his wife prepares to counter it, Anna feels herself torn between winning and the truth. The heavy base of the tumbler distorts the tabletop where it sits; the printed train map bulges, the Eastern Rail line swells and then splits. At the edge of each fractal, the route bends and eludes her. She is thinking where to start when the woman interrupts her. She points at the wine glass, 'We figured money laundering. And you?'

Anna glances at the kitchen and nods to say it's true. It only might be. She'd never thought of that. But it feels good to know.

Chapter 31

The incline is steady in places, much steeper in others, and in the mid-morning humidity, she is beginning to slow down. She has no way of knowing how far she's walked, besides the ache in her legs and the length of conversations she is replaying. But she must be getting close now; the foliage has thickened, and the monkeys are growing louder.

They are somewhere up the mountain, at a distance, still, but clearer. They are territorial and vicious. It is easy to provoke them. Hope told her that an oversized backpack would do it. Anna reaches around and squashes hers as flat as she can make it.

Today, the road is empty. The heat is intense. She hasn't seen another hiker since the turning at temple. Where the road ahead bends, a tall fence guards a platform with a skip, an open manhole, and a bundle of piping. The ancient plastic has perished and waits patiently for burial, weeds teasing their ridges, reaching up through the gravel. The scene reminds her of the village, shallow graves amongst rubble. Twice they'd struck a sewage pipe and split the makeshift shovel.

She continues up the pass, and as she turns the sharp corner, she notices a man some distance behind her. He's too far away for her to see his features, but he is looking straight at her. She's just surprised him, Anna tells herself. Neither had expected the encounter.

She feels him watch her round the hairpin, until the bushes slip between them. The road is winding but predictable. She'll be seeing him again.

She tries to keep herself calm, but Anna feels her pace quicken. He is no one; he's done nothing, but that nothing makes her nervous. There is no one else up here. Anna knows that he knows that too. She scans ahead for the entrance to the pathway up the peak. If she can get far enough ahead, he might not see her take it. Perhaps he will miss the signpost and continue straight past it.

If he has kept the same pace, Anna guesses she has now put two corners between them. If she can make it one more, she might never need to see him. She wishes she'd paid more attention to his clothing. She won't let herself slow down, not for water or directions.

The monkeys are quiet, now. They have called off the ambush. From the treetops, they watch, calling odds on the ending. Or perhaps something has spooked them. Anna misses their chatter, the company of witnesses, grim but reassuring.

The track steadies for a kilometre and is cooled by a canopy of leaves overhead. Anna weaves between patches of sunlight that break through, keeping to the shadows, grateful for the cover. She traces the curve of the road ahead, eager to spot an opening. It is further than she'd expected. The trees either side are thick and dark. She prays she hasn't missed it.

When she reaches another hairpin bend, the road twists with a sharp incline. Deep cracks mar the surface, torn like damp paper where the mountain has shifted beneath it.

As Anna turns the corner, her heart leaps at a familiar image: a wheelie bin and concrete staircase she recognizes from the directions. She almost runs when she sees it.

The route maps by the entrance are too faded to be useful, but that doesn't matter—from here, it will be a single track to the summit. Tucked quietly behind the signs, half hidden by foliage, is the Lion's Rock Country Park sign. She is safe now; it says, the mountain will protect her. Kallum had meant for her to come here. *That's where you find the Hong Kong spirit.* She should have thought of it sooner.

As the sign shrinks behind her, Anna settles into a rhythm. The handrail ends, and soon after, the steps start to crumble. There are stretches of bare track now, sandy earth, and loose rubble. For a while, she enjoys a new feeling of freedom. These are the routes that she wishes she'd been able to show off to her mother, without railings and a smooth concrete path that knows better. *Are they safe though? Don't go missing!* She'd been too cruel to reassure her.

But soon, Anna's thoughts begin to drift back to the stranger, wondering if he's found the entrance, and trying not to glance backwards. She continues up the trail, repeating over and over, she must not look behind. Her quads are burning but she ignores them, pushing harder up the mountain, but her mind keeps racing to the road, recalculating the distance. He might be quicker than she thinks. Perhaps he'd slowed down on purpose, hung back to let her think she has a chance to get away. She isn't moving fast enough, and she feels that he knows it.

She tries to reconstruct his features, and when she has them in her mind, she begins to transcribe him. Five seven or five eight. A black T-shirt; yes, she's certain. But was there nothing more distinctive? She isn't sure; she barely saw him. She searches for a detail, as they snigger at her statement. A thought enters her mind: she will never report him; there is nothing he could do up here that she had hope of surviving. She looks around at the boulders. And dark spaces behind them. She must not let him drag her. She must stay close to the path, make it hard for him to hide her.

She turns a corner and the trees open to the side of the mountain. The road is somewhere below her. Climbing higher above the pass, Anna remembers a similar vertigo. The feeling of an edge, a dubious precipice, like the bedrock beneath her was starting to fracture. She remembers the tingle, the anticipated sinking, pleading with Lottie, knowing her dad would do nothing. But the higher she climbs, the more the feeling mutates. A memory squirms inside her, refusing to settle.

Lottie turns from the window, 'It won't make any difference.'

'It might though, if he knows your friend is going to be there.'

'Kallum's your friend.'

'Yes, but your dad doesn't know that.'

'He won't ruin a story for some random local teenager. It doesn't work like that. It's his job not to tell them.'

Through his rear-view mirror, the driver is listening, decoding their dialogue, waiting for a signal that will sway his decision. When Anna notices, she nudges Lottie.

'Just tell him we'll get out here!'

'I have! He isn't stopping! This is illegal!' she tells him. She knees the back of the seat and he tuts, but Anna sees his eyes flick towards a gap in the lane beside them.

'But there'll still be a story. Police presence will make it bigger.'

But they both know that without police, the chance of bloodshed will be higher.

Lottie bangs on the headrest. The driver yells and slaps the steering wheel. His patience is wearing thin. He didn't anticipate aggression.

They usually pay and contest it after. Couldn't they just have made it easy?
He swerves into the opening. Anna types a message to translate, then deletes
it.

'So, you won't even try?'
'I've told you. I will ask him.'

The vertigo turns into nausea. Anna rests; her calves burning.
She leans against a rock and hears sirens in the distance.
Lottie told her she would ask him. Anna hears it now: she'd
really meant it. Her dad would make the phone call. But he
couldn't make them listen. She sees him slip the phone back
into his pocket. *Tell your friend to stay away, Lotts. They know*
already. We can't trust them.

Each boulder feels taller than the one that precedes it. The
mountain fights against her efforts as she claws at the hillside.
They mirror each other's determination and resistance. The
incline conspires to slow her, but the closer to the summit she
gets, the more impatient she is to reach it. She stops only twice:
when the path splits into two, and again when a dragonfly
hula-hoops around her. It hovers for a moment, powder blue
against the mountain, and—for a second—it is the insect from
the bus ride to Fanling. Then it loops over a crag, back into the
past, and Anna turns back the summit, afraid she'll disappear
with it.

In 2014, a group of students had hung a banner up here
during the protests, and in 2016, a tourist had strayed beyond
a danger sign. But Anna hadn't seen the banner, because she
hadn't known to look for it, and she didn't know the tourist who
had fallen to his death.

The late morning heat is searing. She is getting lightheaded.
Part of her worries that she won't make it to the top. But
something else keeps her going; something like the feeling that

she had already made it. She is already up there, looking down over the pass, waiting for this version of herself to catch up.

The path dips into a trough before the final incline. It stretches ahead of her towards the shoulder of the peak. Anna's calves are burning, from the sun and from the climb, and she uses her hands to pull herself up over the rocks.

At the summit, the city below her is silent. Only traffic moves, tiny speckles of static. They weave between towers that spring up like accidents; blue to the west, and yellow crescents to the east. There's a quarry, and shipping crates that spill into the water, and a giant mole hill that pushes up through the middle of the district. Junctions peel around it like the wings of an insect. It settles on a quilt of turfed pitches and public gardens. Swimming pool irises blink in the light. Anna's own eyes are still stinging, not quite adjusted to the brightness. Anna traces the train line. She wonders now if she'd ever looked up from the carriage, ever gazed at Lion's Rock without knowing she could climb it.

The ocean curves to the east. She recognizes trawlers and the cranes from Tsing Yi, the IFC at the waterfront. It is dulled a little by the smog, but she imagines its colours. On another, clearer day, it would be beautiful, like a postcard. She wonders how many lives are inside this single image and how many stories intersect here and tangle. Anna realizes then, she must be looking straight at him. She is closer than ever and still she can't see him. Distance hides the detail. She presses her thumbs and forefingers together into a diamond and holds it up to the picture, a tiny pinhole to focus through. Shifting it slowly, she isolates pixels: a fourteenth-storey window, a tennis court, a phone mast. But the edges of the images blur at her fingertips, and when she widens the frame, they are lost inside the whole. The light weakens when a thin cloud slips over the sun. Sweat cools on her skin. She drops her hands and stares out across the dull panorama, the backdrop for a city that changes with her mood.

The sweat stings her eyes. She'd believed the police would help them. *Tell your friend to stay away, Lotts.* Kallum had told her not to trust them. They'd left the city to consume itself, one side clawing at the other's already shrinking margin. In a city ruled by watches, they'd let the minutes elude them, let the city feel the weight of life beyond the deadline.

The silence is alarming, reconfirming Anna's distance— from home and from the past and from the city far below her. She misses Lauren and Lottie and her mother and Kallum. She inches out onto the overhang, sits, and swings her legs out over nothing. Her toes tingle. She feels the stirrings of an urge to lean forwards. Dizziness swells; she hasn't eaten since yesterday. She reaches into her bag and searches for a package, the pork bao she bought earlier outside Tai Wai Station. It is cold now, and greasy. The monkeys could smell it, and she won't take the chance on the way back down the mountain. She peels back the damp paper and takes a bite of the casing; its insides are salt-sweet the colour of copper. Below her, a minibus veers into a layby. She listens to the rumble, and something stirs inside her. As she chews the bao, she peers at the centre—fragments of tendon and jelly and gristle. The sticky dough clogs her throat and tries to choke her. Anna gags. There's something missing. She won't find it up here.

She needs to go back, from the city to Tai Po, to the wishing tree, the layby, the boy in the road.

Behind her, stones crunch and there's the sound of heavy breathing. Anna turns to see the stranger. He is pointing at his camera.

'If you want? And I can send you.'

It is kind of him to offer. Her reflection shifts on the lens, but his click decides for her. She smiles for him twice, with Hong Kong in the distance. Caught inside his camera, she is someone else entirely.

Chapter 32

Adverts for moon cakes line the walls of Kowloon Tong. In her absence, a barrier has been erected between the two sides of the walkway—one side for Central and one for the New Territories. There is no marked distinction between people on either side, but Anna likes to imagine that there is: people who are going somewhere and people who aren't.

Here, ribbons of commuters tangle at junctions, and impulsive shoppers change direction without warning. Overcrowded bakeries tumble out into the mainstream of traffic. When she swerves out of their way, a volatile banker walks into her suitcase and sparks with expletives. The main tunnel hisses, though Anna can't see a single person speaking.

She stops at the barriers, struggling with the turnstile, an impatient queue building up behind her. What possessed her to bring a suitcase here at this time?

> '*De-mon-tra-tion,*' *Cheuk Yiu sounds out the syllables.*
> '*Demonstration,*' *Anna beams at her progress.*

It is months since the protests; Kallum's face has healed, though the new front tooth still stands out against the others.

'That's right. And do you know what it means?'

The child shakes her head.

'I think you do. Can you guess?'

Her face remains blank.

'Okay, do you remember the protests?'

The child glances instinctively towards her mother's office, but Christine isn't home. Her fringe bounces as she nods.

'Well, they were demonstrations. Do you know what they were all about?'

'The peoples are kicking the suitcases of people. And Article 23.'

'What?'

'They are kicking the suitcases of the peoples from the mainland. The locust thing.'

'What do you mean?'

'The peoples from China.'

'I know what mainlander means. I'm asking what you mean about the suitcases.'

Cheuk Yiu shrugs. But Anna doesn't really need her to answer. Her own mother had tried to tell her about parallel trade across the border. She said they really were quite violent. *And Anna had dismissed her.*

The man with the suitcase is still apologizing, when an announcement tells Anna that this train is for Lo Wu.

The hair of the woman in front tickles her face, and when the train arrives, her platform-sneakers creak as she rushes towards the bench. But a man with an overloaded trolley bag beats her to it, and the woman spends the journey scowling at him and the cargo, her eyeline half-hidden behind petrol-tinged lenses. She resembles a bluebottle, grotesque and persistent.

He won't shift from the space until the terminal station; he's heading for the border, destined for Shenzhen.

There's no space for Anna to stash her suitcase, so she grips it between her thighs, squeezing tighter as it rocks with each ripple in the tracks. She hates the sight and the feel of it, the weight as it tips, and she despises the contents, the damp stink of Chung King. The cleaner, if there was one, had given up trying to shift it, and when Anna had dragged it from the doorway, her boarding pass and the receipt for her deposit were still wedged behind it. She'd wanted to abandon it, and start a rumour that she'd disappeared, never made it out of that stairwell. But the suitcase is her mother's, she's only borrowed it for the trip, a luggage tag from Dumaguete still stuck along the edge. DGT and their surname, a long expired barcode. She picks at the corner, but the sticky residue is worse. The carriage judders. Anna reaches down to stop it from sliding and feels something hard and rectangular tucked inside the pocket. Her fingers know immediately the feel of faded leather; the journal her mother had bought from the markets.

Really though, what are you even planning on writing? Or are you hoping it's antique?

The edges are wavy and crusted with sea salt. As she opens it, a few grains of sand fall from the binding. Anna slowly turns the pages, skimming backwards in time, reading over her scribbling. The first few entries are sparse and acutely superficial: to show she didn't need a notebook to make sense of the city. But then pride had taken over, the pages begin to darken; the more she'd resisted, the more compelled she was to fill them. Thoughts she'd held for so long were finally offloaded, and these thoughts had sprung others, and she was powerless to stop them. So much bitterness and resentment contained in those lines. And so much contradiction. She realizes now, this is what it must have felt like to be around her. A thick, oppressive presence, like humidity before a rainstorm that clung to their clothing. Her eyes linger on her phrasing, sarcastic and scathing. Like her mother must have then, Anna longs to erase them. She wants to tear up her words, forget she ever believed them. She closes the cover and slips it back into the pocket. Burying it deep inside the lining, where no one will find it. She thinks of her mother, listening to her derision, her negativity and cruelty, and doing her best to fix it. *I thought you might like to use it. A little memory of our trip.* All the while wondering why Anna had bothered to invite her.

Through the window, concrete hexagons fall away into hills. As Kowloon becomes the New Territories, the woman's glower drifts towards Anna. It's as though she knows what Anna is missing, the final detail she can't quite settle. At Tai Wai, the carriage drains, and those who remain inside chase the departing passengers out onto the platform with their gazes. When she looks back, the woman has gone; she'll never see her again.

Anna approaches an empty double seat at the back of the carriage. When she sits down, another face that has been staring turns away. They slip into a tunnel, darkness consumes them, and she finds herself counting white glitches in the wall. But then her eyes readjust, and the inside of the carriage becomes outside. She notes, first, her own face staring out but then another, much smaller, floating in the distance above her right shoulder. Her face is pale, but the other is ghostlike, and the sockets where eyes should have been are empty. On the other side of the carriage, he faces his own window, and through parallel reflections, they stare at one another.

Between strip lights, the images brighten and fade. His thin hair is greasy, and layers of glass make his flesh smooth and waxy. But as she studies him, Anna realizes her own face must look the same; equally mask-like, empty, and bloated. Her eyes drift back to the foreground, her own hollow reflection; those same staring pupils, she watches herself watching.

The pressure squeezes tighter. There is daylight somewhere ahead. *You want to find it? It's in the past.* Anna braces for the exit.

The space stretches longer between stations. At each platform, a new smell wafts into the carriage; recycled air at Sha Tin, and dry leaves at Fo Tan. Here, huge boards of stencilled flora deck the platform, blocking snippets of greenery that try to push through. She might remember them from before; she can't picture what's behind them; and as vague edges begin to form, the train departs, and she forgets once again. Tai Po Market is diesel, hot headaches, choi sum. Tai Wo is the grubbiest. Through the window, she traces familiar oil streaks and dust. As the train slows down to stop, the man with the trolley bag rises, and Anna realizes now he isn't bound for the mainland. His wife has come to meet him, and beams into the carriage; when the doors open, she launches forwards and together they drag the handle. Anna watches them weave through the bodies towards the barriers, proving Anna wrong, without knowing it or caring.

The urgent beeping rouses her, and she steps out after them. *You're not going back home?* Three years shrink around her.

She should have stayed and insisted. She should have called Claudi. *Miss Anna, you should have told me.* She aches to go back there. She wants to shout across the chasm. If she had, he'd be safe now, there'd be no answers to uncover.

For several moments, she is paralyzed, unable to decide on a direction, but the movement of people forces her to the turnstiles.

A tap and the barriers usher her through. The other side has changed almost beyond recognition. Tai Wo Plaza has been refurbished for the new Sha Tin—Central line. She glances towards the stairwell. The vendor cart has been wheeled away; there is nowhere left for him to hide.

Outside, below the station, the 64K is expecting her. She takes a seat on the bottom deck, with her back towards the window. And as they thunder past his village, she barely glances over. At the junction, a man in a rolled-up vest thrashes flies from his neck with a rag. The wail of his radio streams in as they pass. She doesn't try to guess the lyrics, but wonders if the man believes them. Beyond the roundabout, trees loom like sentinels either side of the road, guarding the sidewalks. But something is pulling her out through the window.

It is a feeling like instinct, an idea she's buried. It grows stronger at the corner, and by the layby, it is deafening.

A camphor-skinned youth is lying on his back, overlapping the border where the curb retreats into a layby. What remains of his face is still and angled straight at the sky. Anna twists to see through the window of their taxi. A high school uniform; sand shorts and white shirt. Red seeps into the collar, creeping down towards the pocket.

And Anna looks away, convinced she doesn't recognize the boy she knows she does.

As they pass the parked minibus, the driver's cigarette wags, and Anna feels his eyes find her through the two planes of glass. His fingers are still gripping the sun-faded steering wheel, as he waits with the rest for the sirens. Sirens—Anna knows, now, are already too late.

Chapter 33

She remembers an evening, a dull kind of darkness, intersected by silk trails and thick with mosquitos. It blurred the edges of her thoughts and the path through her village.

Plastic dust sheets rattle in windows of breeze block, steel rods jutting like pikes from its roof. She'd left the girls at Mid-Levels as soon as it was dark. She hadn't even bothered to make up a reason. She just couldn't stay with them, their laughter scratching inside her skull.

Sometimes, in the patches of absolute darkness, there'd been the fear she might fall from the raised concrete walkway.

There are snakes in the bushes. Anna knew what she'd seen: a tail disappearing, a flash between reeds.

The girls hadn't believed her, until one morning they'd awoken to find a man waist deep in the grasses. When they got closer, he cried '*Snek!*' and ushered them past, thrashed the stems with a cane, flailing wide, and laughing manically.

Yes, the grasses around the village were full of them, vipers and keelbacks writhing in the shadows.

Some nights, a strange sound had left Anna frozen at the corner, a whistle or a rustle, a dark snap in the bushes. But that particular evening, her footsteps were steady.

She will scare them away, the vibrations are heavy.

Anna glances up. A woman's silhouette has reached the streetlamp on the corner, her outline embossed like a stencil against the blackness. She looks like a maid, but is too far ahead for Anna to be sure. Her pace is tired and laboured, like she is counting her steps. Anna grips the hooked handle of her umbrella and listens to the tap of its pointed metal tip on the pebbles. In the pools of cold lamplight, it might look like a weapon.

Drainpipes clutch the edge of the path. Beneath the lamps, they're almost luminous, streaking across the village like headlights in a long exposure photograph. Anna tracks them into the grate that gurgles as she passes and shivers at the vanishing shadows of a rat tail. She skips over the channel that floods when it rains.

They haven't spoken for weeks. No message from Kallum. She'd terminated Cheuk Yiu's lessons when she discovered the recorder. She'd found a new school to work for, far away from him and Claudi.

In the end, she'd never go there; she'd leave Hong Kong before the start date.

When Anna had terminated the tutoring contract, she'd heard nothing form Christine, no demands for a reason, no accusations or explanations. Anna had never planned to give one and considered it over. But somewhere inside her, a deep anger was burning.

She looks down at the umbrella swinging from her fist. The thought swells in her stomach. She feels the stirrings of a twitch. She knows it is ugly, but it fills her all the same; she wants the maid to see her and, for just a second, be afraid.

Now, back here in the daylight, she almost misses that darkness, a blanket to disguise herself, to disappear under.

The midday sun is blinding. Any shade is thin and scattered. She must get back to the old rooftop. And this time, no one will follow her.

The breeze picks up, and Anna's trousers flap around her ankles as she winds through the village, the path starting to steepen. Her two weeks is almost over; two weeks since she last came here. No one is behind her. She won't look back. She needs closure.

Exposed skin starts to prickle, expecting a fang in the tendon. She steps quicker along the path to let the snakes know she is coming.

The house seems closer this time. Anna pushes the hot metal. The door resists for a second, then resigns to her intrusion. But as she starts up the first staircase, she feels a dull nagging. She sits down on the steps and takes her phone out from the pocket.

'Wai?'

The sound of Claudi's voice comes too quick and surprises her. The sound is too intimate, too close, too familiar.

'Claudi, it's Anna . . . '

In the background, she hears voices, the distant laughter of a gathering.

' . . . Sorry to call you.'

Inside the speaker, the laughter swells, Claudi joins and then hushes them.

'I can't very hear you. Anything happen?'

'No, it's okay. I just wanted to apologize.'

'Wai.' She says again. It's neither *yes*, nor a question.

Anna hangs up and continues up the stairs, past the first floor, past the second. This time, she doesn't stop; the silence is thorough and reassuring. At the third floor, the door to the roof is open, exactly as she'd left it.

A familiar panorama of dusty peaks surrounds her. But it no longer feels like home in the way it once had. She crosses the tiles and sits in the centre. Through the wide, tinted windows in the perimeter wall, she glimpses the juniper moss of lower slopes, studies them like paintings through the glossy veneer.

One late afternoon, she'd been up here, dozing in the sun, when a thud struck the window behind her. As her eyes readjusted to the light, she searched for the source of the sound. There, lying motionless, was a tiny, sky blue bird. Moving closer, she noticed other shades besides the blue: butter yellow, beads of ebony, and pristine flecks of white. Its soft, teardrop head was resting at an angle. For several moments, she was frozen, half dazed by the sunlight, confronted with such perfection, and suddenly responsible for its rescue. Then, its tiny chest quivered. She'd crouched, wondering how to help it, watching it fading.

She looks over, now, at the spot where she had covered it with the cracker box. The waxy smear on the glass washed away by a rainstorm.

Her gaze drifts further, through the window, out over the village. She follows the path down, through tangled plots and dry earth, before it slips behind the houses that border the road. The road churns steadily behind them, through the bottom of Lam Tsuen Valley. Anna can't see or even hear it, but she knows it is there. Leaning back, she shuts her eyes and lets her face find the sun. Blood orange light leaks through her lids.

Shielded from the breeze, she realizes the heat of the afternoon. Soon, her cheeks and forehead begin to prickle from the rays. A ridge between tiles is digging into her coccyx, but she can't make herself stand and go back inside that hallway. Instead, she leans back, lowering her shoulder blades to meet the ceramic. At first, the smooth surface feels cool, but then the afternoon warmth seeps up into the skin. Anna shivers as it spreads, stretches out her arms, and lets the sun soak into her pores.

She lets the warmth and the calm take her over. Soon, she no longer feels the ache of ridges. She wishes she could have brought him up here, safe above the traffic.

Behind the wall, she is tucked away from the breeze and listens to its whispering just above her head. But as she listens, she notices a steadier thrum hiding inside it, a sound like a generator, distant but sustained, a motorized churning.

Staring up at the sky, she thinks of the injured bird. She'd described it to Claudi, who searched in Cantonese. What she typed translated as 'flycatcher'. At first it seemed to fit, but the more Anna stared, the less she believed it. The colours were too pale. But she hadn't imagined it.

The hidden sound is undeniable now, coiling tighter and tighter. The wind drops and unveils it: tires in the distance.

The vibrations grow louder, rattling through the tarmac. Anna hears them find the bedrock and the stretch of dark earth beside it. The rumble moves closer, through the village, through piping, old lead, smashed terracotta, and cracked plastic bindings. It crawls through soil and bulbs too deep to surface, rotting amongst rubble, still waiting to germinate.

The sound reaches their block. The vibrations intensify, they rumble through gravel, find clay, and then concrete. They reach thick tarpaulin, loose foundations, ground sheets. The terrapin's water tank quivers on the surface.

The sound rises through the floor, iron rods in the walls and through breeze block and the first storey ceiling. She is unable to escape it. The roar is furious in her ears. It finds the second storey and the third. She clenches her fists, knowing any second, it will reach her. Her skin has fused with the tiles. Every nerve cell is screaming.

The sound explodes onto the roof and her eyes are forced open.

A piercing white sears her retinas. She feels tears come to blind her, and Anna lets them flood. She'd come up here to escape herself, for the stillness and the quiet, but instead, she'd found a place where her thoughts were at their loudest. When the lids touch together, tears slip over her cheeks.

She'd kept the flycatcher's body up here, safe from snakes on the ground; but three days later, when she'd checked, something else had claimed it from the sky.

Chapter 34

A taxi is parked by the sign for San Tong village. The driver leans against the bumper, smoking, waiting patiently for no one. He looks peaceful and content; if her mother were here, she might have asked him for a lighter. Like that time outside Dumaguete airport, when the attendant had tried to fine her. It was *little-things-like-that* that made her excited to be returning. *Home or Hong Kong?* Her mother had laughed at Anna's question.

'I guess it is your home, now. And there's this Kallum you're rather fond of.'

But Anna decides to let it go. It's been a good day, sentimental; it's okay, for once, to feel some resolution before an ending. As their taxi pulls out of the gates of the villa, her mother turns for a final picture, but the acceleration blurs it. There's the smudge of a chicken coop cut in half by phone lines, and the corner of the taxi door; she says she'll sort the good ones later.

It occurs to Anna, now, the picture must still be on her hard drive; a folder within a folder, waiting patiently for deletion.

The driver watches Anna emerge from the village and spits his cigarette into a grate. He climbs back in, and Anna joins him. He doesn't wait for a direction.

'MTR. The station.' She calls from the back.

As she boards the train, she listens to the pre-recorded warning. She'd re-memorized the Cantonese, but the words are already fading. Like those phrases at the wishing tree. They'd repeated them over and over, scribbling phonetics above translations, anglicized the sounds, made rhymes, and then forgot them.

They tie their wishes to the strings of oranges and fling them high into the branches. When the string catches, they swing there with the thousands of others.

Her mother marvels at the tree. 'I'm amazed the weight of them doesn't kill it!'

It had. This one was plastic. But they'd pretended it was real. When they'd looked up again, their wishes were lost above their heads, a guess at a future tangled amongst the rest.

As the train moves slowly back into daylight, Anna turns to the opposite window for one last glimpse of Tai Po, but sound barriers block the view. And then they are moving too fast.

Somewhere, just beyond them, is a taxi, and a highway, lives weaving into straight lines, and waiting for the city.

Epilogue

Behind a sun-faded steering wheel, his face is expressionless. The trinkets on his dashboard judder with the road. His fingers tighten around the grooves they have worn into the leather. Seventy-seven days without pay, but it is more than that; this is personal. He accelerates towards the layby. Their eyes meet through the windscreen, too quickly for the boy to register. A shout, too late. A flash of red. The thud will stay with him.

Waiting on the runway, Anna stares out through triple-glazing. The dark is dense and broken only by illuminated signs. From here, it is impossible to judge the distance to the ground. The more Anna stares, the less sure she becomes. She scans for a reference, something familiar for comparison, but there is nothing, only dotted lines painted on tarmac.

She closes her eyes and imagines their faces, the boy and the driver, but the features keep shifting. They could be anyone, or no-one, and maybe that was right. Two strangers and a third who had forced them together, weaving their lives into a story they'd never read. The driver might be out there now, between the village and the harbour, stalled before traffic lights, impatient with the morning.

When Anna opens her eyes, they settle on a backlit arrow. She tries imagining it first as no taller than a street sign, then towering like a gantry, but neither seem to fit. She leans closer to the window and scans the length of the plane, the tunnel between the head rests and the curved inner frame. Parallel gazes stare out at the scene; from identical windows, they wrestle with its dimensions. As the arrow shrinks and grows it pulses brighter against darkness. Then the engines begin to hum, the hum thickens to a rumble, they lean back against their head rests and it guides them to the sky.

She looks out across the lights flickering far below them, blinking shut before her eyes can count them. Then she realizes they aren't flickering, only passing behind buildings, disappearing for an instant as their plane revolves around them. Gazing down at Hong Kong, they plot their stories on the canvas as contrails thicken into cloud, and they disappear into the blackness.

Acknowledgments

I owe a huge debt of gratitude to everyone who has helped shape the *Widening of Tolo Highway* over the past eight years . . .

First, to all my friends in Hong Kong, past and present, for your warmth and openness, and for sharing your city. To Lotte and Claudi, especially; this story would be empty without you in it.

To my editors at Penguin, for your faith and wisdom, and my reviewers, for your time and generosity.

To Adam, Rachel, Agi, Honor, and Richard, and everyone at the University of Sheffield, for your unwavering support, enthusiasm, and guidance.

Next, to my friends and family . . . Luce and Lizzie, for beach days and roof nights; Soph and Dan, for keeping me grounded; Nan, Cazzy, Joe, and Rebecca, for reading (and re-reading) so many drafts; Dad, the greatest storyteller, for those Monday morning pep talks; and Gaynor, for, well, a number of things.

To Siǎn, the strange and wonderful, for the beautiful cover art.

To Gaz, for Tom Waits and Hunter, for when the going gets weird.

And to Dave, my everything, for everything.